BOUND TO THE CROWN

LAST OF THE BLOOD GUARD
BOOK ONE

SIMONE NATALIE

This is a work of fiction.
Names, characters, places, and incidents either are the product of the author's imagination or are used fictitiously.
Any resemblance to actual persons, living or dead, events, or locales is entirely coincidental.
Copyright © 2023 by Simone Natalie All rights reserved.
No part of this book may be reproduced or used in any manner without written permission of the copyright owner except for the use of quotations in a book review.
For more information, address: SimoneNatalie_Author@hotmail.com
First digital edition February 2023
Cover designed by Mayflower studios
Edited by Hot Tree Editing
Interior Illustrations by Drillustrations

*For Danny, my very put-upon husband.
Thank you for being the bringer of coffee, snacks and fuzzy blankets.*

*None of this would have been possible if you hadn't been there to spur me on.
('cos I'm lazy AF)*

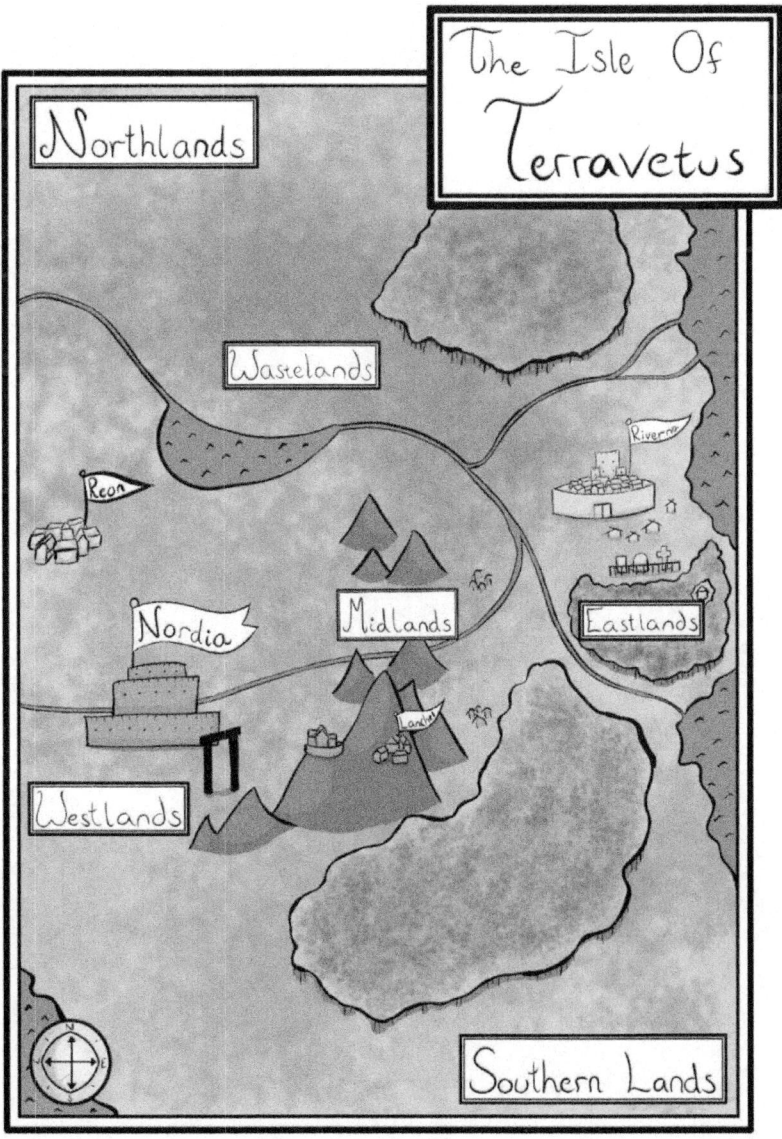

Chapter 1

The hedge witch stared down at me from over the edge of the grave.

Her unseeing white eyes were narrowed and glaring in my direction as I dug the tip of my shovel deeper into the ground, pushing down hard so that the weight of my body forced the steel blade in deeper. I staggered a little when the tension gave way, but it was no struggle to lift the shovel and add another pile of black dirt to the wooden bucket at my feet. The witch could stare at me suspiciously all she wanted, but I wouldn't falter. I was stronger than any other woman or man she could have hired, and I wasn't going to hide it.

When the pail was overflowing, I dropped the shovel and wiped the sweat away from my face with my sleeve. I tugged hard on the rope attached to the rim of the bucket, and a bell rang out above, from on top of a wooden tripod, signalling to the witch that it was full.

The witch turned the crank mechanism and slowly dragged the bucket up and out of the hole. She tipped the contents onto a large mound before throwing the bucket back down at me, ready for the process to begin again. I dodged it, darting away quickly in frustration. For a blind, hard-of-hearing old witch, she sure had a good aim, and she had clearly taken a disliking to me for some reason. I felt a little hurt, because I couldn't think of anything I had done in the last seventy-two hours of knowing her that could've caused this type of venom. I looked up, fixing her with a fierce glower in return for the pointedly aimed throw. She ignored this and resumed her intense supervision. I could almost feel her gaze burning into the back of my neck as I turned away and continued my work.

This certainly wasn't the best job I had taken on over the last six years, but it also wasn't the worst. I could put up with a feisty witch. It was better than…

Well, it was better than what I used to put up with.

BOUND TO THE CROWN

In my time as an agency worker, or "renter" as they were not-so-fondly dubbed here in the capitol city of Riverna. I had seen my fair share of difficult employers. I had taken on almost every role offered to me since I started at the rent house nine months ago. The pay was abysmal, due to the large commission that the owner kept, but there were benefits that outweighed the negative. A roof over my head, two meals a day, freedom to choose what jobs I worked and at what times, and maybe most importantly, it kept me too busy to dwell on things that were dangerous for me to dwell on.

Plus, as a renter, no one cared where I came from or where I was going, and I didn't need any paperwork or identity forms.

The people of Riverna turned their noses up at renters, thinking that only desperate, criminal or destitute people would work under the conditions of a renter house. Well, maybe that was true, but customers came flocking nonetheless whenever a job needed doing, from common witches to the Riverna royalty.

Just then, the witch emitted a dreadful hacking noise from above. It cut through the eerie silence of the graveyard, startling blackbirds loose from their nests in the gnarled trees. I dared a glance up and jumped out of the way just before she spat down at me. It wouldn't have hit me, but it came fairly close. I swore under my breath and slammed the spade into the dirt with force, so that it stood upright.

"What is your problem?" I shouted up at her in annoyance.

Silence.

Her wide eyes trembled and then focused anew at some point just behind me.

"Do you ever talk? Or even blink?" I asked. "I know that you *can* talk," I said.

I had overheard her speaking to Freddy, the rent house owner just four nights ago. I had been working at the bar when the witch came looking for a new grave digger. I heard her clear as day, complaining that the last man was too weak, and I heard her all the more when she had cackled loudly at the suggestion of a woman taking it over.

Here I was though, and I was anything but weak.

The eyes of the hedge witch locked onto mine then, with a startling precision that almost had me questioning If she was really blind at all or playing a part to appear more intimidating. I immediately felt ashamed. While it was true that I had met plenty of witches who had altered their appearance or voice to seem more *witchy*, it wasn't fair of me to presume that of all of them. I could understand it though—no one trusted a potion from a young pretty unmaimed witch. They all wanted their tinctures from old, wise hags.

The witch remained as silent as… well as the grave, I suppose.

"Is it fun being a witch? Good pay?" I asked, switching tactics in an attempt to relieve some of the discomfort I felt.

I filled the bucket again, making sure to level out the ground beneath me, feeling very thankful that it was a clear night, and not completely chucking it down with rain as it had been the night before. I shuddered, remembering the knee-deep mud and the cackling from the witch when I had fallen face first into it. She probably hadn't expected to see me back tonight.

"I suppose there are some pretty disturbing tasks associated with your job," I continued, aware I was mostly talking to myself at this point. "Then again, does it get much more disturbing than digging graves in the dead of night?"

I ventured a look up at the witch, who was still stood silent, hunched over and staring intently, as though I hadn't spoken a word. I carried on with my task, not letting her taciturn temperament deter me.

"I suppose you do the sitting-in with the body before it goes down here though?" I pondered "I'm not sure I could do that."

A loud cackle exploded from above me then, causing me to jump in shock and wheel around to find the hedge witch looming over me. She was bent so far over the edge of the hole that it was a wonder she didn't topple right in. Her straggly grey hair danced in the crisp breeze, framing her long, pointed face. Her thin mouth was curled up in a laughing grin, with the tips of her yellowed teeth poking out between her lips. I caught the glint of a red gemstone dangling from her left ear. She certainly looked the part of a wicked witch.

"You couldn't do that?" She snorted. "You couldn't sit with the dead?"

I stared impassively as the witch croaked and cackled above me, her wrinkled face crinkled up in mirth.

"I know *what you could do*," she continued, "and I know exactly what you are." Her voice was raspy and hoarse, perhaps from lack of use. "I know what you *have done*."

"Goodness me, I wasn't sure you could talk," I retorted, feigning disinterest in her cryptic words. A small bud of panic burst into life in my chest, and I had to look away, suddenly unable to meet the witch's white stare.

Say no more, I thought desperately.

"You are a lie," she spat menacingly, heedless of my silent plea.

I frowned and dug my shovel back into the dirt with venom, attacking the ground, the witch's words made me feel sickeningly exposed. I suspected that they were generic, spoken to scare and unnerve me and with no other purpose than that. The witch didn't know me, and she had no idea what she was saying, but I couldn't stop the panic from blooming.

I heaved the spade back up and tipped more dirt into the large bucket.

My hands were calloused, cracked, and full of splinters from the worn wooden handle. It was to the point of being almost numb, but I was used to this kind of manual labour, I focused on the pain, trying to block out the grip of fear that was threatening to overwhelm me. I needed to minimise this. I needed to shake it off now, before it grew too large in my mind to control.

"I think we could have eased into this friendship with a bit more small talk first, but you do you, witch," I said flippantly.

"You are a lie," she persisted, ignoring my attempt at humour. "Everything about you is. A. lie!" She practically yelled that last word in an odd, wretched voice that I was sure she was putting on.

I let out a long breath.

The witch couldn't know anything about me. She couldn't know how hard the word "lie" hit me or how close to the truth it was. Only two people alive knew: myself and Mags. Mags wouldn't betray me to anyone, not even a fellow witch.

This had to be some tactic, a part of her whole scary hag "shtick." She was simply throwing out hits to see what struck.

After all, who in this world hadn't lied about their life at some point? What renter wasn't running or hiding from something? This witch disliked me, and she was saying anything she could to try to unnerve me, I could respect that, but I wouldn't let it get to me.

Still, I couldn't help but wonder…

I swore nervously under my breath as I filled the last bucket of the night.

"My best friend is a witch, you know," I confided, testing the waters to see what information the hag may have on me.

In actuality, Mags was my *only* friend and a fairly famous witch around this area, so it wouldn't be surprising if they had heard of one another..

The hedge witch revealed nothing.

"Well, I'm just saying," I continued, "I get what you're trying to do. You have to keep up that scary persona, but it's not necessary with me."

More frustrating silence.

I sighed, resigning to take comfort in the quiet. The witch may have stayed her tongue to preserve herself. It was likely she knew nothing and didn't want to give herself away. I tugged the rope one last time.

After the crone turned the crank to tow up the final bucket, I used the ropes and wooden beams to clamber my way out of the grave. Once topside, I flopped onto my back, staring up at the night sky. Stars winked down at me, I shut my eyes and breathed in the crisp night air. There was something comforting about the smell of fresh earth. The mild breeze felt cold and refreshing as it blew through my sweat-soaked hair, sending a comfortable shiver down my back. I lay that way for a moment, focusing only on my breathing and the very distant sounds of chatter and merriment that drifted to me on the air from the city walls.

A small leather purse fell beside my head, clinking as it hit the grass.

"You have blood on your hands, girl," the witch whispered from nearby, shattering my moment of calm as absolute panic ran through me.

Like the sleep deprived fool I was, I hastily checked my hands, then laughed aloud at my own ridiculousness when I realized she hadn't meant it literally. The panic withered as quickly as it had come. I was sure now that she was just trying to scare me, no matter how truthful her speculating words were. If she truly knew my past, there would be more hurtful things she could say.

"It's always there, I can see it," she huffed as she began walking away, clearly irritated by my laughter. She stopped to stoop down and take up both of the oil lamps, snuffing them out with two sharp, quick breaths. I chuckled at the spitefulness of it.

"I will be impressed when you tell me something I don't already know, witch!" I yelled after her, rolling onto my stomach to watch her hobble away down the overgrown pathway.

Had she known that I didn't need the light from the lamps to see in the dark? Perhaps she just didn't care if I could or not.

Regardless, I had to give her some respect, because this was no easy work for anyone, especially not a woman of her age.

I snatched up the bag of coins and chased after the hedge witch before she could get it into her head to lock me in the cemetery.

"See you tomorrow?" I asked nonchalantly as I brushed past her at the high wooden gates.

She grunted noncommittedly. "Maybe."

As we reached the fork in the road where we two would usually part, I noticed her hesitating slightly and looking around, her head tilted to the side as though she was listening out for something.

"What is it?" I asked her, seriously. I bunched my fists and scanned the woodlands around us, preparing for a fight as my thoughts automatically jumped to the worst possible scenario.

"Something dark surrounds you," she said eventually. I met her white gaze, and she looked for a moment as though she wanted to say more. "Be on your guard."

With that, she turned and made her way into the forest beyond the graveyard, disappearing into the darkness and leaving me behind to head in the opposite direction, towards the city lights.

I felt slightly winded.

Three days into this job and the witch was speaking to me now, giving me warnings and calling me out. Maybe this was the beginning of a creepy friendship?

I shuddered. I had once thought about becoming a witch myself, and Mags had confirmed that I had some affinity for it.

Witches got a lot of the reclusive jobs, watching over the dead, maintaining the graveyards, making potions and ointments, tending gardens, and looking after animals, all the while living in isolated cottages or out on the road. Almost anyone could call themselves a witch, and perform the basic roles, even if they weren't a blood witch like Mags, who could use magic.

It wasn't any good though. I didn't want to end up being the person that the desperate ran to when they needed help, or even worse, the person everyone blamed as soon as something went wrong.

That wasn't a job for me.

Chapter 2

The moon was barely visible in the dark sky, obscured by chalky clouds. The night was young though, there had only been two graves to dig tonight, and after being almost seventy-four hours awake, I was thankful for the early turn-in.

The graveyard was on the very edge of the Kingsland of Riverna, and it was a fair walk through the slums to get back behind the main city walls.

Houses in the slum were thrown up from whatever material people could get their hands on, wood mostly but also some flint and stone. It was overcrowded and festering with rats and decay. Forgotten and ignored by the richer city beyond it. I walked along the muddy, slippery pathway, enjoying the occasional blast of heat that emanated from the small firepits along the road

People gathered around them cooking, laughing, crying, and sharing food and gossip. Even at this late hour, the streets were crowded.

Most ignored me as I walked past, as my dirty face and ripped clothes weren't out of place here. I disregarded them just as easily for the most part, but it wasn't always possible to turn away from the poverty. I found it especially hard when it came to the children.

Dressed in rags made from pillowcases or flour sacks, they were all too small and too hungry. They should have been tucked up in beds, but instead they were hanging around the fires as though it was the heat alone keeping them alive. It hurt me to look at them.

I followed a bend in the well-trodden pathway, taking me close to one of the wooden houses.

In the open doorway stood a young girl with matted hair and a drawn face, her body all skin and bones. Her feet were bare and cut. I startled her as I appeared from the darkness, and she retreated further into the doorway. From inside I could hear the sound of a baby screaming and raised voices.

With a resigned sigh I dug into my purse and pulled out four coins. Silently, I handed them to her.

She looked up at me with wide eyes and approached me cautiously. Her hands shook, and she hesitated a moment before taking the coins. The girl then quickly darted back, disappearing behind the door. As it swung shut on me, I froze. There was a hole in the wood that had been hastily patched up with a broken piece of multicoloured glass, and in it, I could see the reflection of a tall, hooded figure standing directly behind me.

I spun around, but there was no one there. I scanned the area anxiously, assessing the shadows between houses, and the dark smoke that blew from the firepits, but I could see nothing.

Maybe I was hallucinating now?

I shook it off and tied the purse back around my belt, cursing myself for its lightness. Food would have been safer for the girl than coins were, but I had none on me. I had to stop giving my coin away, or the people would begin to take more notice of me soon.

The city loomed in the distance, a beacon of glowing lights, half concealed behind the towering stone walls.

The Blackmoore Castle rose out above all else, a large looming shadow that cut into the sky. Its majesty mocking the destitute villages and settlements that spilled out below it.

As I left the area, I could make out the red and yellow flags of Riverna dotted all along the battlements of the capital. They flapped violently in the wind, illuminated by great braziers.

BOUND TO THE CROWN

I nodded to the group of guards stationed at the main gates, who paid me no attention beyond a dismissive wave that allowed me entrance into the city.

Most businesses along the way were closed at this hour, but the renter workhouse where I lived was lit up and bustling as always.

The rent house itself was a tall, crooked building with thick black beams. It tilted alarmingly and looked very much reliant on the bakery next to it to keep it up. The small shop looked very put-upon by the five-storey rent house.

It was full to the bursting with men and women for hire and was owned by an old lady who went by the name of Madame Fredericka. Only she and her mother knew what her real name was though. We all called her Freddy.

I had met Freddy nine months ago in a dirty hotel tavern. She watched me beat a man half to death before spending my very last coin on a small shot of whisky. Something about that exchange must have endeared me to her, as she'd promptly offered me a job. I'd accepted of course. What else was there to do? I still had no idea what she saw in me, a twenty-four-year-old runaway with an anxiety disorder and a nasty habit of hitting first, asking questions later. Or why she offered me a place here. I was thankful for it though. I was less…manic when I had a purpose.

The ground floor of the renter house was a pub that also functioned as Madame Fredericka's booking room. If you had money and a need, then a renter house was the place to be. From ladies of the night to farm workers, you could hire a person for any job here, and since a renter house usually attracted its employees from the stateless and the poor, you weren't likely to see much complaint.

It was tough work, but it suited me well, for now.

Marlo was on the door tonight. A short, rotund man with a mountain of hair on his chin and barely a wisp of it on the top of his head. He didn't look like much, but he would have a punter on his arse before they even knew that they were misbehaving.

I whistled as I walked past the line that went from the renter house to the end of the road. I nodded at Marlo and slipped in. The pub was heaving with people, mostly men. It was loud and hot, and the air was full of smoke. The low ceiling had the tallest men bowing their heads uncomfortably. There was a rumour that Freddy had added wood and plaster board to make it that way. "Nothing more vulnerable than a man forced to bow," she would say.

I preferred my men at knifepoint.

As I forced my way across the floor, I heard Freddy's shrill voice boom above the noise.

"My coin, you sneaky bird!"

A thin, disembodied and bejewelled hand appeared from nowhere to meet me. I unhooked my purse and counted out five bronze coins, leaving only one silver and one bronze in my bag. I dropped them into the palm, and when the hand didn't withdraw, I pushed it away.

Then, suddenly, Freddy was there, materializing from behind a group of unwashed men like magic, which of course it was. Her face was barely visible from beneath her mass of curly white hair, but her sharp brown eyes stared at me threateningly. I wasn't physically scared of much in this life, but that look sent shivers down my spine. I reached in the bag and pulled out the last bronze coin. She blinked and plastered on a warm smile as I placed my coin into her hand, her real hand, not her glamoured one that had already floated off to meet some other poor soul in debt.

"How's about I do you a deal, bird?" she said with a twinkle in her eye.

My name here was actually Cera, but Freddy had never called me that, she addressed all the female renters as "bird". I would be offended, but "bird" was much tamer than the name she gave to all of the men.

There was such a fast turnaround in this business that it would be impossible to memorize names, I supposed. Not that the name I used was the one I was born with anyway.

I raised my eyebrows.

"You can keep this coin if you go relieve Valerie from the bar?"

I opened my mouth to protest immediately, but Freddy's face suddenly fell into an over-exaggerated frown, she pointed to the bar, where a renter girl, who looked no older than sixteen, was taking orders. She had purple smudges under her small, blue eyes, her clothes were drenched with what I could only guess was a mixture of sweat and ale. Her hair was falling out of its messy ponytail, and she looked frazzled as customers barked their ordered at her.

"Poor bird's been on shift since yesterday's rush and all through the night. I usually shut the pub for a few hours in the morn, but angry punters are thirsty punters."

"And you are never one to miss an opportunity." I mumbled.

The girl did look done-in and close to tears. I watched as her hand shook as she pulled a pint, spilling half of it onto the floor. She raised her arms in apology at the angry cries of protest. She was too exhausted, and not fit for the work. Maybe the customers would tip more in appreciation of a better barmaid? I could make up for some of the wage that I had lost to Freddy.

With a sigh of frustration, I ran my hand through my tangled hair and snatched the coin back from Freddy's palm. "I'm doing this for the coin." I snapped, wanting to make it absolutely clear to her that I had no sympathy for the renter girl.

Because I didn't.

The moment I threw up the wooden latch and stepped behind the bar the girl turned to me, her eyes large with hope, she looked up at me like I was her savour, it made me want to push her down in panic. Instead, I held up the latch and nodded my head at it meaningfully. She hesitated only a second before pulling the sopping wet tea towel out of her belt, throwing it down on the bar and escaping under the hatch and up the stairs beside it.

It Freddy was to be believed then the girl must have been on shift since the lunch time rush the day before, that's a long time without a break, even for me.

A roar of appreciation went up from the men that gathered on the old, crooked stools that lined the bar. "New blood!" One cried. "I've been here since midnight and barely had a decent drink!"

"I wouldn't be shouting that about if I were you." I said as I grabbed a pint glass. "What will it be then?" I asked him.

"Your finest lager!" He demanded, putting on an affected accent. I nodded and pulled the pint, giving him more head than was necessary, in retaliation for how they had all treated the girl before me. Then I thought better of it, tilting the glass at the last moment so that it evened out. I was doing this for the money.

"What's your name then?" The old man asked as I slammed the glass down.

"Noneya"

"Nonya?" He repeated, confused.

"Yeah, None-of-ya business." He guffawed at the cheesy pun and slammed his coin on the bar, I pocketed the change, and he didn't protest.

The next hour flew by similarly, no one gave me any trouble, which was surprising for the early hour, and a little disappointing as there was something oddly satisfying about throwing a rude person off of their bar stall and getting Marlo to throw them out.

I began to zone out while cleaning glasses and mopping up the sticky drinks that had spilt earlier in the night, until my ears pricked up at a rowdy conversation happening at the far end of the bar.

"I swear on my life!" One man yelled, standing quickly and knocking his chair to the floor in the process. I sighed and walked over.

"Calm down fellas or I- "

"-I swear, she ran away and Joined the blood guard…" The guy continued. I felt a shiver run down my spine and I lost my breath for a moment.

The man swaggered drunkenly and grabbed a hold of the collar of another, who was looking at him with a doubtful sneer. "I swear, Rich, that's where she's gone."

He said, his voice cracking "My only girl" He sobbed as he shook Rich's collar weakly.

"Paul, man." Pleaded Rich, gently. "Even if she has run all the way to the Westlands, they don't let just anyone join the blood guard, especially not a little easterner like our Kel."

"That's what I'm saying, they are going to kill her, Rich."

In a daze I walked away from the conversation, putting as much distance between myself and them as possible. Even after all of these years, those words still sent the fear of the gods through me. I felt stunned for a moment, and I tried to shake off the nervous feeling in my gut.

The blood guard.

The elite guard of fighters from the west, a battalion of solders that were unbeatable and unwaveringly loyal to their king... whether they wanted to be or not.

They were everything I was running from, yet even in Riverna I couldn't escape their infamy.

"Bird!" I jumped to find Freddy standing in front of me, looking slightly concerned.

"I've been yelling at you, girl. When did you last sleep?" She asked.

"It's been a few hours," I said vaguely. Freddy raised her eyebrows but said nothing. She turned to expose the person behind her, a middle-aged man I had seen around the renter house a few times.

"He's going to take over for you," she said by way of explanation as she pushed the man urging him to go under the hatch. I nodded and made my way out towards the staircase, thankful to be done.

"You should stay, bird," said Freddy. "Why's that?" I asked.

"There is a celebration at Blackmoore Castle," she explained. "The king wants women to dance and men to humiliate." I shuddered at the thought of working at the palace.

It explained why the renter house was so busy though— they must be taking up all the staff.

"That's not happening, Fred," I said firmly.

Freddy eyed me head to toe.

"Clean yourself up first," she said, ignoring my comment. "You're an absolute state!" With that, she turned away and disappeared into the crowd once more.

I made my way to the staircase that led to the rooms above. I raced up the rickety steps, skirting around a couple of other renters that I knew by face only. I got to my room and turned the key as fast as I could.

I breathed a deep sigh of relief as I slammed the thin wooden door shut behind me. Almost on cue, the city bells rang out the hour. The deep clanging bells tolled once, twice, four times in total. I swore under my breath as I pulled off my muddied boots and threw them under my bed. Four am. I hadn't slept in almost eighty hours. I had gone longer than that before, but only once.

My entire body ached, and I could only imagine how bad I looked, I already knew how bad I *smelt*.

Grave digging was physically demanding. None of the other workers had wanted the job, but I had jumped at the chance. It was solitary, and it was safe. Even with the old hedge witch watching over me.

However, I could admit that I had taken on a few too many jobs lately. I was exhausted and shaking and clearly beginning to see things.

In the mornings, I helped load and deliver milk around the city, around noon, I mucked out stalls for a horse and cab company, and then in the last of the daylight, I gathered herbs and plants for Mags and worked in her shop before heading to the graveside for the evening.

I did it for the distraction as much as for the coin.

I hated to admit it, but as much as I needed this money, I was working myself to death.

I peeled off my muddy sweat-soaked clothes and threw them into the washing bowl. I would scrape the muck off them later, ready to wear again tonight. I pulled the last coin from my purse and added it to the small collection in my trunk under the bed.

I dared a quick glance in the mirror as I got back up. My tangled chestnut brown hair that I had messily hacked to my shoulders last week was caked in grime. Golden eyes stared back at me from a sharp angled face covered in dirt, with a large scar running above my left eyebrow. However, if someone walked in now, they would not see the same reflection as I did, they would not see my true reflection. They would find themselves staring at a woman with strawberry blonde hair and watery blue eyes.

If I looked hard enough and long enough, then I could see it too.

It had been about five years since Mags had cast the glamor to change my appearance, five years since anyone other than myself and her had seen my true face.

And six years since I had...

I took in a fast, sharp breath and shook my head, trying to shake the thoughts away with it.

I knew I looked strange, jolting about, but it was one of the techniques Mags had taught me years ago, back when I couldn't rein in my panic attacks or push away the memories of my childhood training. Sometimes these techniques worked, and sometimes I came undone. That was the odd thing about grief and fear, it could rise up inside of me without a moment's warning, and if I didn't take control of it, then *it* took complete control of me.

The talk about the blood guard had me feeling rattled.

I busied myself with filling my clay washbasin. The water was shockingly cold, and while I missed the luxury of a warm bath, here I felt lucky enough just to have a tap in my room.

I scrubbed off the grime that had accumulated over the last three days using lye soap for the stubborn dirt.

Once washed, I threw on a clean nightshirt and collapsed onto my hard wooden bed. Sleep came quickly and with it came the dreams.

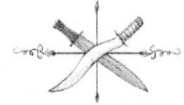

I could hear my little brother crying from his bedroom down the corridor. He must have had another nightmare. I didn't know why Mum agreed to move him out of the nursery already. Four was too young by far, and he was so soft. Just today he cried when the cook killed one of his favourite chickens and then refused to eat it. I had warned him not to name them. He was far too gentle for his own good.

I should check on him.

I could hear that familiar cry, high-pitched and just a little put-on. He did it for my benefit, I was sure.

I don't think I ever cried as much as him when I was small.

Dad taught us to be "as cold as marble and as sharp as Flint." He always used to say that, since it was a play on our name. But

Cian was gentle and sweet, tender-hearted, and a little bit silly, as any small child should be I suppose. I couldn't help but admire how he naturally resisted Father's hard tongue and even harder hands.

I got to Cian's door and found it shut, which was odd, because it was never shut. I pushed hard on the thick wood, but it wouldn't budge.

A shiver of panic ran through my body.

"Cian?"

I pressed my ear to the wood "Cian?" My voice came out sounding muffled and odd. I pushed against the door again. Nothing.

His cry got louder then, so loud that it hurt my ears and reverberated uncomfortably in my chest.

Frustration and fear pounded fast through my veins.

"Cian, open the door!" I demanded, but still my voice was too quiet. He wouldn't be able to hear me.

I slammed my body into the door with all the strength I could muster, but it didn't so much as shake. I jimmied the handle frantically and scratched at the hinges, trying anything to get inside, anything to get to my baby brother. I had to protect him—it was my job.

Suddenly something flooded at my feet, warm and thick. I stood back in disgust and glanced down to see crimson liquid pouring out from under the door frame.

It looked like blood. It smelled like blood.

My scream was silent, my panic uncontrollable now. I bashed on the door with all my strength and twisted the handle until it came off in my hand, useless. I was too weak. I couldn't move the door. I couldn't get in.

I couldn't save him.

"Cian!"

I awoke to familiar, gasping, all-consuming panic. Guilt made me senseless and desperate. I threw the blanket back, jumped from the bed, and ran to the window before I knew what I was doing. Taking large gulps of air, I swept my fingers through my tangled hair manically and obsessively, trying to soothe away this wretched feeling.

It wouldn't go. It was no use. It grew more overwhelming by the second.

He was dead, my beautiful baby brother was dead, and it was because of me. Because of my mistakes and my own cowardice. I was sure of it—at least I was almost completely sure. Nothing could reverse time, and nothing could take me back to six years ago.

The inevitability of it all made me cry out. I sobbed and let myself sink to the floor, shutting my eyes tight and muttering comfort words under my breath. I bunched my hands into fists and crossed my legs, struggling against the fight-or-flight urge to pace or run, knowing already that there was nowhere on this earth that I could go to escape my own gutlessness.

Instead, I counted to fifty, to a hundred, to a billion if it would distract me. The dream had been fiction, a twisted nightmare, I knew this. It was a fact. I needed to repeat it to myself.

The episode ended, finally, how it always ended.

With reluctant acceptance and then reassurance. Telling myself I did what I had to do by leaving that place, that it was for the best. His fate would have been worse if he was alive. Better he was dead and free than alive and trapped as I had been.

And yet, there was a persistent hope, a tiny flicker of a flame in my naïve little heart, kindled and nestled and refusing to snuff out even after all these years. Whispering to me that he might still be alive, reminding me that I had fled before the execution date. Nudging me and goading me to return. I banged a fist hard against my chest, as if to knock away the gnawing feeling, the false hopes. There was nothing waiting for me back in my homelands. Nothing but death… and the guard.

Soundlessly, numbly, I stood. I wiped away the tears, my face set like stone, and walked back to the bed. I climbed under the thin, coarse blanket and stared up at the stained ceiling until, after countless minutes, sleep claimed me again.

Chapter 3

A loud knock woke me.

Half asleep, I rolled out of bed, barely registering the bright sunlight that shone through my dusty windowpane. I unlatched the door and glared daggers at Freddy.

"That's a bit better I suppose" was her only greeting as she took in my straggly hair and cleaned face.

"Come on, the king wants a girl to sing for him, and I have no one left for that job but you."

"Ask Mariette," I said in a haze, naming the most popular prostitute in the renter house and the only name I knew. "She can sing well enough."

"The girl is tone-deaf, and as I said, everyone else is already there, including Mariette. The king's mistress has borne a male heir, and the celebration has been going on for days. There is plenty of money to be had in it."

"An heir from a mistress?" I asked, confused.

Freddy looked at me conspiratorially. "Well, its common knowledge that the foreign queen is sickly, and the king plans to marry his lady once the queen has conveniently died."

"Common knowledge, huh?"

"Well"—Freddy smirked—"common to those with a *common* interest."

I sighed, refusing to take the bait and ask about any twisted schemes she may have planned.

"So, the job?" she pressed.

I ran a hand through my mess of hair, frustrated. I avoided the gentry and aristocracy as much as I could. Freddy knew this, so she had to be desperate.

"Find someone else, Fred," I said as I moved to shut the door, only to find Freddy had jammed her foot between it and the wall. Her face was stern, and her eyes bored into mine.

"There is no one else," she said.

I stared her down, my face a mask of stone. A moment went by like this, then her frown fell.

"I need to keep the palace, bird. My rivals are breathing down my neck, and if I lose the palace, then my highest paying customers will go along with it."

"So, hire another girl, just for tonight. There are many a singer busking the streets who would love the chance."

"You," she spluttered, losing her cool for a moment. "You know I won't employ just anyone off the street, I need reliability, I need a good, respectable worker."

"Respectable? Why in Kingsland did you hire me then?" The silence grew as we both stared at one another, neither willing to back down.

"Fine," she spat. "Do this job, and you can keep all the wages and the tips. Just this once."

I faltered.

I lived day by day, and being able to get a leg up would help. I'd been in the renter house nine months now, and eventually the time would come to move on. That would be a much easier task with coins in my purse.

"Fine," I conceded. "But I won't take this kind of job again, so hire some new blood."

"Good." Freddy seemed to sink a little with relief. "The kings-men are waiting down in the bar now. Change, but don't leave them waiting long. They are in foul moods and have probably drunk more than is good for them." I nodded and shut the door.

What had I gotten myself into?

I ran to the trunk under my bed and freed the key from where I kept it, tucked into my hair with a hairpin. The latch clicked, and I threw it open.

Inside were remnants of old jobs, homes, and kingdoms. I was careful not to keep anything in there that could identify me.

I pulled a forest-green gown out from the very bottom of the trunk. It was slightly faded with age and covered in dust. But the style had recently become popular in Riverna again, so it would do. I stepped into the dress and slipped my arms through the short, gathered sleeves. The front panel of the dress hung down over the skirt and needed to be fastened in place. I found black velvet ribbon in my drawer and threaded it through the hoops, pulling the front panel up so it was flush with my torso. I tied the ribbon tightly, only struggling at the top where it needed to be laced right under my arms. I made my way down to my hips, tightening and adjusting. I had no stays or hoops to wear under the dress, so the shape wasn't quite right—but good enough for a renter girl. I slipped my dagger into a secret pocket that I had sewn into dress previously.

I combed and plaited my hair, then rolled it into a bun, securing it at the base of my neck with pins.

I slipped on my boots, hoping the dress would cover them.

Walking into The Blackmoore Palace looking like a street urchin would do me no favours. I wanted to blend in as much as possible. I had no makeup to rouge my cheeks or lips, but I was presentable enough.

BOUND TO THE CROWN

The entire dressing process took less than twenty minutes, but by the time I descended the staircase, the king's men were yelling at Madame Fredericka, their voices so loud they could be heard over the roar of the pub. I clenched my fists, frustrated by the thought of having to appease the kind of people I had spent the last six years avoiding. Loud. Entitled. Stupid.

Dangerous.

I threaded my way through the punters, moving silently and slicing through the packed room with no resistance.

They were angry that the palace had claimed all the workers.

People were calling out impatiently for cleaners and babysitters, factory workers and escorts. Some threatened to take their business to the renter house on Town Street. However, Town House charged a lot more, had stricter rules in place for punters, and hired practically anyone off the street. This discouraged most of the rabble looking for hard, cheap workers.

By the sound of things many of them were finding solace at the bottom of a tankard.

I spotted Freddy and the kings-men at the far side of the bar. Three men for one renter girl?

The king's men were an odd trio. There was a tall older man with thinning, messy white hair and stubble wearing a basic crimson tunic and leggings and a younger man with a head full of thick copper hair adorned in all the finery of the palace. Medals and ornaments shone from shoulder to shoulder and the entire length of his sleeves. He wore the royal colours of crimson red and canary yellow just like his elder, but his tunic was made of velvet brocade, and it shimmered under the dusty pub lights.

It was he doing the majority of the yelling. I already had him marked as a pompous arse.

The third man was dressed apart from the other two and stood back slightly. I would not have placed them together at all if not the elder man's turning to talk to him. He sported simple black clothes under a thick riding cloak. His long brown hair was tied back neatly with a ribbon and his wide golden-brown eyes flashed from behind the black cloth mask that covered the majority of his face. A practice common among assassins-for-hire, so they could go about in public without losing their identity.

But that didn't make sense to me. Why would they need an assassin to fetch a renter girl?

His body language seemed relaxed, and his stance was almost awkward and juvenile, as though he hadn't finished growing into his long limbs. However, something about the hardness of his mouth and the tension in his jaw told me he was on guard. I noted the sword at his hip—it was longer than the weapons the other two men wore.

He was tall enough to have to bend his head.
I would watch him.

"Oh, here is just the girl," cried Freddy as she saw me approach. Her usual calm was replaced with a slightly manic expression. I raised my eyebrows but said nothing.

"This is Cera." She placed a hand on the small of my back and pushed me forward.

"This is Sir Prue and Sir Halsted," she said, pointing first to the younger guard and then the elder.

"His royal majesty prefers brunettes" was all Prue said as way of greeting, all while eyeing me from head to toe.

"Does it matter how I look?" I asked incredulously.

"It certainly helps," he replied with a smirk.

"In that case, I had better not do it." I turned to walk away, but Freddy pushed harder, joined by two of her floating hands, which each gripped an elbow. I found her uncharacteristic insistence alarming.

"It must be you dear," she stressed, giving me a pointed stare. I frowned.

I glanced up at the elder man, Halsted, but his face was unreadable. I turned to the masked man, looking at him pointedly, but he did not meet my gaze, and no introduction was forthcoming.

I was beginning to feel like this was a huge mistake. Freddy was pushing this too hard. Was she showing her hand, or was this really just a simple singing job she needed filled desperately?

I had a way of reading into things and always expecting the worst, and I usually made it a point to never be coerced into doing jobs that I did not want to do.

I'd had enough of that to last a lifetime.

Looking now at the three men and the unusually manic Freddy, I felt odd and unsettled. My mind went suddenly to the shadow near the edge of the cemetery and the witches warning. Perhaps I should take it to heart and leave. I could feel the familiar panic creeping in at the edge of my mind, as my suspicious thoughts jumped to any and all possible conclusions. Some ridiculous, some more plausible but still concerning.

In only the few minutes it had taken to be introduced to these men, in my mind I had my whole life packed up and ready to flee. Part of me was embarrassed, but I had indulged my cowardly tendencies for the last six years, there was no reason to hide from it now.

I could be across the border and into the wastelands in less than a week.

It was the perfect place to be forgotten, but it was also full of cutthroats and crime with no policing. I preferred organised chaos over full blown disarray. Plus, there was Mags to think of—she had already followed me so many places, abandoned so many plans…

BOUND TO THE CROWN

"Bird?" Freddy pressed.
"Coming," I answered firmly, feigning calm.
 I think it was past time to get paid and get gone.

Chapter 4

The drive to the palace was an uncomfortable one.

Opposite me sat the pompous guard, Sir Prue, in a four-person carriage lined entirely in red velvet. The two other kings-men rode on horses alongside us, and I caught glimpses of them trotting along from out of the small, curtain lined widow beside me.

Sir Prue did not shut up. He waffled on for the entire journey, telling me about what the king was like, how the king himself had given him two of his medals, how the "foreign" queen was stuck up and a bore. How hard it was to get good workers. I looked out the window the whole time, making a point not to engage him, but apparently my interest wasn't necessary. It was almost a relief when we reached the gatehouse. The horses slowed as we passed through the large, white stone walls into the outer courtyard.

The sun was full in the sky now. It bounced blindingly off the white-stained bricks and the ornate marble fountain carved into the shape of a merwoman embracing a lover that took pride of place in the courtyard.

I pulled the sash down on the window closest to me and stuck my arm through to unlatch the carriage door. Sir Prue looked at me reproachfully.

"That is the job of the footmen," he complained as I pushed it open. I shrugged and jumped down onto the mounting block just as an out-of-breath footman placed it. The sooner I got inside, the sooner I could get my money and go. I was already regretting my acquiescence.

I felt a tug and realised my dress was snagged on a wheel spoke. I yanked at it hastily, and it tore, exposing my boots. I swore loudly in frustration.

Being in stately places like this one made me feel flustered and impatient. I wasn't even inside yet, but the anticipation of the kind of people I would meet within the castle walls already filled me with dread.

It reminded me too much of home.

Military men and knights were parading around the outer bailey in full uniform with swords held aloft, and I could make out more soldiers patrolling along the battlements above. The sound of their synchronised footsteps pounding down on stone pavement filled me with nostalgia and discomfort in equal measures.

The castle itself was a fortress, with turrets and towers of white brick that seemed to disappear up into the clouds.

The carriage door on Sir Prue's side clicked shut, and I looked back down, realising that the probably-an-assassin was in front of me, watching.

He unmounted his horse, handing it off to a waiting stable worker. I met his eyes with a challenge, and the corner of his mouth went up in amusement. He leaned forward and untangled my dress from the stirrup effortlessly

"A talented singer and graceful as well—I can see why Freddy recommended you," he said. His voice was filled with humour, and I frowned at the mocking tone.

"You should see what I can do with a knife," I warned, flashing him the hilt of my blade concealed at my hip in the folds of my dress. He practically beamed at this and dipped his head in acknowledgment before stepping back. I noticed again how young he looked. There was something annoyingly friendly and almost familiar in his wide, mischievous smile. Still, I didn't appreciate being openly mocked. I needed to let this kid know that underestimating me would be a mistake. He was no longer the only assassin in this courtyard.

Prue and the older guard, Sir Halsted, led the way up stone steps and into the inner courtyard and from there into the castle itself.

At some point as we passed through corridors lined with tapestries and portraits, the assassin disappeared, melting away into the stonework as though he had never been there.

The halls were busy, and we passed many courtiers as we walked. They were dressed in a strange mix of conservative finery or titillating nakedness with no in-between. We passed a room where a group of women sat on a rug in front of a large fireplace, giggling and watching a naked man dance. They themselves were dressed head to toe in gowns of a similar style to mine, restrictive and lavish, mostly in shades of red and yellow.

The further in we went, the more chaotic the scenes became, the louder the orchestral music.

I was somewhat surprised to see a look of distaste on Prue's face as a curvy woman, wearing only a bedsheet, flitted past us laughing. He saw me staring.

"Revels are one thing, but I for one cannot wait for this debauchery to calm," he said.

"Prue will feel much better once the false queen is gone and the rightful queen is on her throne," explained

Halsted. His words seemed in earnest, but when I caught his eye, he winked at me conspiratorially.

"That sounds a little like treason," I muttered, surprised. None of them seemed to hear me though.

"I am just concerned," explained Prue. "It isn't secure, a child born out of wedlock. It isn't *secure*."

Halsted grunted, but I wasn't sure if it was in agreement or dismissal.

Where I came from, people wouldn't have dared talk about things such as this, not in the corridors of the palace anyway. I wondered for a moment if maybe this king was more lenient on his people, or perhaps gossip was more favoured in this court.

Finally, we reached the end of the corridor, and I was faced with two large doors made from beautifully carved wood. Four more guards stood before us, and they waved us in without a word. The sounds of string music and laughter were almost deafening, echoing around the large throne room. Men's voices rose in slurred song.

The smell of cooked meat was heavy in the air, making my stomach growl, and I homed in on the long tables, filled to bursting with platters of food and bottles of wine. Lit with candles and decorated with flowers and vines in varying shades of blue. My stomach growled again as I stared at the pastries and cakes. I watched as a drunk man wrapped in nothing but a Riverna flag dug his hand into a large exquisitely decorated cake, dripping with chocolate. He ate the decadent mess straight from his hand, laughing as he dropped some onto the marble floor.

I took an involuntary step forward, eager to try some of the food myself, only to stop when a spindly hand grabbed my upper arm forcefully. I looked at my assailant. An older woman glared down at me. Her face was long and pointed, and her black hair was pulled tight into a bun at the top of her head. She wore no jewellery, but there was something very stern and regal about her. She had huge black eyes and delicate, thin lips.

"The rented help do not eat," she said calmly. "Is she for the king?" the woman asked the guards over my head.

"I am here to sing," I answered firmly.

Her eyes flicked down to me, and she gave me a once-over, taking in my shabby look, torn dress and large boots. She looked disapproving but let go of my arm regardless.

"Good luck," whispered Halsted, I turned to him, and he looked sincere. Both he and Prue bowed slightly to the woman before turning their backs and moving to speak to an attendant who stood at a podium by the doors. The attendant looked frazzled. He had a bright pink wig on his head that had slid too far left. I watched as he crossed something out on a list that looked like it would hit the floor if unrolled.

"I am the Lady Scarlet, his majesty's head of household." The woman introduced herself, raising her head proudly and shooting me a superior look. She obviously expected me to be impressed. I took a pointed glance at the chaos around us. Lady Scarlet didn't seem the type to be proud of an orgy, but I suppose even an orgy needed to be planned.

"You will not speak unless spoken to," she continued "Even then, do not speak out of turn. Do not offend His Majesty, do only as you are asked to do, exactly as asked. Sing until you are dismissed and then you may see if any others want your services, with the king's permission."

"Look," I said. "You don't need to worry about me. I am singing, I am getting paid, then I am getting out of here." Lady Scarlet's eyes narrowed sternly, and her thin lips melded together in disapproval.

"You will stay until the revel is over or until you are dismissed," she repeated.

I shrugged, and Lady Scarlet seemed to think that was confirmation enough for now.

"Sirs Prue and Halsted have signed you in at the door, so now you are to go through the great hall to the throne room, anon. Wait to be called forward, go to your knees and do not move until told. Then you may join the orchestra. His majesty misliked the last singer, so I suggest you do better than her."

I sensed that I didn't want to know what happened to the last singer. Lady scarlet held her hand out for me to go ahead. The rooms were set out in three tiers, each open to one another through wide gold filigree doors. This being the first, and the great hall came next, which was full of dancing couples swirling and gyrating chaotically. Most of them looked dead on their feet, and I remembered Freddy saying the revel had gone on for three days already.

The walls were mostly glass panels framed with brassy gold. I could see beyond into the court gardens, where gardeners dressed in overalls and large wicker hats were tending to purple tulip gardens, trimming shaped topiaries and sweeping up a river of pink blossoms that had fallen from the trees. It was a stark contrast to the chaos inside. The ceilings above were dominated by crystal chandeliers, all wider than the carriage that had brought me in.

I made my way through the great hall, silent as a ghost as I weaved through the dancers.

The shift from great hall to the throne room was alarming, and as soon as I stepped over the threshold, all the warmth of the room before vanished to cold. My body tensed, and I felt hyperaware of the space around me. A large circular room with white marbled floors and a blood red dais that looked as though it had been carved from ice.

I turned all my attention to that dais where the Throne of Rivera sat and upon it their king.

I wasn't sure what I was expecting, but a short, thin man with wispy white-blond hair and wrinkled skin was not it. I had met the old king many times before, the nephew of this one. He had been very young, not even fourteen, when he inherited the throne from his father. A short, bloody reign ensued.

Henri wore a huge robe, much too big for his tiny frame. It was deep red and trimmed with gold. He sat back in his throne that looked as though it had been carved from the same white marble of the floors, shot through with gold and silver veins that sparkled under the chandeliers.

Sitting next to the king, on a significantly smaller throne, was a woman I could only presume was the "sickly" queen. I felt a twinge of sympathy as I looked at her. She was a small thing with long, elegant features, her light brown hair was pulled loosely away from her face in a plated braid, and a thin circlet of gold shone around her brow. Her head was down as she stared at the floor. Thin and small, she looked barely grown.

I approached the dais and went to my knees before them, not wanting to draw this out. I didn't wait until I was summoned forward.

King Henri looked at me with hooded eyes as he swayed slightly on his throne, clearly struggling to stay awake. He said nothing, and I was greeted instead by a small round man with puffed-out cheeks and dark hair that stuck to the sweat on his red face. He was dressed in bold colours, pink, red and orange, with a large, exaggerated collar. He was likely a jester or entertainer of the king.

"Look my lord! Another renter girl has come." He stepped over to me, bent down to my level and laughed loudly in my face. Spittle flew and narrowly missed me. His exaggerated smile faded when I neither flinched nor complained.

"What slum did they dig you from, rented girl?" he asked, looking me up and down as though he was disgusted by me. I ignored him and instead noticed the man stood at the king's right, a man I knew to be the old king's seneschal, and by the looks of it, he had managed to keep his job somehow.

"Leave her be, Thistle," said the seneschal. To me, he asked, "Your purpose here?"

"I am here to sing," I said. At this, the queen looked up from her feet and searched my face with large, pale blue eyes. She looked sick and weary, but her beauty was remarkable.

The seneschal smiled falsely and looked to the king, who was busy downing the last dregs from a bone tankard. He looked oblivious, frail, old and easy to kill. I pursed my lips, frustrated by my own murderous thoughts. Those days were long behind me.

"At last, we have a new singer. Do you wish to hear this woman, my king?" asked the seneschal. He was greeted with silence as the king motioned for an attendant to refill his tankard.

"I wish to hear." The queen spoke up. The seneschal frowned oddly, as though he wasn't used to hearing the queen voice her wants, but he nodded at me nonetheless before standing back.

"You may rise," the queen instructed gently. At this, the king suddenly roared and threw his tankard to the ground in front of me. It broke into pieces, scattering bone fragments at my feet. I took a fast step backwards to avoid the sharp shards.

"I say rise! Not you!" he bellowed in a voice that didn't sound like it could come from such a frail body. The queen flinched and nodded. Unmoved by the display, I stared at the king, who was now panting as though he had run for miles.

"Well, rise," he commanded me. His watery eyes were unfocused and rolling around in his skull as he spoke, as though he was trying hard to look at me but couldn't figure out where I was. By the time I stood, he was slumped back in his chair, seemingly asleep. The room was silent in their uncertainty for a moment, and even the orchestra and the dancers had stopped. Then the rooms filled with the sound of the king's loud, uneven snores.

For another beat, everyone was still, then the queen spoke.

"What songs do you know?" Her voice quivered slightly, and I felt the small bud of unwelcome sympathy bloom larger in my chest.

"What would your majesty like to hear?" I asked.

She glanced nervously over at the unconscious king.

"Stanza seven is my favourite. It should be in the book." She motioned to the orchestra behind me.

I nodded and turned to join the large orchestra, made up of at least sixty men and women and consisting of many instruments, some I had never seen before. Pipes, flutes and stringed instruments made from wood and bone and animal sinew. Two grand pianos, one stained white the other black, faced one another.

They were all seated in the great hall, raised on a wooden dais that looked as though it had been knocked up for the occasion.

I realised then that from the throne room you could look down on the other rooms, seeing them almost in their entirety. It must be on a slant, angled up. I could see the dancers waiting and swaying from drink, and exhaustion, the food tables beyond with people gathered around. All were staring forward at me, waiting for the music to start. I stepped up onto the dais and took my place near a podium where the singer before me had obviously stood. I flicked through the programme until I found stanza seven. I read the music and soon recognised the tune. I had heard it somewhere before.

I nodded at the frazzled instructor, who began the music right away.

The familiar notes lifted my heart. It was comforting, painful, bittersweet. I must have heard this song in my childhood.

Quietly at first, I began to sing. The notes were low to start and hard for me to hold onto, but as the verse moved into chorus I got the hang of it, and the lyrics flowed through me. The song was beautiful, a romantic tragedy. I had not sung in a while, and I had forgotten the joy it brought me.

When this song finished, I flipped the page and continued singing. This song was a bawdy tune, something to dance to, and I found myself wanting to laugh along with the cheeky lyrics.

Time flew by as I went from song to song. We reached the end of the programme, and the instruction signalled for me to go back to the start, a slow, quiet ballad about a widow mourning her young husband.

Suddenly a loud, vulgar snore ripped through the song, causing several people to jump and then laugh nervously.

The spell was broken, and I remembered where I was and why. The king continued to snore, and I realised most of the room was empty. The exhausted partygoers must have taken their chance to slip out while the king slept.

The queen stood from her throne and clapped enthusiastically, solely. There were tears in her eyes, and I felt a small bit of pride at having touched her.

The conductor tapped at the podium sharply and began to play music again, this one an instrumental.

I stood, listening politely, but impatiently as I watched the seneschal oversee a group of men lifting the intoxicated king and half carry, half drag him out of the room.

Thankfully that seemed to be the signal to end the party for good, and the music faded out. Of the few dancing couples that remained, many had simply fallen to the floor where they had been stood and were now fast asleep, or perhaps unconscious.

The musicians began packing up around me, complaining under their breaths about calluses and bleeding fingers. The speed at which the room began to empty and the servants began to clean was actually quite impressive. The renters formed a dishevelled line towards the podium near the door that I had spotted earlier. They collected their wages and were gone as quick as possible.

As I stepped down from the stage, I narrowly missed being knocked off my feet by a child with a sweeping brush. They raced the length of the room, gathering the dirt.

The sun was burning in the sky now, turning the room into a sort of greenhouse. I moved to join the line, anxious to get paid and get gone.

Suddenly a large arm shot out and curled around my waist from behind, pulling me into a soft, too warm body.

"Don't hurry away yet, renter. I have need of your *services*," hissed a voice in my ear, I grimaced at the hot, wet breath on my neck and the sickly voice of the king's jester. Without hesitation, I grabbed the slippery fingers and bent them back as far as they would go. I smiled as I felt the satisfying crack of the bones snapping. I turned quickly, twisting the arm round as I went, and kicked the man's legs from under him. Thistle was half on the floor. He yelped and cried out in pain, begging me to let him go. For a moment I considered breaking his arm also, but I released him as I began to sense the shocked gaze of the musicians upon me. Thistle cradled his hand and spat profanities at me from the floor as I walked away wordlessly, stepping down hard on his leg as I went.

My satisfaction was short lived as I could hear hurried footsteps behind me, getting faster and closer. I stopped dead and cursed myself in frustration. I knew that resisting would only make it worse.

"Stop her!"

Chapter 5

As I got to the back of the ever-decreasing line, I found my way barred by the queen. Her black eyes were glowing with excitement. For a moment I forgot myself and just stared at her, confused. Then I remembered myself with help from a well-timed cough, no doubt from the newly reappeared Lady Scarlet. I had a feeling she could sense trouble out like a bloodhound. Slowly, reluctantly, I went to my knee, hoping that my show of submission would help this interaction move along faster.

"That was quite a display of strength," said the queen. "What is your name?"

"Cera," I answered.

"No family name?" she pressed, I remained silent. "An orphan, perhaps?"

An orphan I almost certainly was, but I simply shook my head.

"Your singing was beautiful," she continued, unconcerned. "I would like to hear more."

"Thank you," I replied, hoping she wouldn't push the matter. The quiet stretched, until the queen, no doubt sensing my reluctance, placed a hand on my shoulder and said, "Come to my entrance room, I would like to listen there."

She then turned and walked away, leaving Lady Scarlet to grab my upper arm forcefully. I cursed under my breath, already knowing what was to come.

"If you want to be paid, you will stay until dismissed," Lady Scarlet hissed in my ear as we began an awkward shuffle of coercion and reluctance behind the queen.

I noticed as we walked that this queen was universally misliked. The remaining guests barely acknowledged her, bowing slightly, moving away quickly. She had no attendants, no maids, and no one but the lady and me followed her through the sunlit halls.

We passed many frantic attendants looking dishevelled and tired, carrying stacks of dirty trays or mops and buckets.

Lady Scarlet kept a grip on my arm, like she thought I was going to run. Which, to be fair, I was considering.

But the idea of going through all this ridiculousness, having to bow, and then not even getting paid left a nasty taste in my mouth.

We wound our way down many corridors, out through a small, pagoda-covered courtyard that led to another corridor inside, up a wide staircase carpeted with worn-down rugs before reaching a large, gilded door. After an awkward amount of time, the doors were opened by a guard, and we walked into an opulent entrance room.

"Leave us now, please," the queen addressed lady scarlet, who let go of my arm, bowed slightly and walked out. I had a feeling she would be standing behind that door until I left.

"Follow me." The queen led us through into her bedroom. She went straight to her canopied bed and sat down on the edge, fanning her skirt out gracefully on the embroidered covers.

The door shut quietly behind us then, and I heard the click of a lock, but I refused to look behind to see who else was with us. I could already guess who it would be.

The queen levelled her gaze at me.

"Your name is Cera?" she asked, her voice shaking slightly, her tone more genuine than when we were in the halls/ "Freddy sent you here?" she asked. I nodded slowly, apprehensively.

"That's right," I said, "and I am beginning to guess that you don't actually want me to sing for you."

"Correct," she said, confirming my suspicions. "Freddy said you were quick, so let me get to the point," she continued as she leaned forward. "I am in danger."

"Yes, you are." I agreed simply, without hesitation. It wasn't hard to see that her reign would be a short one if things carried on the way they were going.

"I am not wanted by the people of Rivera, nor by its king. I am a failure, I suppose. But then, I wonder if I was sent here specifically to be a failure." Her voice cracked a bit as she said this, and her hands were fidgeting wildly in her lap. "I have sent letters to my brother, the current ruler of my homeland, for help. I asked him to send his men to escort me home. However, he has denied me." She paused for a moment, as if trying to process her brother's abandonment all over again. I felt sorry for her. She had clearly been thrown in above her head and used as a pawn in her brother's political games. "He said it would start a war if I were to leave," she continued, "Presumably, it would also start a war if I were to be killed by my husband. I suppose my brother doesn't mind that as much." She sniffed and swallowed hard, fighting back tears. The young man in the mask who had helped collect me from the renter house slunk out from behind me then and wordlessly handed the queen a black handkerchief. She stared up at him apologetically. "Sorry, Kohl. I know I said I would try to be brave," she said with a regretful smile.

His dark golden gaze met mine then, and I forced myself to look back stoically, my face blank. I had guessed he hadn't gone far. If he had expected me to be shaken by his presence, then I was happy to disappoint. I smiled slightly, and he furrowed his brow.

"I don't particularly want to die," she carried on after wiping her face. "I need someone to help me. I *need* help." I looked pointedly at the very tall, foreboding man standing right next to her "Someone inconspicuous," she elaborated. "My guard cannot be compromised. He is all I have from my homeland, and my husband does not know about him. I need someone who can be with me all the time."

It was then that I began to understand and piece together what was happening. The king had not sent for me at all. I hadn't imagined the way Freddy pushed me into this job. None of this was about singing or keeping up with demand. It was about the queen.

"You want protection." It was a statement.

The queen's face lit up. It looked more childlike than ever. "So you will do it?" she asked. It cannot be a man, you see." She inclined her head to her masked guard. "It must be a woman and a fighter. Freddy said you were the strongest person she had seen, man or woman."

What an idiot I had been. I knew there was a chance Freddy was watching me. I knew she was giving me jobs usually set aside for men. What a fool. "Please understand this has not been easy to fix," the queen continued desperately, obviously sensing my anger. "I will make you richer than you can imagine. All my gold, trinkets, jewels. Everything I have in my possession here can be yours. All I need is for you to keep me alive long enough for my brother to see sense." I looked at her doubtfully. "He does love me. I'm sure he will come around."

"How sure are you? if he knows how you are being treated, why hasn't he intervened?" I asked, sceptically.

"I don't think he wants to risk a war," she said. "I know he will do something, but I think he is just waiting for the right time, waiting until…" She trailed off, unsure.

"Until you are assassinated?" I finished "So he can go to war pretending to be the great hero, liberating this city of its murderous king?" I guessed.

"No!" she cried "I don't think he wants me actually killed or why would he have sent his man to protect me?" She gripped the masked man's sleeve, holding onto it as though he was her lifeline.

"We think he has to wait until a public attempt is made, just enough so that he can invade and collect her with reasonable cause," Kohl said, speaking up for the first time.

"Reasonable cause?" I laughed "What about that is reasonable?"

"Look, I don't know what the plans are. Maybe the king will divorce me if I ask. He is desperate for an heir, and now he has one, potentially. I don't know if my brother will save me or if my fate is already written and this is all in vain. I do know that I am in want of a permanent guard, someone that has no allegiance to my husband, someone strong, like you. Freddy told me you would be that person."

I shook my head solemnly and took a firm step closer to the locked door behind me. I felt for this woman. I couldn't help it, she was desperate enough to run to Freddy, and I could see the fear and anxiety she was trying to hide. I could see it in her ridged shoulders, in the way she rocked slightly back and forth as she sat, in her furrowed brow and the smudges under her eyes, but I wasn't in a position to help her. I could barely help myself.

"He doesn't look like much," she said quietly, looking down at her small, shaking hands. "King Henri." She looked up again, tears streaming down her cheeks unchecked now. "But you don't become king here and stay king without having a lust for violence and bloodshed." Her voice wobbled. "He isn't kind. The things I have seen him do…" She trailed off and looked up at me in earnest. "I am scared, Cera. I am scared to move, scared to sleep, scared to eat. I cannot do this anymore."

"I need time to think," I heard myself say.

"There is no time," Kohl snapped, his voice sharp. "I cannot let you decline this offer," he said meaningfully. The queen looked uncomfortable, her eyes flicking to the thin blade at her guard's hip.

Ah, of course.

I couldn't help it—I laughed aloud at the threat.

"My lady, If I decide to decline, there is nothing your friend could do to stop me."

"Good." Kohl let his cloak drop back, covering his blade. "I hope your confidence is rooted in skill and not ego."

"I haven't agreed to anything at all," I reminded him.

"Neither have you declined."

We were at a standoff. He wasn't wrong though. I hadn't declined. I knew that I should, but something was stopping me. I needed to analyse my hesitation. Was it sympathy? Was it my self-destructive tendencies? Or did some small part of me still crave violence? I couldn't deny that it had felt amazing to break thistle's fingers earlier. I had a nasty habit of wanting to show everyone how capable and strong I was. It was in direct contrast to everything I was fighting for.

Suddenly a bell tolled loudly from somewhere in the depths of the palace, and as though on cue, there was a sharp rap at the door.

Kohl slunk away into the shadows. The queen rubbed the tears from eyes and brushed the wrinkles out of her skirts. "Enter," she cried once satisfied. After a beat, I moved to the door and unlatched the lock.

In stepped two female attendants carrying gold trays. One was stacked with food and the other a teapot, water jug and several cups.

The sweet fragrant smell was like a kick in the stomach to me.

Wordlessly they placed the trays down on the footstool at the end of the bed, bowed their heads ever so slightly, and went to walk away.

"Wait," the queen barked. They came back reluctantly.

"Both of you, taste the food and drink the tea."

This they did without hesitation, one breaking off a small amount of pastry and popping it into her mouth, the other pouring a drop of tea into one of the glass cups and sipping it.

The queen stared at both of them in silence, time stretching for what felt like an age.

I watched the teapot, mesmerized by the steam curling from its dainty spout.

Eventually, the queen waved her hand, releasing the attendants, who both scurried away.

I locked the door behind them.

"I fell very sick last week after eating a meal. I mistrust them now," she explained, as though I needed an explanation to the obvious.

The trays were stacked with crunchy parcels made of flaky pastry, coated in nuts, drizzled with honey and stuffed with soft, silky cheeses. The pot was filled with a light orange, citrus-scented tea, and next to it was a glass decanter of deep red wine.

The queen held her hand out in invitation, and I practically fell on the food, taking large bites and drinking a cup of tea it one go. It burnt my throat.

Why did I do this to myself? Deprive myself of basic needs until I felt ill. It was a habit forced in my childhood training that I just couldn't break.

Always testing myself, always pushing myself to the limit.

Never good enough.

I bit into the soft parcels, and the pastry melted in my mouth. The cheese was sharp, but the sweet honey balanced it out.

"Eat as much as you like, eat it all."

I looked up at the queen. Her tone was filled with concern, her brows furrowed as she watched me eat. I didn't like the show of worry on face. I finished the parcel I was eating and left the rest.

"So, what now?" I asked.

The queen glanced at her guard, who had reappeared from his hiding place, then back up at me, eyes hopeful

"If you agree—"

"—She must," interrupted the guard.

"*If* you agree," the queen continued, looking at her assassin pointedly. "Then by all appearances, you will become my lady-in-waiting. A renter girl with a beautiful voice, it will be easy for others to believe I formed an attachment to you, that I want to take you under my wing. In that guise, you will be able to be by my person at all times. I will teach you what to do—most of it is smiling, bowing, and agreeing with whatever the higher court members say."

All the things I hated.

"I can't pay you much to begin with," she admitted nervously. "I get a very large stipend, of course, but my husband watches it carefully. You *will* be paid though, and when I am back home you will have all you can dream of and a place at court, if you wish."

The job was high risk, the kind of job I avoided at all costs. However, the money was tempting. I had almost nothing stored away, and I couldn't go back to the renter's house and Freddy, not after a betrayal like this. Not now that I knew for sure that she had been watching me. Could I? No. The beauty of the renter house was that I was in control and inconspicuous. Maybe if Freddy hadn't been so secretive, then I would have felt differently, but she clearly thought the threat of this assassin would keep me in line, and that didn't sit right with me. I took a quick look around the room. The silver hairbrush on the queen's nightstand alone would be worth more than triple what I had saved away in my pockets.

If the queen survived, or even if she didn't, there would be money in this kind of job. Money enough to be done. Money enough to be completely free of these lands. I could get off this island, go across the seas to a completely new world and never have to think about the blood guard, or my past again.

"I have many questions," I said finally.

"We have time to answer them," the guard replied.

"What happens if your brother never comes?" I ask.

"Then I will escape," said the queen with passion "There is nothing here for me. I would rather be poor and inconsequential than rich and abused."

I scoffed. "Spoken like an entitled fool who has never been poor and starving."

She hung her head, and for a moment, I felt ashamed for my harsh words.

"If… when you leave, take me with you. I can't sell your trinkets here," I said, gentler.

"Of course, you are free to come and join my court!"

"I don't want that. I don't want to be some sycophant to your brother king. I need your word that I will be free to go wherever I wish."

"Of course," she said, sounding offended by my disbelief. I looked to the guard, and after a time, he nodded also.

I had all but agreed. They knew it and so did I, but there was one more thing to do. I had to see Mags, I had to get her thoughts. I had to know her opinion.

"I need to get my belongings from the rent house," I said.

"We will arrange for someone to bring your things," said Kohl.

No way in hell was some random person going through my trunk.

"That's not happening. Let me go back and settle my affairs. It won't take more than an evening."

"No," said the guard firmly. I looked to the queen instead, frustrated by how stubborn the guard was being. I wasn't going to be ordered around. I could understand their apprehension, but it was wasted here.

"Why would I run? Just let me get my stuff and say goodbye to my friends."

She seemed the soppy kind, the kind to have a lot of empathy. And sure enough, she looked up at the guard. "I'm sure we cou—"

"No. Everything you need will be collected."

"Or you could just believe in my word that I will come back. There needs to be some trust between us," I said.

"Trust is earnt," replied the guard through gritted teeth.

"That's true," I replied, nodding. I stepped over towards the window and looked out. Sunlight danced off the water in the ornamental lakes and ponds that permeated the colourful gardens below. It was beautiful.

"That's very true," I said again. "Trust is earnt."

Then I jumped.

Chapter 6

I sat on a worn cushion with my feet soaking in a bucket of foul-smelling hot water. It had been thrust on me by Mags the moment I stepped into her hut. I had learned by now not to question her. She busied herself around her small home, muttering to herself as she searched her stacks and stacks of dust-covered shelves, shuffling through bottles of all colours and sizes. They were all filled with dubious contents that I told myself, with as much conviction as I could muster, were dried herbs, chutneys and syrups.

"A witch visited me," she said suddenly as she pulled a small bone from her hair and used it to stir something suspiciously chunky in a rounded pink jar before placing it back onto the shelf.

"Oh, a friend of yours?" I asked.

"Of yours." She smiled slyly.

"Mine?"

"Yes, an old dead-watcher, a hedge witch and nothing more. She sought me out and told me to give you this." She pulled a small leather pochette tied with a little brown ribbon from her pocket.

"I daren't say no. She seemed very stubborn. It has no malicious energy, so I think it's good to go, whatever it is." She tossed it over to me, and I caught it, examining the small purse in my hands. The old witch didn't seem to have any good feeling towards me, so I have no idea why she had sought Mags out. There was no point trying to figure out how she knew Mags or how she found her. Witches, true witches, had a way of just knowing things. Five years ago, Mags had found me in the middle of the forests that bordered the midlands. Half-dead, completely starved and consumed with my own grief and shame, I hadn't wanted to go on. I didn't have the strength to. Then came Mags with bones and sticks in her cornrowed hair, a robe of sage green, decorated with buttons, knitting needles and all manner of herbs and bric-a-brac. She had the warmest smile I had ever seen and purple eyes that twinkled like they were filled with stars. Someone else might have been scared of eyes like that. But to me she was a vision. She had kneeled in the dirt with me, stroked back my hair and tears and whispered words of comfort in languages I had never heard. Then when I was calm, she had taken my hand, looked me dead in the eyes and said, "I have seen you coming. I have waited for you." She knew my real name, and she knew who I was and what I had done. She'd taken me in and saved me.

I'd stayed in her home until I could no longer stand the debt I owed to her. But she was always near, regardless.

Every time I moved to a new town or city, she would show up sooner rather than later. In a shop or a tent, and once in a hut made from sticks. I took as much comfort in it as I did guilt.

Mags sang under her breath as she sat down next to me on the cushion. I listened, realising after a while that it was the first song that I had performed for the queen earlier today. The one I had recognised. It was still familiar to me now, but I couldn't place it.

"How are your feet, Cera?" Mags asked when she reached the end of her tune.

"Fine."

"You shouldn't jump from windows without wearing proper footwear" She laughed.

"It's fine, Mags." I didn't ask how she knew, and I would never admit to it aloud, but I had misjudged the distance quite badly. I thought we were only two floors up, but the palace must have been deceiving, like in the throne room, because it had been a very long drop, and I hadn't landed as gracefully as planned. It wouldn't have been so bad if I hadn't also had to run away the very moment I hit the floor to make sure no one caught me.

"So, what do you think?" I prompted.

"About the job proposal? Of course you should do it. It is your destiny." She said this so simply, as though we were talking about the weather and not a complete change in my career path.

"Just like that, huh." I laughed "I don't believe in destiny." She smiled knowingly.

"Believe in it or no, it comes unbidden," she said.

I rolled my eyes. *Witches.*

"You have already made your mind up to do it," she said. "I saw that same look in your eyes when you told me your plans to move into the rent house, and before that when we moved from the port town to Riverna."

"Don't you ever get tired of following me around?" I asked her, feeling guilty.

"No." She looked at my cryptically. "Every step you take leads us closer to where we need to be." I shot her a quizzical look, and she leaned in closer.

"Be warned though," she continued, her face suddenly serious, her dark purple eyes piercing mine. "This path is a difficult one."

"Yet, you would still bid me gone?" I asked, matching her tone and letting a little of my apprehension show. She nodded.

"I would. I do, and so does he." She looked pointedly in the direction of the doorway where the queen's guard now stood, looking fairly unimpressed and slightly out of breath.

"Oh, hello," I said, surprised to see him.

"Hello?!" he repeated incredulously.

"Would you like some tea?" asked Mags.

"No, I would like to wring her neck," he said, staring daggers at me. He didn't look very composed now.

"That's not nice," I observed.

"I'll get some tea," said Mags, rising and going to the kettle.

"Have you come to escort me to get my things?" I asked innocently. "Wait, how are you here, anyway?" I wondered, suddenly wary. There was no way he could have followed me from the palace. I was too fast.

"Did you really think I would bring just anyone off the street to help guard my queen?" Kohl laughed. "I have been following you for weeks."

"Well, I don't like that," I said, completely stunned. Weeks? My skin prickled in discomfort. How had I not noticed Freddy and this kid-guard plotting and scheming around me for *weeks*? *What* a failing. Mags was pouring saffron tea from a crystal kettle into painted porcelain cups, seemingly unconcerned by this revelation.

"Did you know?" I asked her suspiciously.

"Of course."

"Thanks for sharing that with me!"

"It must have slipped my mind." She shrugged, unworried, and handed the cups to me and the guard, who sniffed his suspiciously.

"While I remember, I should inform you that he is not alone," Mags continued. I looked to the guard, who was now staring at Mags in some surprise. "There is another watching."

"How could you know?" he asked her.

"I am a witch," she said simply. I looked back and forth between them both.

"Is this *watcher* here too?" I snapped. Kohl did not meet my gaze.

"My ally is a shadow," he said eventually. "He is not meant to be here, and the secret isn't mine to tell." Well, that was ominous.

I was alarmed, and beginning to second guess the choice I was making here. I was very aware that the benefits didn't seem to outweigh the cons of this job, and that my reasons for doing it were murky at best, and completely fucking destructive at worst.

Yet, something about being around Mags always calmed me, like she knew exactly how everything would pan out. If she wasn't alarmed, then I would try not to be. I trusted her.

"Best get going the both of you," Mags said cheerly, interrupting the growing tension. "Your queen is alone, is she not?"

Kohl sighed and made his way to the door, stopping and gesturing at me impatiently.

I hugged Mags goodbye, and she reminded me of the pouch I had been gifted. It had completely slipped my mind. I grabbed it from the cushion and tucked it up into my sleeve.

"Will I see you soon?" I asked her, suddenly feeling apprehensive.

"Soon enough."

I leaned in, lowering my voice. "This feels like a misstep."

"You don't need me to make your decisions," she chuckled affectionately, knowing I needed more confirmation of my actions. "What do you think is right?"

"I think I have stayed here in these city walls longer than I should have, and it's time to move on," I said steadily. "I also think a good part of that is because I don't want to uproot you again." Mags smiled at me in the silence, her eyes crinkled and bright. I had no idea how old she was. Her face was a mystery—she could be twenty, she could be fifty. The longer you stared at a person like Mags, the more you would see. Right now, I saw the woman I had grown to think of as my family, my sister, my confidant. And it unsettled me how much I was unwilling to move on from her comfort.

"I will be along, Cera, don't you worry," she said finally.

"I will get away to see you again, soon," I promised, hoping it was true. She nodded and walked with me to the door, ushering me and Kohl out into the sunlit streets.

The guard looked at me mistrustingly before downing the last of his tea and handing the cup back to Mags with his thanks.

"Take her to get her things, boy. She will be loyal to those that are loyal to her," Mags said sternly. He didn't look convinced.

"We are almost there anyway. You can be my chaperone," I said sarcastically.

He grunted his acquiescence and slunk down a side street without another word.

"He's a one to watch," I muttered. Mags laughed, took a tight hold on my hands for a few seconds and then backed away inside her hut.

Halfway down the road, I was met with a carriage in my way, I backed off to give it room to pass, but instead the door was opened next to me. Halsted popped his head out.

"I'm under orders to collect you," he said with a smile. I rolled my eyes but stepped up anyway. Prue was in the carriage also. He looked at me awkwardly.

"Seems our queen has taken a liking to you, girl," Halsted said when I settled in opposite him, and the carriage began its rickety journey along the cobblestones.

"She liked my voice," I said, noncommittally.

"I heard it too, very beautiful. Just make sure you watch yourself, what with the new heir and everything." I looked up at him. It was clear he thought he was sincerely giving me advice.

"I don't know about royalty or successions," I said. "I do as I am paid to do."

It took a half hour to get back to the renter house by road and not a word was spoken the rest of the way. For a moment, after getting out of the carriage, I felt a wave of apprehension come over me and maybe a little regret. I could probably stop this now and stay at the renter house where I was safe and somewhat happy. Where I didn't have to answer to anyone or put myself in mortal danger. Yet, I couldn't shake the image of the queen's dismayed face from earlier, filled with tears and the heartbreak of her brother's abandonment. I wondered if that was how my own brother had looked after I left him to his fate…

I quickly stomped into the renter house, not allowing myself to follow up on that thought or dwell on things that I couldn't change. Halsted and Prue followed me.

Freddy was standing by the bar. She glanced up as we walked in. I shot her a look that could kill. She laughed as I stormed over to her.

"The puppet queen herself," I hissed. She cackled and took a long drag from a pipe resting between the fingers of her glamoured dismembered hand.

"Cheer up, bird, the rooms at the palace are much nicer than mine." She blew scented smoke into my face.

I wanted to slap her. She had known what she was getting me into the whole time.

"Do you sell out all of your workers for a bag of coin?" I asked bitterly.

"I don't see it that way," she said, stubbing a long finger—a real one—into her pipe to get it lit again. She lowered her voice. "There was a job needed doing, and you were the best for it, the best by far."

"You could have told me, I would have…" I trailed off, and she smiled at me knowingly. I would have run the moment anyone mentioned working as a guard for royalty. Even as I thought about it now, I was filled with panic.

Neither I nor Freddy said another word, so I went to the stairs. Halsted followed me up, but Prue stayed down, and ordered a pint.

It took me no time at all to pack my things. I pulled the trunk from under my bed. Shifting through I grabbed a pouch containing a lock of Cian's hair. I had taken it from his first curl when he was only a baby. It was an old family tradition, meant to bring good luck. I pressed it to my lips then dropped it round my neck. In a bag, I placed my wretched father's favourite book, one he had handed me the night I left. His last hidden letter, an order to me, was still folded up within its pages. I had almost burned it many times since leaving my homeland, but somehow, I'd never managed to go through with it. The only other possession I had from home was my mother's family talisman. A silver crow and dagger. I wore it around my neck always. I added some toiletries and my hairbrush to the bag, then kicked shut the trunk, leaving everything else untouched. It was time to start new. Too many sentimental things would only hold me back, or worse, expose me.

I went to grab my clothes from the drawers, but Halsted took my arm to stall me. I shook him off violently, and he looked at me, shocked by my strength. I glared at him, daring him to touch me again. He stepped back, jokingly holding his arms up in defeat and nodded his head at the drawers.

"Don't bother bringing any clothes. Lady Scarlet will only burn them," he explained.

I huffed and slammed the drawer shut again. I went to my bed where I retrieved a strip of leather from under my pillow. I rolled it open to check the small knives and tools secured inside. Satisfied, I rolled it up again and shoved it down into my boot. Halsted made no move to stop me.

"That book..." He hesitated. "If that book is important, then don't bring it. Put it somewhere safe," he said.

"There is nowhere safer for it to be than on my person," I said, refusing to be affected by his consideration. He stared at me as if he understood.

And with that I was ready to go. I took one last look at the room I had called my home. It made sense that I was leaving. I knew the time was coming anyway. I had stayed far too long here. Getting comfortable in one place was dangerous for someone like me. The only thing I regretted was that I hadn't already set this in motion myself. I was about to go on to do the riskiest thing I had done in six years. Who knew if it would turn out to be the right decision, or one I would regret.

It had been almost six years since I had stepped through the white border and into the west-lands. I had been starving and half-dead, having travelled from the east land of my home, through mid-land where I didn't feel safe, and on again.

I had lived alone on the streets for a while then. Hunting for food, selling what I didn't eat, taking each day as it came. I couldn't deny that I preferred the life of a renter worker to scrounging on the edge of existence. It had felt somewhat steady, almost like actually *living*.

With one last look, I walked from the room for the last time and back down into the pub, closely followed by Halsted, who had not rushed me through any of my sentimental goodbyes.

"Bye, bird," Freddy said when she saw me. She held her long arm out towards me. Did she want me to kiss it? Did she want me to *thank* her? I took her hand uncertainly. She gripped me hard and pulled me into an awkward hug. I felt something heavy drop into my hand. It was a drawstring purse. I looked up at Freddy, surprised.

"Good luck, Cera," she said. "You're going to need it." There were a lot of things I could say. I could get a little sentimental or a lot mad. After all, she had sold out to the palace. But part of me recognised a strong woman doing what she could to survive, and if I let myself get used by her, then it was nobody's fault but my own.

She nodded at me and took another long drag of her pipe before turning away towards the bar. A couple other renters watched me from their tables as I left. I didn't bother saying goodbye, I didn't know them.

Me, Halsted and Prue remained silent for the carriage ride back to the castle. It was getting darker now, the sky turning golden, and I watched as the sun hovered over the tops of the dilapidated homes. Shadows ran over roofs and through the cracks between the houses. We rode past a market where vendors were yelling loudly, competing with one another to get their wares sold before pack-up time.

I held my bag tighter to my chest as we left the market and the houses behind, driving up the winding paved roads to the castle. A horse appeared next to us, and Kohl rode upon it, half hooded. I saw him for a split second before his horse sprinted ahead.

Lady Scarlet waited outside the palace doors for me. Her hair was more frazzled now and her dress slightly black at the hem. I almost felt sorry for her. Did the woman ever sleep?

Chapter 7

We descended the carriage.

"The rent girl as requested, my lady," said Halsted.

"She was no trouble," said Prue. He wobbled slightly as he walked over to us, and I wondered how many pints he had managed to chug down with Freddy while he waited for me.

"If that's all, then I'm back off to the barracks." He didn't wait for a reply before heading off towards the gardens. Swaying, he tried to pat one of the horses tied to the carriage as he passed them but missed and swiped at thin air.

"Thank you, Sir Halsted," said Lady Scarlet, turning a blind eye to Sir Prue's antics.

"Take her to the queen's rooms in the east wing. There will be a maid there to meet you. Tell her to get those clothes and burn them!"

Halsted shot me a knowing look and winked.

"Girl," Lady Scarlet continued, looking at me sternly but not unkindly. "Make no mistake that her Majesty will tire of you fast, but if you are lucky and behave well, you could see yourself in another role here." She raised her head proudly, obviously thinking this idea would appeal to me greatly.

I nodded politely, not trusting myself to say anything, and followed Halsted back to the queen's rooms.

Now that we were alone, it became apparent that he was very chatty indeed. He took great delight in showing me around and introducing me to maids and servants that we passed on our way. The majority of the courtiers were all asleep it seemed, and the palace staff were still busy rushing about, cleaning up the carnage left from the king's revel. Now that I wasn't standing alongside the queen, they were all very interested in meeting me. They nodded their heads politely when I was introduced and chatted to Halsted at length about the chaos of the party and the messes they had to clean.

"Through there are the laundry rooms." He pointed down a small corridor of white stone. Steam billowed out the room at the end, and I could hear the sounds of chatter.

"The kitchens are below us. You get to them from outside. There is an entrance hidden in the great hall too, but that's only to be used when serving at parties," he continued. "Up the stairs here are the rooms for the royal household, that's where we live here on the grounds, and the guard barracks, where I sleep, are at the back of the palace." He looked at me with a smile. "If you are asked to stay here when the queen is gone, then you will be living up the stairs. For now though, you are to stay in her chambers."

Mercifully we finally reached the queen's rooms. The guards that had stood outside the door earlier were still there, along with an older woman with grey hair pulled into a side braid. She held a grey bucket filled with towels, linens and soap.

Without a word, the guards opened the door, and the woman signalled for me to follow her in.

"See you around, renter," Halsted called friendlily as the doors shut behind me.

I followed the maid to a room on the left, away from the room I knew to be the queen's. We walked down a long dusty corridor, and she stopped to open windows every few steps. The dust danced in the golden light, making me cough. Finally, she picked a door and unlocked it. It creaked in resistance as it opened.

The furniture inside was covered in a layer of dust, and the room was dark and looked as though it hadn't been used in years, but someone had been in already and lit a small fire in a stone hearth. The woman went to the window and pulled open the thick red velvet curtains, letting a little more light in.

The space was small but opulent, with a four-poster bed, a chaise lounge and window seats.

I could see a brass claw-footed tub, half hidden behind an open door with steaming water rising out of it. The furnishings were all upholstered or stained in deep reds and bright yellows. I looked at the bed longingly. It was plush and heavily blanketed, a far cry from my lumpy straw mattress at the rent house. For the first time, I was starting to think I had made the right decision. I wanted to collapse right away and sleep until noon. It had been a very long time indeed since I had last slept in a bed similar to this.

"Please disrobe, my lady. A chamber maid has filled your bath for you. It will still be warm."

"Thank you," I said, needing no more prompting before stepping into the bathroom. The floor was tiled and cold, but the bath looked amazing, and thankfully there was a fully plumbed toilet. I could have laughed. I'd had enough of chamber pots to last me a lifetime.

I heard the woman talking and investigated. I popped my head around the door just quick enough to see her slink off, and the queen stood in her place.

"I thought you might prefer a bit of privacy," the queen said, coming over and placing the basket of towels at my feet.

"When you are done, ring the bell by your bed. A maid will come to dress you." She looked as though she wanted to say something else. Her hands fidgeted together.

"I thought you might like to sleep tonight, but it's probably best you join the dinner," she said eventually.

"It might not be pleasant," she elaborated.

"Why?" I asked.

"Well…" She stilled her hands "The king is going to show his heir off to the congregation tonight."

Ah.

"His lady is still abed, so thankfully, she won't be there."

"Does she usually eat with you?" I asked.

"Oh yes, her father is an earl and very rich. Their family are exceptionally popular. They have more rooms in this palace than I do."

"Is it typical for rulers here to choose an heir of any child they have?" I asked, curious.

"It's not common, but it has been done. Rulers here have the absolute word of the law, so it cannot be disputed. The king's own grandfather was an illegitimate heir. I think a lot of it is down to popularity. I will say though, the crown does… change hands often."

I nodded knowing that already.

"I'll go now. Dinner doesn't start until moonlight, so maybe you should sleep. I will come get you when it's time." With that, she slipped away.

As soon as the door was shut, I pulled a wooden chair that had previously been at the side of my bed over to the door and wedged it in under the door handle. It wouldn't keep anyone out, but the noise would at least alert me of people attempting to enter. I took a step back from the door, assessing my work, then another until my legs hit the soft bed. I let myself fall onto the soft blankets. My head felt fuzzy and dazed as I breathed in a deep, calming breath. "What are you doing here, Celia?" I asked myself.

What had I gotten myself into? What insanity was this?

Why would I throw myself into danger when I had spent so long running from it. Was I bored? Had I just been waiting for an opportunity to get back into this game of thrones? I had placed myself here willingly. It didn't matter how far removed this place was from my homeland, these kingdoms were all connected somehow, enemies, allies. It didn't matter. They were all intertwined.

Being in a place like this, it stirred up painful memories… memories of my family, memories of what I had done, memories of… him.

Garrett

I hissed out loud at myself, shaking my head as though to shake out the very name from my recollections.

So stupid. Garrett? What had made my mind wander to him?

Garrett, who would kill me with glee the very second he saw me, no doubt. Who must hate me more than anyone else living, even more than the Blood King himself. Not that I could blame him. What a vicious coward he must think me.

What a vicious coward I was.

I didn't have time to reminisce…

Except, lately it seemed like all I had was time. Time at the graveside, time at the pub, time picking herbs by the lakes… far too much time to think.

The further the years removed me from my past, the more it tormented me. The more I dreamed of being there again, I dreamed of the mistakes I made. If I could turn the clock back to that night, with all the knowledge that grief and time had granted me, would I have done things differently? Yes, without a shadow of a doubt. If I could go back, I would never have abandoned my brother or Garrett.

I couldn't go back though, not even to see if my family... No, I wouldn't even speculate on that. I could never go back. It would risk the thing I treasured above all else. It would risk my freedom, my very autonomy, my—

"Are you awake?"

I stilled. The guard had crept up on me. I cursed under my breath and sat up to face him. I saw that the chair remained unmoved from its position under the door. So there must be another way in.

Kohl stood with his back against the wall, next to a tapestry that waved in a very slight wind. A hidden passageway.

"You move like a ghost," I observed, trying to hide my frustration. He smiled at the compliment.

"As do you," he said.

"Why are you here?" I asked him.

"I came to make sure you got to your rooms."

Like I had a choice, like he hadn't practically forced me into the carriage himself.

"And to not-so-subtly warn me that I am constantly being watched?" I asked as I walked to the tub in the bathroom. It smelt like lavender and sage.

"Yes." His eyes took in the chair wedged against the door. I couldn't tell if he approved or thought me silly.

"The queen will introduce you to the king tonight."

"I have already met him," I said.

"She will introduce you to him as her companion, as a lady."

"Are you here to prepare me and teach me court etiquette?" I asked as I began to untie the ribbons of my many-layered dress. The guard didn't flinch. If I unnerved him, he wasn't going to show it. He turned away wordlessly to give me my privacy.

Once undressed, I stepped into the bath. I felt the warmth to my core as I sank in up to my shoulders.

"I have a feeling you already know it well," he said.

"Know what?" I asked, barely listening now as the heat seeped into my bones.

"The ways of court."

I experienced a stab of panic at his words. He made it sound as though he knew all my secrets. Which obviously, he didn't.

"I understand the basics," I confirmed. "However, all courts and kingdoms are different, with different hierarchy, traditions and customs." He made an unconvinced noise at this and walked back into the main room, keeping his back to me at all times. Part of me wondered if I should be offended that he felt safe enough to turn his back on me.

I used the soap to scrub my body and hair. When I was dried and wrapped in a soft towel, I found him again in the other room, waiting on my bed.

"Your Madam Frederika is somewhat of a friend of mine," he said as I walked in. "She has been watching you, and she trusts that you are right for this job. I have been cautioned by her though, of your… shall we say, lack of loyalty." I felt my face go hot at his words. Embarrassment or disappointment, I couldn't decipher.

"Looking out for myself isn't 'lack of loyalty'. It's a lack of stupidity," I snapped.

"Be that as it may, you *will* be loyal to my queen." Something about his wording set me on edge, and I couldn't pinpoint it. It wasn't the thinly veiled threat. It was the way he said *my* queen.

"Do you understand?"

"Do you usually threaten people into doing what you want, because let me make this very clear to you now," I said, stepping closer. He rose from the bed to meet me.

"I am not scared of you," I continued. "I am not threatened. I will fulfil my promises to you, and you will fulfil yours to me. Then this is over, and I will be in the wind."

He regarded me for a second, and then in a movement almost too fast to comprehend, a sword was at my throat. The tip of Kohl's thin blade pushed gently, just under my ear. His eyes bore down into mine, wide and full of menace. I smiled brightly, unable to conceal my glee as my own dagger, at the base of his neck, shone with red blood.

"You're fast," he croaked, clearly impressed. "Faster than me." He stepped back, sheathing his sword at his hip and placing a black handkerchief to the small cut. There was a crest on the square of fabric, but I couldn't make it out.

I wiped my own dagger on the carpet, taking some rebellious pride in the stain upon the intricate pattern. I kept it to hand.

"Dress soon, and we will meet you in the entrance room." He pulled the tapestry back to reveal a large wooden door. I bit down the annoyance I felt at having not checked earlier for such an obvious entryway.

"You will be known as Lady Cera. Paperwork has been forged and purchased for you. Your father is a knight from the northlands." It was plausible, the north and east were allies, Similarly the east and mid-lands were bound together in trade, more than in loyalty.

"And if I am asked about anything?" I wondered. "I've never been in the north."

"Just be polite and vague. I'm sure you have had experience?" Another leading question. I just smiled.

"You know," he began, "I have never distrusted the madam before, but she was wrong to choose you."

"Why is that?" I couldn't help but ask.

"You are too dangerous," he said.

Chapter 8

This queen was in desperate need of rescue. None of the court seemed to care for her favour, they all but ignored her, and even the servants behaved as though they were under orders to misunderstand her requests at every turn. The only servant that appeared to have no bias towards her was Lady Scarlet, who walked behind us as we progressed through the palace halls, her head low in respect and her sharp tongue ready to reprimand any servant that spoke out of turn. Yet even this was obviously due to some strong loyalty to the title that she couldn't see disrespected and not any devotion to the queen herself.

It was hard to watch as the servants physically turned away from the queen without acknowledging her and ignored her greetings. It was hard to be a part of. It felt as though we were being shunned and shamed for something.

It reminded me of home.

It reminded me of my father.

When I was very young, he used to keep bees at our summer home. He was fascinated by their hierarchy. One day, the drones expelled and killed their own queen when she stopped laying the right eggs. At the time, he told me it was very practical of the bees to do this, and I had agreed, but really it had been horrible to watch, and I remember feeling sorry for the queen. It had seemed so needlessly cruel to me. My father had somewhat excelled at cruelty though…

Earlier when I had been in my rooms, the staff was friendly to me. The maid who dressed me was young and chatty. She seemed to almost feel sorry for me having to work for the queen. Part of me could respect the amount of work that must have gone into the defaming of this queen. The people hated her, even when they didn't know her. The maid had put me in a flowing yellow gown covered in hand embroidered red flowers and curled my hair with tongs all the while lamenting its short length and its glamoured dirty blonde colour. Most of the women in Riverna wore their hair long and braided.

As we walked through the halls, I stared at the queen's own golden-brown hair. It was similar to my natural colour. It was long and pulled up into a high bun. She should ask a maid to fix it in the style of the court.

Many courtiers didn't bow as the queen passed, and doors stayed shut to her a second too long before an awkward throat clear from the queen or a bark from Lady Scarlet would spur the guards into motion.

When we entered the grand hall, no one announced our arrival, and the king barely looked up from his goblet as we sat down at the long table.

No one stood.

The queen shot me apologetic looks throughout, which made me feel all the sorrier for her. She obviously knew that we had our work cut out for us. The king was seated opposite the queen at the head of the table, with a woman upon his lap. She had a very small waist, so I couldn't imagine she was the mother to his new son. She giggled and fed him from her own plate, baby-talking to him in a voice high enough to echo over the chatter. Her dark crimson dress was torn slightly at the bust, exposing skin.

The queen said nothing about this display, so I presumed it was a common occurrence.

The food was served, but it seemed to reach me and the queen later than everyone else. I turned in my seat to see if Lady Scarlet was around. Surely she wouldn't allow this treatment? But the head of house was nowhere to be found. The sharp glare of disapproval that I shot the footmen when they placed the queen's bowl down in front of her after placing my own was unheeded.

Soups, pies and roasted meats were served to us. They were all delicious, and I devoured each plate as soon as it was placed. The queen barely ate a bite though. I could see the skin at her collar was pink with embarrassment. It made my heart twinge uncomfortably in sympathy.

"Are you okay, Your Majesty?" I found myself asking her under my breath.

She looked at me and smiled weakly. "I am well. How do you enjoy your meal?"

"Who is this?" The king demanded suddenly. I refused to look up, knowing he must have been addressing me.

All faces turned to us, curious. The queen cleared her throat.

"This is the lady Cera, my new lady-in-waiting. She is teaching me to sing. You heard her yesterday at the revel."

The king grunted at this. "I have not met her," he said. I wasn't surprised at his not remembering me. "Did I invite her to this meal?" he asked.

"I invited her, dear husband."

I felt shivers run up my back, her voice was timid and shaky. I could see her body tense, just waiting for the backlash, prepared for the lashing. It was a feeling I recognised.

"May she stay?" she asked.

His face snapped to mine, and for a moment I met his gaze with a challenge, refusing to be cowed by him, but a little cough from the queen reminded me that I was meant to be playing a part. I lowered my gaze.

"I come from the north, where I have heard much of the opulent court of King Henri," I said, voice low and coy, "… and of the handsome king who ruled over. I know I am privileged to be here." I looked up from under my lashes. Was I going too far? No, he looked pleased with himself, and the woman who sat on his lap was staring daggers at me.

"The queen is much as described also," I continued, less enthusiastically. The queen's head turned to me in surprise, shocked by my tone, but she said nothing.

"Is she? Aha!" laughed a man seated next to the king. "The women from her lands are not bred the same as our women!" He was drunk and disrespectful, but no one said anything to contradict him. Not the king, not any courtier. The woman on the king's lap giggled heartily, once she was sure the king hadn't taken offence. A small rage began to burn up inside of me at this. I had to remind myself that I was here to placate the king and agree with these sycophants, not smash their heads together like I wanted.

"No need to be so shy, girl!" cried the same man, gesturing for me to come closer. Completely unaware of my distain for all of them. "Come look upon your king."

The last thing I wanted to do was get a closer look at that disgusting man. As I stood up, I purposefully tripped over my chair leg, falling to the floor in a crumpled heap as clumsily and grotesquely as I could manage. The queen stood up and gasped, believing I was truly hurt. After a beat, the room erupted in laughter, and a servant came forward to offer his hand and pull me up. I took it, feigning a nervous smile. He led me to stand in front of the king.

King Henri regarded me for a few moments, clearly unimpressed with my looks and disappointed by my lack of grace. The woman on his lap whispered something into his ear, and he snorted wickedly. She looked at me with a snide smirk, to make sure I hadn't missed the jibe.

"So, you are teaching my wife to sing?" the king asked. I nodded and curtsied clumsily. "How is she faring?"

"She has much to learn," I said, I could tell he liked this answer. He smirked and exchanged glances with the courtiers sitting nearest him.

"I bet she does." He stared at me a moment longer, trying to see something to his taste, but the woman on his lap was wiggling and working hard for his attention.

"You suit one another," he said smugly, to the great amusement of the people around him. I bowed deeply.

He flapped his hand at me, and with that I was dismissed. I turned away, relieved that he hadn't demanded I be thrown out. He hadn't exactly agreed to my acting as the queen's lady-in-waiting, but he hadn't forbidden it either.

I'd take that as a win.

As I sat back down, the queen shot me a bemused look. The chatter soon grew loud as all forgot about me and moved on to more amusing things.

The queen stood after the last course was served, I quickly followed, scraping my chair back loudly and pulling the drunk man next to me up. This spurred many others seated close to us to stand also, out of habit, or surprise. Slowly and awkwardly, the other guests at the table rose to acknowledge the queen was leaving. The king frowned, confused by the sudden show of respect.

"I am retiring to my room," the queen said quietly, her head facing the floor. He nodded and waved her away with his hand in the same way he had dismissed me. Everyone at the table, excepting the king and the woman in his lap, was standing now. They dipped their heads as the queen left.

I curtsied low to the king and left also, after a pace, with my head down respectfully. I followed her this way, for any passer-by to see, until we were in her rooms.

"What was all of that?" she squeaked as soon as the door was shut.

"It's better they think me a complete simpleton in awe of her betters than to take an interest in me as someone who might be a threat to their plan," I explained, sitting on her bed. "Plus, it couldn't hurt for the court to see someone show you a small bit of respect. You should never have let it get this bad!" I admonished.

"What could I do?" she cried angrily. "They were against me from the moment I got here." Tears were filling her eyes, and I could see she was exhausted from the effort of pretending to be okay. She looked like she was about to crumble. I knew that feeling well.

"Didn't you bring any of your own people?" I asked "Why have you no lady maids or staff of your own? This is complete bedlam."

She looked ashamed for a moment.

"It was part of the arrangement of my wedding. It was agreed that I would bring no one and nothing from my homeland. I was to leave everything behind. I was to become a true queen of the east. Even my name was changed. Here, I am Lady Helena. Or was, before we married. Now, all I hear is that I am queen, but this isn't how queens are treated in my homeland. This isn't how my mother was treated, gods rest her soul." She bit her lips and fell silent, a dark, faraway look on her face. "They gave me maids in the beginning," she said quietly, "but, slowly they all left me… through marriage, pregnancy, or illness. One reason after another, and they were never replaced. Not one of them came back. They all misliked me from the start anyway, always gossiping or giggling at me like I was a simpleton every time I didn't understand their ways. What could I have done differently?"

I wondered if she came from a kingdom in the south. The countries there were notorious for violence and had been at war with the eastern kingdoms for centuries. If that was the case, then it was no wonder that the people of Riverna wanted her to disown her old life.

"Power isn't just given, Your Majesty," I said. "It's taken by force, with strength and confidence. You are a queen! The first time a maid giggled at you, you should have had her beaten. Someone has let you down badly, perhaps many someones. I don't know how you haven't found yourself at the end of some plot already."

"There have been attempts" came the guard's voice from the shadows. "I quashed them."

"I don't doubt it," I said darkly.

"So how big is this operation?" I asked. "The men that collected me yesterday must be yours? Prue, Halsted. Kohl, obviously." I said, nodding to the guard as he slunk out from behind a tapestry to stand by the queen's side. "A carrier to get your mail to your homeland? Is there anyone else?" The silence stretched. "Who?" I asked again, impatient.

"None of them are mine," she admitted. "Sometimes guards and attendants do as I ask, and sometimes they don't. Lady Scarlet is a stickler for propriety, and she commands them all. She does as I bid, and no doubt when I am replaced, she will do as my successor bids also, without hesitation. Prue is a functional drunkard—he values money and is easy to bribe. Halsted is friendly and rather oblivious, so he helps me often." That wasn't the impression I had gotten from Halsted, feckless, maybe but not naive.

"Only Kohl is mine. My brother commanded him to watch me from the shadows while I settle in."

"He seems very loyal for one simply ordered to watch you," I observed tartly.

"Well, it isn't a choice," she said.

"Your Majesty," cautioned the guard, his voice low and dark.

"What?" I asked when she looked at him in panic. Obviously, she had said something she was not meant to. But I couldn't unravel anything from our conversation that was concerning, other than their lack of a plan or support.

"What am I missing?" I asked. "If you want my help, you need to tell me everything."

"We want you to guard my queen. We will tell you what information we deem necessary for you to complete that task," the guard snapped.

"I'm not going to be able to protect the queen if I don't understand what is happening. What exactly is the plan here? What do you want from me?" I asked. "Your brother will eventually send people to get you, and what, the king will happily release you of your duty?"

The queen looked down sheepishly. "My brother is still refusing to get me," she admitted.

"So, he has completely abandoned you?"

"I suspect he is ashamed of me and how badly I am doing here."

"So, save all of this bother and run away then, if you are planning on leaving anyway?" I said flippantly throwing back to our earlier conversation.

"Run away?" she cried, offended. "That has to be the *very* last option," she said, seriously. "We haven't even tried to fix this yet. Imagine the shame that abandoning my post would bring to my homeland, to my people who expect better of me. Not to mention it might break our treaty. How could I throw my brother into a war, risking countless lives, just to appease my own discomfort?" How indeed? Her words made my chest ache uncomfortably and my heart palpitate. It sounded very close to exactly what I had done.

"I need to leave on good terms," she continued. "I believe the king would be willing to negotiate, if only my brother would speak on my behalf or offer him something worth the time. The king would never listen to me, but he respects my brother."

"You're too soft to be queen," I said resentfully, letting my own shame colour my words.

"Watch it, renter girl," the guard warned.

"Don't pretend you don't know. Why haven't you done more?" I asked him. "You're her guard, aren't you? You should have acted quickly and violently against every act of disrespect, every whisper of plot right in the early days," I admonished.

"I wanted to win their hearts, like I won the hearts of my people," the queen beseeched. I sighed, almost feeling sorry for her.

"It's easier when they are *your* people. They love you because you are their creature, their blood and their history. Here, you are an outsider, one from a previously hostile country at that. No doubt in the past your people have killed the grandfathers, fathers and brothers in the Westlands, and that is not something easily forgotten. You cannot show weakness."

The queen looked down at her hands, wringing them together.

"Then what must I do?" she asked quietly.

"You can do nothing without more people on your side. You have some sway. You are a princess in your own right from a strong kingdom. Don't expect loyalty. You don't need loyalty, but you need allies. Find out who trades most with your kingdom, find out who would lose the most if they were to go to war. These people will want you on the throne.

Get some ladies-in-waiting. You can't be a queen if you don't act the part."

"The king doesn't want anyone by my side. He—"

"Stop!" I cried, irritated. "Stop it now." I continued, gentler "The king married you because he needs this alliance. He has taken your measure and thinks he has lucked into a meek girl that he can grind down into dust. Into nothing. Show him that you are a queen to be afraid of. You do not need to please him. You need to rule with him or against him. Whatever is easiest."

"He will openly defy me. You don't know him—he is ruthless."

"Ruthless but presumably not stupid," I said. "And you have me to help you now."

They both looked at me, unconvinced. I have no idea how they had struggled on this long without any allies. I had to agree with the queen's earlier thoughts, that maybe she hadn't been meant to succeed at all. In my mind, she had four options: carry on as she was and wind up on the losing end of some plot on her life or run away and leave all of this behind her, living as others live. She could wait for her brother to decide the treatment of her was bad enough that he can no longer allow it, or she could become a queen to be reckoned with, kill off her husband, and take over the country. Personally, the second choice would be mine, but as she wasn't ready for that, the latter was the only valid way forward in my mind.

"I will do what you suggest. I have tried everything else, and I trust you," she said.

Trust? I could never trust anyone like me.

This felt like the kind of emotional burden I was not willing to take on, but I nodded anyway.

"I will sleep now, but tomorrow, tell me your plan," she said.

My plan? Scheming and skulduggery were a part of my past, a past I was in no way ready to drag up. Yet here I was, and I had to admit, it felt good.

It felt familiar and exciting.

And terrifying.

Chapter 9

I lay in my bed, listening to the sounds of the creaking castle. Footsteps echoing, doors slamming, tapestries swaying against the stone walls.

Noises that were painfully familiar to me. My heart pounded in my ears as I focused on breathing in and out slowly.

This entire situation felt far too close to the days of my past. I had been so careful for the six years since I escaped from the East out of the black gates of Nordia. So careful to stay away from people like Kohl and the queen. I swore I would never go back. I swore I would never be put in a situation like that again, and despite being this far away, I still felt dangerously close. Close to the memories of my brutal training, close to the edge of an assassin's knife. Close to my father's cane and sharp tongue, close to my brother's hopeless gaze and my mother's blind eye.

Close to the blood guard.

I had fought my way out of the east. I had lost everything for the chance to be free, betrayed everything and everyone I loved. It was no small price.

This path I was on now wouldn't see me on a road to destruction, would it?

Surely not. Surely Mags wouldn't have saved me and watched over me, trying to cease my self-destruction all these years, just to allow me back there. She wanted me here, and after dragging her from kingdom to kingdom over the last five years, I owed her some faith. As hard as that was to give.

I was in this for me too though, and the queen could be a way out of this kingdom, with a lot of coin.

Yes, I was making the right decision.

I had to be.

Why couldn't I shake this growing doubt though?

I shut my eyes, breathing deeply and steadily until sleep claimed me.

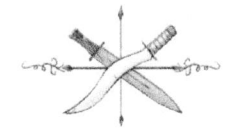

I was in my old bedroom, back in the barracks at the palace. My black dress was torn to ribbons, barely covering me. I sat on the cold stone floor, too numb to move. There was blood on my hands and scratches up my arms. Killing was never easy, but it

wasn't usually physical. It was done in the shadows from afar. Not this time though. It had been face to face, and my target had been unwilling to die quickly. He had been strong for an old man. The look of terror in his large green eyes when he realised I would overpower him, was one I would never forget.

I heard slow, purposeful footsteps on the stone behind me. I knew that tread.

"It was bad," I croaked, my voice alarmingly weak.

"I know. I was there."

I turned to face Garrett, who towered over me. He was handsome, without a doubt. His silver hair was shaved close to his head, his jaw line was chiselled and pointed. He had a dimple in his right cheek that only showed itself when he was smiling or flashing his teeth in anger. His lips were thin but expressive, and his smokey blue-grey eyes seemed to take in even the smallest of details. Right now, he was dressed simply in a black shirt and in black leather trousers. His favourite sword hung on a belt at his waist.

Seeing him looking so poised and calm made me feel ashamed of my state. I pulled at the fabric of my dress and tried to stand. I found my legs had lost their strength, and I fell back. He caught me, of course he did.

"Why were you there?" I asked, my voice shaking as I held back the sobs.

"He wanted me as backup, but I was only to intervene if you were dead."

"So instead, you got to watch. That must have been fun."

He grabbed my chin and forced me to look at him, his face stern, almost angry.

"If I could have taken that from you, I would have. If I could save you from this fate, I would. I would give my lifeblood for that."

I pulled away, and he let me.

"There is no point in saying such things. I don't need saving. We are both of us as stuck as the other."

Garrett stroked my hair, and I let myself be comforted. He smelt like lemon, sage and rosewood. His large fingers brushed through the thick waves of my hair softly, and I could feel his breath at the back of my neck. I don't know how long we carried on this way, but it felt like time had stopped. I didn't dare move, for fear of breaking the spell.

"Your hair is beautiful, Celine." His voice was low, reverent. I couldn't reply. His hands moved from my hair, and the tips of his fingers trailed down my neck and onto the tops of my bare shoulders.

"One day, I will get you away from here," he whispered. I turned to face him, grabbing his hands in mine.

"Don't even contemplate it," I breathed.

His eyes flitted over my face, as though frantically trying to memorise it.

"He can't control what we think or what we feel, Celine, remember that."

"Does it matter? When he can control what we do."

"It matters. It matters more than anything. They can't have me, and they can't have you."

BOUND TO THE CROWN

A clock chime rang out from some cold corridor, signalling the hour and waking me.

I stared up at the ceiling, struggling to catch my breath. My dry eyes stung from tears. I brushed them away quickly and wiped my face on the back of my hand.

I sat up and buried my face in my knees, rocking back and forth and counting to one hundred, trying to calm my racing heart. For a moment I was oblivious to the world around me, all my focus on banishing the dream from my head. That was until a floorboard creaked from somewhere to my left.

I stilled instantly.

There was someone in the room with me, an observer to my heartbreak.

Slowly, so as not to alarm the intruder, I lifted my head and took stock of my surrounding. My eyes adjusted quickly to the semi-darkness, and almost instantly I spotted a large figure, stood next to the tapestry that concealed the secret entryway into my room. The very one Kohl had used before. I hadn't bothered to block it, presuming Kohl wouldn't leave it open if it was compromised.

The figure was a man, cloaked all in black from head to toe, face obscured by the shadow of his hood.

It wasn't Kohl, I was sure of it. Kohl wouldn't bother sneaking around in silence. Not now. No, it was someone else entirely. Someone who was here either to threaten, harm or observe me and I had no patience for it right now.

"Get out," I said. My voice came out shaky with emotion, when I had meant it to be intimidating. The shadow was still and silent.

I kicked my legs off the bed, while grabbing my dagger from under my pillow.

"I'm not here to hurt you." The voice was a low growl from the gloom.

"Do I look like I care why you are here?" I laughed humourlessly. "I don't like spies," I spat. "Are you Kohl's man?" I heard him exhale in amusement. "Not his man, then?" I surmised, irritably. I stood and began edging closer, my dagger out ahead of me.

"Did you have a nightmare?" the intruder asked in a whisper as I approached.

I hissed sharply, embarrassed to have been seen as weak. I lunged but the man was much quicker. He had my sword hand gripped in his. He squeezed hard, but not hard enough to cause pain. I moved to rip his hood off with my other hand, but he stepped just out of reach. "What do you want?" I barked.

The man lifted his head, so that I could make out the shadow of a sharp jawline.

"Nothing. I was just… watching."

Creepy shithead.

I pulled my arm free from his grip and swiped the air with my dagger again. I heard a low chuckle before the man lifted the tapestry and turned away. He held it open for a moment, and looked back, as though he was going to say more. But after a beat he let the tapestry drop and disappeared from my sight. Leaving me staring at the woven fabric.

I considered following him, but what was the point? All the air was knocked out of me, and my face was still wet with tears. If he had wanted to cause me harm, then he would have done it while I was fast asleep.

Fucking Kohl!

I should have nailed that door shut.

I turned away and kicked at the foot of my bed in frustration, painfully stubbing my toe in the process. I took a deep, calming breath, which turned into several, but they weren't making me any less calm.

It was still dark outside, with only the dying light from the crackling fire to brighten the gloomy room, glittering off the expensive furnishings.

I wouldn't sleep again, not tonight and not for as long as I could help it.

I roughly pulled on the first outfit I could find folded up in the wardrobe that wasn't a dress. It looked like riding gear. Once suited up, I upended my pillow and took its case. I was furious and embarrassed, I wondered if Kohl had sent this person to make sure that I didn't run away again? The complete snake.

Quiet as a shadow, I left my room and flitted through the queen's apartments, pacing up and down erratically, grabbing trinkets and expensive ornaments and dropping them into the makeshift bag. A small snuff box, a silver candelabra, the lace tapestries that protected the varnished walnut writing tables.

The nightmare I had of Cian the night before was still fresh in my mind, but tonight's dream was worse because it was a memory, something that had actually happened It was twisted and distorted in my memory by the passage of time, in the strange surreal way that dreams often were. But it was based on real events, events that I had replayed in my head a million times.

Garrett had never called me beautiful though. He hadn't stroked my hair or told me he would free me. Had he?

The recollection of that night was inexact and distant to me now, but I remembered the assignment like it was yesterday. I had been ordered to kill the mayor of a small town to make way for a man more willing to see things the king's way. The mayor had not wanted to die, and I had not wanted to kill him. It had been violent, and many times during the act, my heart had felt tight with horror. I remember vividly that at one point I had laughed hysterically in the man's face. It had been unconsciously done, caused by the trauma of the deed I was committing and the repulsion I felt at committing it.

That familiar panic was taking control of me again now, the sensation that I had done something terrible that could never be taken back, no matter how much I wished it. This was what I was good at though, killing, stealing. Running.

I hesitated, then placed my hand on the queen's door handle, my mind on her silver brush. I hadn't so much as turned the knob when I felt the familiar cold of steel at the back of my neck.

"I knew you had no valour," Kohl spat from behind me.

"I'm surprised you took so long to apprehend me," I replied.

"I wanted to see what you would do, but the moment you dared enter my queen's room, I would have removed your head from your body."

"You would have tried." I bent forward quickly, away from the blade, while kicking back and knocking the guard from his feet. I grabbed his sword hand and quickly slammed it repeatedly against the wall until he let the blade go. It clattered to the floor.

His other fist connected with my face. I took the hit, then headbutted him square on the jaw.

"Fighting isn't your forte." I laughed cruelly. "Stalking and poison might work well for you, but fighting—" He darted down for his sword, but I slammed my boot onto it, crushing his fingers under the hilt. He looked up at me with wide, furious eyes. His thick hair was dishevelled from the tussle, and his lips pursed angrily.

"Are you scared now?" I asked. "You threatened to kill me if I didn't give you what you want. Now you find you cannot. What will you do?"

"I could have killed you just now at the door. I could have sliced your throat!"

"Then you should have," I said, lifting my boot and releasing him.

"What do you want? What are you doing?" he asked as he cradled his bruised hand. "I can't make you out. I spent weeks watching how you live, everyday working yourself to death, never getting any richer because you gave what little money you had away. Are you a glutton for punishment? Or are you simply mad, living every day making the same mistakes again? You could have a chance to do something good, to help someone. But instead, you throw it away for some silver that you won't even be able to sell here."

"Doing good? What good would helping your queen do?"

"She *is* good," he implored, as though it should be obvious.

"*She* is stupid, and *you* are blinded by infatuation." For a moment he looked shocked and disgusted and incredibly young, but he didn't try to deny it. "You aren't discreet about it." I laughed.

He was silent for a moment.

"What about your witch or Freddy?" he asked quietly. "They think you are something special. Don't you care about disappointing them?"

"No, I don't," I lied. "And I don't understand that way of thinking. I especially don't understand it from you, who must have grown up surrounded by users, abusers and scum. Why would you sympathise with this queen? Why would I care what anyone thinks of me? I don't care about your expectations of what a good person is or isn't or what I should or should not be."

"I think you do," he said, "and you know nothing of my life or how I grew up."

I found myself faltering then, having to purse my lips tight to stop from screaming what I knew. It may not have been exactly the same, but you didn't become an elite soldier without having to go through your share of pain and trauma. At least he presumably had free will, which was something that had been robbed of me.

"Help us," he insisted.

"Why?"

"Because you can? Because why not? What have you got to lose? All this skill and you waste it."

"I like wasting it," I said pettily. "I don't want to be some hero. I just want to be free to squander my life if I want to."

"Then take the bag and leave. I saw something in you that just didn't exist."

"You saw what you wanted to see." I sighed. Kohl shook his head in frustration. The faint light from the braziers cast shadows over his rounded face and high cheekbones. His long dark eyelashes touched the tips of his cheeks as he looked down at the ground, dejected and disappointed with me. He was so young, and despite his outward appearance, and rough words, I could tell he was naïve and hopeful. In that moment, I felt like he was just a lad thrown in at the deep end, trying his hardest to figure out what to do next and who to trust. I couldn't help but wonder why he had been given such a large task.

I sat down on the floor next to him. The all-consuming panic that had caused me to act so irrationally had subsided now, and the fight was seeping out of me. We sat in complete silence until the first rays of morning light began to touch the room.

"I will stay and help," I said, resigned. "But don't mistake who I am, or why I am here. I give my word now that I will help your queen until she is either with her brother or her husband is dead. But I have no loyalty to you. I am not trustworthy."

"You are just scared," Kohl sneered. "Scared to be held accountable."

He stood and grabbed his sword from where it lay.

"Go back to bed and keep the trinkets if you want. They don't belong to us."

I watched him going, thinking about his use of the word "us" and wondering if the queen was maybe as in love with him as he was her.

It wasn't until after he had left, that I realised I hadn't even asked him about the hooded man.

Chapter 10

Not long after I got back to my rooms, a maid came and dressed me ready for breakfast.

I followed her down into a large dining room. It was empty except for attendants, who stood to attention by a long table of silver trays, piled high with steaming food.

My mouth watered, and my stomach growled as I took it all in. There were trays full of spiced rice with currants and nuts, steamed fish covered in citrus fruits. Glazed buns and sugared fruits. Trays of poached tomatoes and boiled, salted eggs. I looked at the attendants questioningly, wondering if I served myself or if I was supposed to sit at the table and wait.

I couldn't see any plates, so I took a seat. After a while, a few other members of the household entered the room.

This must be a dining room for popular members of the king's court.

Finally, the queen walked in alone, and I stood as she approached. I shot dark looks at the others who had gathered around. A few faltered under the direct eye contact and arose also. Yesterday, I had told the queen not to sit down at a table until everyone in attendance had acknowledged her. It was a sign of respect, and she needed to force it now, no matter how awkward it felt or how long it took. She stood behind her chair at the far end of the table. She cast me a few uncertain looks, and I glared at her when she began to nervously wring her hands together. She immediately stopped and raised her delicate chin. Her long hair was down, with small sections braided with yellow ribbons, in a similar style to that of the other woman in the room. She was wearing a gown in the Riverna colours, patterned with delicate hand stitched autumn leaves. Her circlet crown rested on her brow. She looked the very picture of a queen. Slowly, everyone who had already been seated stood, and those that had been dallying around came to take their place behind their own chairs. There were some mutterings of confusion, but it happened nonetheless. An attendant hesitated before stepping forward to pull out the queen's seat for her.

"Eat, please," the queen announced, as though they had all been waiting for her. The attendants took up the platters and began serving food. I tried the rice and fish and ate as much as I could without feeling sick. The room was silent except for the clattering and scraping of cutlery.

Just then, a young woman strolled into the room, and every chair was hurriedly pushed back to allow its occupants to stand, every chair except my own and the queen's.

The woman was only a little older than the queen, and her black hair was curled up on top of her head in an elaborate braid and threaded through with gold ribbon, the same colour as her gown. The skirt of which was so full that she could barely fit through the door. It was embroidered with moons and stars. A few people clapped as she entered the room, and by the paleness of the queen's face, I could guess who this was. It must be the king's lady.

An older, aristocratic woman ran to meet the newcomer with her arms outstretched.

"Oh, congratulations, my lady!" she fawned. "You look so well!"

"Very well," agreed another courtier. "Should not you be resting?"

"I couldn't sit around in that bed forever," the king's lady replied with a tinkling laugh.

I looked at the queen, who hadn't stood at least. She busied herself at eating her breakfast. I wasn't sure if ignoring the king's favourite would garner her any sympathies, even if I could completely understand her motive behind it.

I stood and approached the queen, as the rest of the diners flapped and fussed over the lady, all anxious to be in her good graces.

"Helena?" I ventured, using the name she had given me. The queen looked up at me, her eyes wide. It was clear she felt uncomfortable and hurt.

"Let's play the game and kill them with kindness," I whispered. "We don't always have to do what they expect." I raised my eyebrows, looking towards the lady, and the queen seemed to take my meaning. She gracefully dabbed at her mouth with a napkin and then rose to greet the king's lady.

"Dear Lady Duna," she said, sickly sweet. "You are practically glowing! It's hard to believe you were abed only a few days ago." The lady Duna turned to the queen, looking confused, but she smiled pleasantly and inclined her head in thanks for the compliment.

"I can't wait to meet my husband's child," the queen continued. "Unfortunately I missed him yesterday, but I will be sure to set aside time today." It was clear that Lady Duna didn't know how to take this change of tactic from a queen that had all but ignored the threat of her up until now.

"I am so glad to hear you take an interested in our child," she replied.

"Well why wouldn't I? Your child and any that I might have would be siblings, after all." Lady Duna was shocked silent at this. Helena placed a hand on the lady's shoulder. "You should go back abed after you have eaten. You don't want to strain yourself. Rest assured that the king will be well looked after during your confinement. Lady Spree's daughter was comforting him only yesterday." She inclined her head to one of the other women in the room, who blushed furiously.

"My daughter is very tender-hearted," she said with a light laugh.

"Indeed," said Lady Duna, clearly annoyed.

The queen turned to leave then, after bidding them all to enjoy their breakfast. I followed her out of the room, and once we were a dignified way from the dining hall, she stopped and clung onto my arm, shaking slightly.

"That was a bit fun, actually," she admitted.

"You were good at it," I laughed.

"I wonder if Kohl saw me from the shadows somewhere," she said.

"No doubt." I smirked, amused.

"Where should we go next?" she asked enthusiastically.

"It's liberating, isn't it?" I said. "Not having to be silent and demure all the time."

We spent the day making sure the queen was seen by her people. We stayed far away from anywhere that the king might be, or anyone else with the power to naysay her. At lunch, we ate in the library, and several attendants bowed to her before serving the food, which was an improvement.

Lady Scarlet walked past us a few times while we were about our business. She always looked at me meaningfully, and I couldn't tell if it was with approval or disdain.

I didn't see so much as a shadow of Kohl until the end of the day when we were dressed for dinner and sitting in the queen's rooms. My maid had dressed me in a silk forest-green gown, embroidered with brightly stitched birds, trees and red berries. I had my dagger concealed at my hip.

"I don't want to go," the queen insisted. I had to stop myself from rolling my eyes.

"Queen Helena—"

"Ugh, I hate that name," she said.

"Queen, then, we had such a great day today. Why don't you want to continue on? This is important."

She crossed her arms against her chest, and I had to stop myself from laughing. She looked like a child having a tantrum. Kohl stood beside her, silently.

"Don't you have any opinion on this?" I asked him, hoping for reinforcement.

"I think my queen is right," he admitted.

"Why?" I protested.

"You made progress today. It would be a shame if one dinner ruined all of that."

I sighed. "What do you think will happen?" I pressed.

"I think the king will be there," the queen said, "and he will talk to me like dirt and then tomorrow at breakfast, everything will be back the way it was."

I wanted to reassure her that it wouldn't happen, but I had to admit that there was a chance.

"Look, for every step forward there are going to be a few steps back," I said. "But consistency is the key to this."

"I think if I show myself off too much, the people will just hate me more," she said, looking down at her hands. She wrung them together nervously. "I keep wondering about what you said."

My mind raced, what had I said?

"That my people only loved me because they were *mine*. I have never had to win someone over with my charm alone, and I am worried that I could overplay my hand." I felt an instant sting of guilt. I had said something to that effect, hadn't I?

"You won me over," I said. "And that is no easy task." The queen laughed.

"I didn't win you over. I threatened you and manipulated you." There was some truth in that…

"Your guard then," I said. "He has come all the way here with you, and I know he would lay his life down for you." The queen sighed at this.

"Well, he really doesn't have the choice," she said. I remembered that she had alluded to that before. Kohl grabbed her hand in his, but his quick attempt at reining her in came a second too late. "He is part of the blood guard. He has to do what my brother commands. I think he would literally die if he tried to resist."

Blood guard.
Part of the blood guard.
My veins flooded with icy panic.

Chapter 11

The effect her words had on me was instant. I felt as though my entire body had lurched sideways sickeningly. My heart raced, and I couldn't catch my breath. Outwardly I tried my best to be calm, to fight the almost overwhelming urge to run from the room without looking back. I stood without meaning to. Pure panic and adrenalin flooded my system, making it hard to stand still, making it hard to breathe. I ran my hands through my hair.

"You know it?" Kohl asked. I looked at the guard who stood by his queen, watching her so diligently.

I could picture in his eyes how I must look to him. Pale as a ghost, shaken to my core. It was no use. I couldn't get control. I could feel everything I had worked for slipping away through my fingers. I could almost taste the warm wind of the capitol of the western lands on my tongue for how close I felt to it now.

Had I suspected this all along? I must have known—deep down, I must have already been aware that this was a possibility. What other reason could there be for me being so easily taken in? What other reason could there be for not asking more details, not even asking where the queen was from? I had been so careless. I had presumed the queen's homeland to be somewhere in the north, as I knew that the west had recently allied with them. But she wasn't from the north. She was from the Westlands. from my home kingdom of Nordia.

I must have seen the signs because they were so glaringly obvious to me now. The way both the queen and Kohl spoke, his habit of saying "my queen" as it was a custom of the west. The way he moved like a shadow—he'd been taught in the same rooms I was taught in and by the same teachers. Their slightly darker complexion that matched my own. I knew immediately that if I were to brush his hair away from his forehead, I would see the scars from the silver blood crown along his brow.

Scars that matched my own.

This revelation took only a moment, though it felt like an age. I pulled myself together as best I could.

"I have heard of them, of course," I said. My voice shook, betraying me. Kohl's eyes narrowed.

I looked at him anew, with curiosity. I searched his features to see if I recognised him. There was something familiar about his face, but I couldn't place it.

"Clearly," he said, his voice hard.

"When my father was in charge, they were pretty monstrous, it's true," said the queen, misunderstanding my reaction. "But my brother commands them now, and they are more…" she trailed off, clearly not convinced in the point she was trying to make.

"It's more humane now," she finished.

The blood guard. The legendary guards who signed away their lives to the king of Nordia. Becoming his puppets, having to obey every request asked of them.

It was a commodity exclusive to my homeland. An army of elite soldiers that helped cement Nordia's reputation as a kingdom to be feared and respected.

The legend went that the ancient King Cerntra spared the life of a witch princeling during the great wars; in return he was granted any boon he desired. The king wanted loyalty above all else, so the witch crafted him two crowns of silver, one for his own head and the other to be placed upon the head of his men to test their loyalty. Once worn the wearer would forever be bound to the king, loyal and obedient. Unable to turn down any request.

BOUND TO THE CROWN

It was a great honour to be chosen as a member of the blood guard, something coveted, because only the strongest were asked to wear the crown.

But everyone knew what it meant really. It meant you were enslaved. Your very actions were no longer your own.

So, this young queen that I had been getting to know and care for was from my homeland. From Nordia.

Then she could only be little Princess Odelia.

The youngest child of the king and queen of the western lands. The queen had died only days after the girl was born.

Princess Odelia had been only eleven years of age when I left, and now she was still barely a woman yet already married off to a king and thrown in over her head. At only seventeen.

And I was the fool that had agreed to take her back home. Back to the brother that had abandoned her and back to the world that I had spent the last six years blindly running from.

In Nordia, I had been a puppet for my father and for the old king. I shuddered in horror at the memory of the men who had forced me into the role of assassin and spy. I had killed and betrayed the people I cared for just to get away from them both. I wouldn't go back now.

No fucking way. There would never be a coin purse large enough to convince me.

Yet, I couldn't pretend that the thought hadn't crossed my mind before. I had passed many drunken nights considering just that. Fighting between the urge to right my wrongs, and the terror of returning and being controlled again.

In the end, fear would always overrule any sense of duty I had. Fear of accepting the reality that my family were most likely dead and the fear of staring into the eyes of those that I had selfishly double-crossed. Perhaps worst of all was the fear of facing Garrett, who would no doubt kill me on sight for what I had done to him. For what I took from him. Kohl watched me carefully. I had many years of hiding my feelings, but I was struggling now. I sat back down on the bed and met his gaze as steadily as I could.

As he observed me, I felt a small pang of anxiety that he would suspect something of me or even worse, recognise me.

But Mags had sworn that I would be unrecognisable to anyone who knew me before, and I trusted in her power.

Besides, after what I had done, he would have already tried to drag me back to Nordia if he knew me, or maybe he would have tried to kill me the moment he set eyes on me. I bet all the blood guard had orders to bring me back, dead or alive.

You didn't turn on your own people and get away with it. Not in Nordia. And no one escaped the blood guard, not alive anyway.

"I have heard of them, obviously," I repeated when the silence grew too long. "I don't know much, but I know they are formidable," I said weakly.

"Well, I am just a princess," Odelia said. "I can't control the guard." She looked quickly to Kohl then, placing a hand on his arm. "I never would, even if I could, you know," she reassured him.

I doubted that. I was sure she would never set out to try to control him, but it would happen, even if she thought she was doing it for his own good.

He nodded slightly, but I could see on his face that he knew the truth too. The power to control another being was seductive and irresistible, and Odelia would give in to it, sooner or later. Good intentions or no.

I needed to get out of this room and out of this castle. This changed absolutely everything.

"I've put you off now. I can see it clearly," Odelia said sadly. "Please, just take tonight to think about everything. If you want to leave in the morning, you can."

"My queen?" Kohl warned.

"No, Kohl," she said firmly. "I don't want to force her to come back with us. Look how pale she is." I felt embarrassed to have been so obviously shaken by the revelation. To them it would seem like cowardice.

Well, it *was* cowardice.

"You don't seem the type to be put off by the threat of the guard," Kohl said, and he sounded genuinely disappointed. "You were never afraid of me. I would have thought you would be intrigued and maybe even gloat a little."

"Gloat?" I asked genuinely confused. Kohl smiled slyly, the suspicion dropping from his round face. "You trounced a member of the guard, and that's no small achievement."

I let out a shaky laugh.

"That's true, are all the guard as easily bested as you?" I joked, but my words fell flat as my voice trembled, betraying my feelings.

"They really aren't that bad," Odelia said, "The guard work for the crowned king, not me. When we are back in Nordia you will barely even see them." Her eyebrows were drawn together in concern, and she was wringing her hands together in her lap. Her tenderness frustrated me. It made it harder to leave her to her fate here. But that was what I had to do.

I met Kohl's eyes, to discern what he was thinking. They were blank.

I couldn't find words for a moment. Odelia looked at me beseechingly, silently pleading for me to stay and help her but not pushing me to answer.

BOUND TO THE CROWN

I stood and turned away from them both. I only hesitated at the door for a moment before wordlessly stumbling from the room.

I stopped in the hall and took a look around, my gaze resting on the large windows. I genuinely considered leaving right now, but I was physically exhausted from all the information and emotions swirling around my brain. I could feel a panic attack gathering in my chest.

Instead, I staggered into my room and collapsed on the bed.

The blood guard.

Everything I had been running from.

I stared at the ceiling, trying to focus on my breathing. In…out…in.

Mags must have known. She knew everything.

Yet she still wanted me to help the queen.

Well, she was wrong this time!

I wasn't going to even consider this. I had no craving for retribution or forgiveness. I wasn't going to put myself in this situation. It would be insanity.

I sat up, suddenly determined to leave right now.

But I fell back down into the soft bed just as fast.

Princess Odelia had been a very sweet child. Her and my brother had been close in age, and they often played together.

My family was a wealthy and powerful one in Nordia, and there had been talk of betrothing them to one another when they came of age. Until my father showed his traitorous ways and put paid to that.

I smiled despite myself thinking of the child I had once known.

She was sweet still.

My smile dropped.

Chapter 12

I woke gasping as a hand clamped hard over my mouth. I looked up to see Kohl above me, a finger pressed to his lips.

"What the hell?" I hissed quietly. He shook his head and pointed towards the door where I could hear raised voices.

"Unhand me!" came a cry from the hall. I threw back the covers at the sound of Odelia's raised voice. I could tell she was furious and terrified. Kohl let me get off the bed but gripped my elbow to still me. I turned to him questioningly, and he shook his head, pointing towards the tapestry where the hidden door was. He wanted us to abandon the queen?

"Are you mad?" I asked in a hushed tone.

" We can't help her if we are captured too," he whispered pleadingly.

A scream from the other room forced my feet to move. My heart pumped hard in my chest, and adrenalin flooded through my veins. I heard Kohl hiss my name in warning, but it was too late. I yanked open the door to find Odelia being manhandled to the floor by two kingsmen. A small crowd of people looked on, including the king and his lady, Duna, who held a sleeping baby in her arms.

"Let her go!" I demanded. All eyes turned to me, including Odelia's tear-filled ones.

"Cera!" she cried. "They are accusing me of kidnapping the baby."

"She was found in your rooms, you filthy western liar!" said Lady Duna. She smirked down at the queen, enjoying the display.

"This is obviously a false accusation," I snapped. "Someone is trying to frame her."

"Are you calling the mother of my heir a liar?" The king asked. He gestured for his guards to apprehend me. I shook them off violently and headbutted the nearest one, who crumpled down to the floor in a heap, out cold. The king stared in shock a moment before yelling for more guards.

It took eight of them to hold me down. I knew I was making matters worse, but I was indignant.

I couldn't understand why this king was making such a stupid move.

"Are you sure you want to risk the outbreak of war on the word of a social climbing—" Before I could finish, a guard kicked me in the jaw with the heel of his boot. Blood filled my mouth, and I spat it onto the leg of his polished iron armour. Odelia was sobbing on the floor now, and her face was pressed roughly into the carpet by a kings-man. I felt overwhelming guilt at not having listened to Kohl. He was right. I could do nothing for her in this position.

"The renter girl will be executed for this treason, but let her starve in the dungeon cells for a while first," the king announced. "Lock the queen away in a tower until we can get to the bottom of this."

I shot Odelia an apologetic look as she was dragged from the rooms.

I scowled up at the frail king and spat again. Blood splattered over his pointed leather shoes.

"You are an idiot," I hissed. "You will start a war over this. Can you and your army defeat the blood guard? The king's face contorted in rage.

"Someone shut her up!" he ordered. "Now."

I struggled against my captors but not quickly enough. Four hits of a sword hilt across the back of my head and the world went black.

Chapter 13

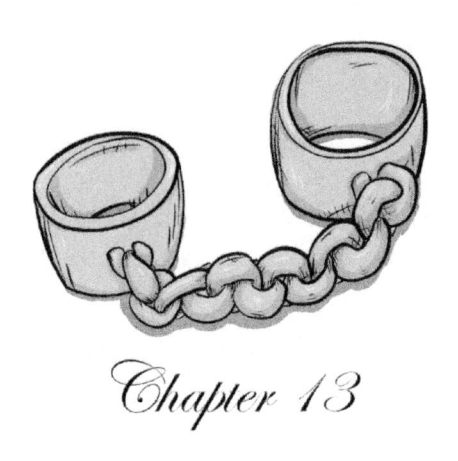

"Any more bright ideas, renter?" Kohl appeared at my bars, materialising from the cold shadows as he always did. He couldn't hide the slight smirk on his face, nor the guard's blood dripping from his blade.

"I said I was strong, but I never said I was smart," I retorted from my spot on the hard floor. My body was completely numb with cold, and my hands were red, raw and bleeding from the shackles chained around them.

"Clearly," he agreed. "Your flaw was in thinking this court was the same as whatever court you received your education in." He looked at me pointedly, but I wouldn't take the bait.

"The people here crave chaos and violence, none more than the king. He doesn't want a strong queen. He wants to have his way, always. Like a child. All you did

was give him a reason."
"Are you here to scold me," I snapped, "or to free me? I am genuinely curious."

"Free you. Why else would I be here?"

"I suppose you need every ally you can get," I suggested.

"I would have left you here, personally," he said "But the Princess is fond of you. Besides, as you said, you are not smart, but you are strong. Strength is essential now."

He took a large ring of keys out of his belt and began trying them on the door. When he found one that fit, he pulled them open. He turned into the darkness behind him then.

"Did you find a key for the chains?" he asked. I couldn't see who he was speaking to. Suspicion flared in me, and I stood quickly, losing my balance on my injured foot and falling into the wall. "Who is here?" I asked him.

"The ally I told you about," Kohl said simply. "It was time for him to step in, so we are going, now."

My heart pounded in my ears. "I don't want to be a part of that then," I said firmly. "Give me the key and go."

Kohl stood and looked at me, confused. "This was the plan. You are not backing out now."

"Leave her" came a rough male voice from the darkness. I could just make out his shape standing back against the wall, but no features. The light from the braziers barely touched him, and my eyes were struggling to adjust.

"I can't leave her. The princess has insisted that she come too."

The stranger stepped into the doorway. He was covered head to toe in black. Black breeches with black, blood-marked boots. A leather strap full of small daggers, bottles, pouches and arrow tips was strapped around his chest, and a woven cloak covered his shoulders with a large hood that hid his masked face in shadow. It was clearly the same fucker who had invaded my room the other night.

"Will you be trouble?" he asked, turning his hooded gaze in my direction. I hesitated only a moment.

"Yes."

He reached for me. I had expected it, of course, but he was faster than I was prepared for, and the chains held me back. I faltered under the weight of them, and before I could stop it, I was in his arms, cradled close against his hard body. I blinked up at him in surprise, wondering how I had ended up here so quickly.

"I will ask again," he breathed "Will you be trouble?" Something about his thin, smirking mouth made me want to fight.

"Yes!" I said, trying to wiggle out of his grip. When that failed, I lashed out, catching the side of his jaw with my flailing fist.

"Then sleep," he growled before sticking me in the arm with something small and sharp that he pulled from his belt. I gasped and then, as he had suggested, I slept.

Chapter 14

I woke up on my back to find myself staring up at a starry midnight-blue sky. A bright crescent moon bobbed above me, bordered either side by tall, leafy trees.

I was on some kind of wagon. I could hear the crunch of the wheels below me as they trundled over dirt and rocks, and my body vibrated and gently swayed with the movement. I felt strangely relaxed and comfortably warm, bundled up as I was in layers of soft cotton blankets. I shut my eyes and listened to the steady clip-clop of horse hooves and the hushed whisper of many lowered voices.

BOUND TO THE CROWN

A soft, fresh breeze lifted my hair and cooled the feverish sweat on my face. A lantern swayed above me, hanging from a pole. It danced and bobbed in the wind, and the light was almost hypnotic. I found myself staring at it for a long time, my breathing slow and deep.

I woke up again sometime later to the sound of barked orders in the distance. The sun was beginning to peek through the gaps of the trees around me, the moon no longer in sight. Whatever truck I was on came to a jarring halt, causing me to shift down in my blankets. My hands and feet rattled from the chains that were still attached, and I swore at the throbbing pain.

"How are you feeling?" came a voice from behind. It caught me by surprise, and I sat up quickly, hitting my head on the post that held the still-lit lantern. The wagon around me was loaded up with boxes, jugs and fabric-covered parcels. Some had fallen or rolled at the sudden stop.

I turned around to find the speaker was a woman with tan skin and auburn hair sitting at the head of the truck. She was turned in her seat to look at me, a large smile on her hard face. She held the horses' reins in one hand.

"How are you?" she asked again. "You were out for nearly a whole day."

With annoyance, I remembered the events of the night before. Kohl's rescue from the dungeons of Blackmoore castle and the hooded man. I examined the spot on my arm where I had been stuck. It was a little red.

"What did he give me?" I asked groggily.

"Just a green-lock thistle. They have a natural poison in them that aids sleep. It usually wears off after about an hour, but you were out a long time. Maybe you needed the rest." She smiled warmly. I didn't return the smile. I was under no illusion she was clearly here to guard me, otherwise my chains would have been discarded by now. Instead, my joints were raw and bleeding from rubbing against the rough metal cuffs.

I shook them in frustration and instantly regretted it. I looked at the woman pointedly.

"Can you take these off now?" I asked, irritated.

"Well that depends," my guard said, rubbing her chin as though she was considering it.

"On?" I demanded. Her playfulness was irking to me.

"My princess is very fond of you. She has asked that you be sent to her the moment you awake…once I have deemed you no threat." She let go of the reins and clambered to the back of the wagon, sitting next to me in the small space. She grabbed the lamp and shone it into my face, causing me to squint against the painful glare. I growled in annoyance. It was certainly bright enough to see me without illuminating my every feature.

"So," she whispered, leaning down close, unconcerned by my discomfort "Are you a threat?"

"I'm more likely to run away from you than to hurt you," I said, pushing away the light and awkwardly kicking back my blankets that had been placed over me. I felt a quick shock of shame as I revealed my torn, dirty and bloodied clothes. But I refused to hide back under the cover, not wanting to look any weaker in front of this stranger. I was still wearing the forest-green gown the maid had dressed me in for diner. It must have been at least two days since then. I was thankful to still have my dagger and, my mother's talisman, but my heart throbbed painfully with the realisation that I had left my other things hidden in my room. My father's book, the lock of my brothers hair, the odd pouch that the hedge witch had gifted me and my leather tool bag. All I could do was hope that no one would find them, maybe I would be able to get back there.

"Ah, see, that is what I am concerned about," continued my guard, ignorant to my loss. "My princess wants to make sure your contract is fulfilled, and I have *very* strict orders to make sure that happens." She raised her eyebrows at me.

"So, you want me to agree to go along on this little journey of yours? And stay by her side until she gets bored of me?" I asked snidely.

"Exactly."

"From one prison to another," I mumbled. The woman took a blade from her pocket, and with four heavy blows, she cut through the chains at my hands and feet, leaving only the metal cuffs.

"It's a much nicer prison though, isn't it?" she said. I met her eyes sceptically and saw a small amount of sympathy staring back. It would be easy to hate her, but the scars along her brow reminded me that she was trapped in her own prison.

"I'm a nomad. I care little where it is I end up or how I get there," I said, and this seemed to be enough for now.

"My name is Greta." She introduced herself while holding out her hand for me to shake. I took it reluctantly.

"Cera."

"I already know." She smiled. "Stay here, Cera." Greta jumped down from the wagon and ran ahead to another that was stopped in front of us. She caught the attention of a female guard by tapping her shoulder. The woman turned, and after a brief conversation with Greta, she directed her gaze to me. With a sickening lurch of shock, I realised this was a woman I recognised. A woman I knew very well,

It was undoubtably General Vale.

My old trainer.

She looked exactly the same as she had six years ago. The jolt of familiarity I felt when her eyes met mine made my stomach heave without warning. I threw myself towards the side of the wagon and vomited into the dirt. I hadn't eaten anything in days, and retching hurt. I unabashedly grabbed the blanket to wipe the bile from my mouth, then promptly threw up again.

When I was confident that my stomach was calm, I looked up to find four people staring down at me. Kohl, Greta, the general, and the hooded man from the dungeons who had poisoned me.

I still couldn't see his face, half hidden as it was under the dark robes. I felt a stab of embarrassment to be observed by them all this way, especially Vale, who I had looked to as a mentor. I glared up at Kohl angrily, my eyes full of venom. I could blame him for my being here right now. It was as much his fault as it was my own.

He laughed heartily at me before holding his hand out to help me off the wagon.

"You're a state, Cera," he said, not unkindly. I climbed down myself, slapping away his hand as I went.

"She passed as a lady's maid?" asked the general, looking at me in disgust. I couldn't blame her. After a day and a night in the dungeon and another on that wooden cart, my hair was matted, my body covered in dirt and my clothes stuck to me, caked in waste and who knew what else. I probably stunk, but I was used to it now and couldn't tell.

"Barely," Kohl laughed. For some reason, that was the final straw. Before I could be stopped, I lunged forward and punched Kohl full on the cheek bone. I held back from breaking it because like it or no, I had some fondness for the kid. He cried out in pain as the blow knocked him from his feet. For a moment there was stunned silence and then the general observed Kohl on the floor. "Did you deserve that?" she asked him. Kohl rubbed his mouth, then nodded, unable to talk.

"Well, you have some strength, even if you have no style." Coming from her, it was a compliment, but it still stung.

This was the woman who had trained me from a child, since I was first initiated into the guard at only ten years old. The woman who had taught me to fight, to kill, to stay alive. My love and respect for her ran as deep as my hatred of her.

That was how relationships in the guard worked. None of them were simple. It was hard to love someone unconditionally who could be ordered to kill you at any moment. Loyalty didn't matter. Loyalty didn't exist there.

I had proved that rule myself.

I found I couldn't meet her gaze. I knew she wouldn't recognise me, but I still felt the shame of my past actions, and the crushing fear of discovery that made my heart pound and my breath come fast. I felt naked and exposed, like at any moment her eyes would widen with recognition and I would have to face all my mistakes and have to try to explain why I did such a terrible thing.

It also felt uncomfortably bold to be standing here in front of her, pretending I was a stranger, when in fact I had betrayed them all in the worst way imaginable. Though I had been disguised for a long time now, I hadn't ever needed to pretend to be anyone else or to hide my personality and quirks. Kohl seemed familiar to me, but our ages were vastly different, so we wouldn't have trained together. Even if he had known me, it would have been a minimal acquaintance, so it wouldn't matter if I had the same habits of or some similarities to a girl he once met. However, the general knew me well, in the way a teacher would know their student.

She knew me in the way a parent might know their own child.

I gave no reply to her comment and looked instead at Kohl, who was now back on his feet.

"Did that make you feel better?" he asked.

"Cut these cuffs off. Now," I demanded. "That would make me feel better." I held my arms out and tried not to flinch back when the hooded man grabbed them, fast as a striking snake. I gritted my teeth. "You're lucky I didn't break *your* jaw," I hissed to him. "Poison me again, and I will do more than that."

I could see his mouth curve into a smirk under his hood, but he said nothing. His hands were large, calloused and covered in white scars, He felt around the metal cuff, and using a small crescent shaped knife, he sliced through the metal as though it were made of paper. I flinched, expecting it to hurt, but he placed a finger under the cuff, protecting my wrist from the friction. He did this with both hands, and to my annoyance, I found myself feeling slightly pacified by his gentleness.

"They need to be cleaned and bandaged," he said when he was done. He turned my hands around in his, inspecting them. Now that the cuffs were gone, I could see the damage. My wounds were large, scabbed and black. Mixed with old and new blood.

"There is water nearby. We will rest here and eat now, then continue on until sundown," said the general. She looked to the hooded man for confirmation, and he inclined his head in agreement.

I found myself curious about the masked figure. Who was he? Possibly an assassin, but his clothing wasn't the same as Kohl's. It wasn't anything I recognised from my time as a guard.

"Why is he covered?" I asked Kohl as he led me away from the dirt road and into dense woodland.

"Why would anyone cover themselves?" He laughed.

"To hide their identity," I said. Kohl nodded as he snapped branches down out of our way. I could hear the babbling and trickling of a stream before I saw it. Nestled on the forest bed, a shallow but wide brook trickled over moss-covered stones and thick tree roots. I could see brown, speckled fish darting wildly under the surface.

"What do I call him then?" I asked as I sat down on a large rock. I used my hands as a cup and scooped up some river water to drink. It was cold and refreshing.

"Nothing. Stay away from him," Kohl warned as he came to stand near me "You two would not get on."

I smiled. That I could easily believe.

"He shouldn't even be here," Kohl muttered as he scowled down at the splashing fish.

"Oh?" I asked, curiosity getting the better of me. "Why not?" Kohl picked up a small stone and skimmed it across the water, scattering and scaring the fish. It was childlike.

"The princess has been in my charge for over a year now, so I should be leading her rescue."

He skimmed another rock. "And now my job has been taken from me."

"By him?" I asked, surprised. "Not the general?"

Kohl snapped his head in my direction, his usually calm face darkening with suspicion.

"The general?" he asked. "Who is the general?"

I backtracked quickly, realising my mistake. No one had told me her name or her position, and certainly no one had mentioned a general. "Well... isn't there a general leading this team or a captain?" I asked, taking another drink and feigning indifference. "It couldn't be him. He doesn't seem the type," I continued.

"No," he said "Vale, the other woman who was with us just now, used to be a general of sorts, a long time ago. It was just an honorary title. She lost that wh-" He stopped short. "There is no general," he continued. "There is the knight."

"The knight?" I asked, genuinely intrigued. It wasn't a rank I was familiar with.

"Yes, our king's right-hand man, the captain of the guard." Kohl threw another stone, this time with force. "He commands the blood guard."

"The knight?" I confirmed. Kohl nodded then turned away from the river to look at me, his face unreadable, reminding me of how closed off he had been at first. No one but the king had commanded the blood guard before. I didn't know that anyone else was capable of it, not with the same compulsion as the king. "Who is the knight?" I asked, feeling as though I shouldn't push but not able to stop myself. "A lord? A member of the royal family?"

Kohl scoffed. "No, the king would never give so much power to someone he couldn't control. The knight is one of us, our captain."

"And that hooded man, he is the knight?" I guessed.

Kohl was silent a moment, then he nodded at my hands.

"Hurry up and clean your wounds, Cera. We have to go," he said.

I pulled up my sleeves distractedly. This new information confused me. There had always been set roles within the blood guard, with generals who watched over each of them. Teachers, assassins, spies, soldiers, informants, and guards.

But this knight working as a captain of the guard was entirely new to me, as was the notion of any leader of the guard. That rank had only ever been the king's. Watching Kohl now, I could tell it didn't sit well with him, and even I, who had renounced everything and left them all to rot, felt a strange sort of betrayal at the very idea.

I washed my wrists in the stream, cursing under my breath from the sting as I scrubbed old blood from the wounds. When I was done, the water was tinged pink, and my wrists were red and raw. Kohl winced as I did the same to my ankles. They were worse, even more than my wrists, and skin hung off in some places. It hurt, but pain didn't bother me as much as it would a normal person. The kings-men back in Blackmoore castle had amused themselves by pulling me around by my chains while they watched over me. I had a steady footing, but even I couldn't resist being dragged by a group of men without falling.

"Will you be able to walk?" Kohl asked, his voice full of genuine sympathy.

"She doesn't need to walk" came a gruff voice from behind us. I turned to see the hooded man, the knight, standing not far back, leaning against a tree and watching us. I could see his pointed chin, covered in dark stubble and half hidden in shadow. When had he followed us? How long had he been listening?

"Take her back onto the cart," he said to Kohl. I looked to the young guard and saw his face was red. I couldn't tell if it was with anger at the demand or embarrassment at possibly having been overheard.

"Tie her if you have to."

"I won't be chained to that wagon," I said. "I've already given my word that I won't run, and I will come with you to the east." I walked over to him, getting into his space to show how little he intimidated me. "I don't need to be tied up…I *won't* be tied up," I warned. "You can try to scare me by dehumanising me and talking over me, but if your princess really wants me as her guard, then I don't think she would appreciate you treating me like this."

"I haven't treated you badly," he said conversationally, a small smirk lifting the corners of his hard mouth. "And I am not trying to intimidate you, if you find me intimidating then that's on you."

I scoffed at this.

"You poisoned me."

"Green-thistle is an herb, not a drug nor a poison. You would have been awake again within moments had you not been so weak. I gave you the choice back in the dungeons, and it was clear you would have hindered our escape." He stepped forward, filling the small gap between us so that I was staring up into the shadows of his face. I had to fight the urge to rip his hood off. I didn't want him to have the satisfaction of knowing I was curious.

"I placed you on the cart, with the kindness of a blanket, instead of forcing you awake," he said. His voice was deep and rumbling, even when quiet. I imagined that I could feel it vibrating in my chest. "I stopped our procession so that you could eat and tend to your wounds. What have I done that was lacking, or threatening?"

I paused for a moment. The way he spoke made it sound so reasonable, like he had been doing me a favour, but I was having none of it. I wouldn't be gaslighted into believing that I was being treated like a guest, and it made me furious that he was trying to belittle the fact that I was their prisoner.

"And chaining me back to the wagon?" I countered.

"You clearly cannot walk."

"I can ride or sit. I don't need to be chained or tied up."

"Kohl here has informed me that you are exceptionally strong, *oddly strong* was the phrase he used. While I have not seen anything extraordinary myself, I have to trust in his judgement. I am curious, where did you train, and what was it in aim of?" I stepped back a pace and shook my head in denial of this.

"Kohl is mistaken," I said firmly. I looked at Kohl angrily from out the corner of my eyes, but he didn't meet my gaze.

"That is doubtful, so until I have ascertained that you are no threat, you will remain under my watch."

"I had the queen's word that I would be free!" I yelled, enraged. I knew this was how it would go. I had been so stupid to put myself in this position. I never should have taken this job in the first place.

"You will be free, when and if I deem it safe for you to be. You could be a spy."

"*If* you deem it safe?" I hissed. "What the fuck would I be spying on exactly, and who for?" I spluttered, furious with myself for ending up in this situation. It was obvious now that I would have to escape somehow, perhaps biding my time, playing up my wounds and then running in the night? How many days' ride would it be to the black gates of the west, because I needed to be gone before then.

"If you are a spy, you aren't a proficient one. I can see exactly what is going on behind those eyes of yours," he said. I looked up and caught a glint of light from bright eyes and the shadow of a straight nose.

I glared up at him. "Really? Do tell."

He smiled, flashing white teeth. "I think not."

"She isn't a spy. I trailed her for weeks," Kohl interjected. The knight turned from me and approached Kohl instead "She may have known you were following her, and her witch could have told her this."

I found I could barely listen to them. The knight stood in front of me, back turned, and this, more than anything else he had done so far, pissed me off. To see that he felt so unthreatened by me, despite Kohl having given him an account of my strength.

I knew that lashing out would do me no good, I *knew* it was childish, but I couldn't stop myself. Something about him bothered me. I wasn't scared of him, but his arrogance was infuriating. I stared at his large frame, trying to find a weak spot, but his clothes were a shroud.

Impulsively, stupidly, I kicked out, connecting the sole of my foot to where I was sure the back of his knee must be, it was petty and ineffective. Either he had expected it already and braced, or I hadn't hit out hard enough, because he didn't falter as he faced me, his expression stony, well, what I could see of it.

I didn't wait to find out what he would say or do. I struck again, this time with my fist, aiming a hit at his throat, already expecting it would be intercepted. I told myself I needed to check his strength, but really, I just wanted him to feel as annoyed as me. He grabbed my wrist before I could make contact, the movement so fast it was a blur. His grip on my wrist was firm and painful due to the wounds. I gritted my teeth and refused to make a sound. I tried to pull away and found I couldn't. This feeling was new to me. It had been a long time since I faced someone who might be on par with me, let alone stronger. I didn't like it.

"You have some anger issues," he whispered, his voice low, dark, and annoyingly attractive. For a blink, I couldn't move, struck speechless. He adjusted his grip to farther up my forearm, away from the wounds at my wrist.

Then, embarrassed by the realisation that I had been staring, I twisted myself out of his hold completely, frustrated in the knowledge that he had let me do this.

I stared back at Kohl, who observed this whole exchange silently. He looked as nonplussed as I felt. Then I cursed at them both under my breath and stormed away, through the trees and back to the road.

Chapter 15

Once clear of the woodland, I could get a better view of the company. There were four wagons carrying supplies and tents. Dozens of mounted guards and at least double that on foot, all uniformly lined up along the road, clearly unbothered by the thought of being spotted by anyone from Riverna or the mid-kingdoms of Frahlan.

"Where are we?" I asked as I heard footfalls behind me.

"Outside of Gwain. A small hamlet in the east of the mid-kingdoms," said the knight.

They weren't confident enough to follow the main trade route then, instead going through the villages and forest roads. Frahlan, a Kingsland of the mid-kingdoms was allied with Nordia, the capitol of the west, and had been for centuries. It would be unlikely for us to come across resistance from them, but rebels, rogues or even missionaries from the east or south could be trouble. By this point, war between the east and west was probably imminent. They had been on the brink of war just before I left, but somehow tensions had cooled. That obviously hadn't lasted long. Odelia's marriage was likely a last attempt to find some peace and easy trade, however, the west was large, and allied with the mid-lands, it would be almost unstoppable. The north and south were peace-seeking lands, much smaller than either east or mid-kingdoms. It wasn't as clear-cut as this either, with villages and kingdoms along the borders that felt allegiance and kinship to both territories or neither. If a war broke out between east and west, it would involve the entire island of Terravetus, and all the kingslands and queenslands would have a stake in it.

I could see mountains and forests looming above us in the distance. The Westlands and Nordia would be beyond them. The trail through them would be the safest road, but it would take weeks, perhaps months with all these wagons.

There was another route south of here, one I had used before... but it ran along the border of the mid-lands, and the people who settled in the dense forests there were known to be wild and lawless.

No, the mountain trail it would be, I was sure.

I stared up at the snow-capped highlands and felt a stirring in my heart. Those mountains led to home. I shut my eyes against the unbidden memories of endless blue lakes and roaring fires. My family held a seat in those mountains, and we had spent many a long winter there in the brutal cold. I remembered dark nights lit by glittering candles and fireplaces as large and deep as caverns. My parents would throw weeklong parties to stave off the cold, filled with luxuries and excess and the most powerful people.

I remembered the fresh, clear ice and lush winter blooms. I could picture the manor grounds now, and my little brother running around with our dogs, bundled up in thick leather coats, cheeks pink from the cold, golden-brown hair messily peeking out from under his hood.

I never stopped before to think of what brought us to those mountains. The elite status? Or perhaps my father had angered the king again and waited out for his favour to be restored, as it always was eventually, at a cost.

I sighed and opened my eyes as I felt an angry tear trail its path down my cheek. I looked up and found that the knight was staring down at me curiously. His hood had been pulled down now, but his face was still covered by an assassin's mask. Grey eyes flitted over my face. I felt a shock of embarrassment but refused to draw attention to myself by wiping the tear away. I hoped he would mistake it for sweat.

He followed my gaze to the mountains that I had been reminiscing over just moments before.

"They are beautiful, aren't they?" he breathed softly.

"Are they?" I replied impassively. "They look like a wasteland to me."

"No doubt to some they would be," he continued, unperturbed, "but hidden on those mountains are springs and valleys that only the most powerful men of the east can access."

"Most powerful or most wealthy?" I mumbled, thinking of my father's manor.

"That's the same thing, isn't it?" he asked, casually resting his hand on the hilt of his sword.

"You think power and wealth go hand in hand then?" I asked. "Was it wealth that secured your position as the king's knight?"

He smiled at this, the corners of his mouth turning up. He leaned down over me. "What do you think?" he whispered. "Am I not a skilled enough swordsman on my own merit?"

"I could best you," I said boldly.

"Few could, so you must rate yourself highly. Shall we test each other?" He was teasing me now, and I didn't care for the shift in tone.

"You *do* test me," I growled as I pushed past him roughly. I heard his low chuckle as I walked back over to the guards. General Vale stood with a large company around a bonfire. A rack of wood had been knocked up, and a large pan hung by chains from it. I peeked over the rim to see that the cauldron was filled with water from the stream, some meat, bones, vegetables and herbs picked from the road.

A couple guards were unwrapping fabric and jars and adding the contents into the pot.

I didn't dare look too closely at anyone gathered here. These were the people that I had grown up with. I didn't want to ruminate on who was here and who was not.

I had been an elite warrior, which meant that after training, I had worked very often on my own, but I still knew almost all the guard back then, though there would be now of course.

More than anything, I was scared of seeing *him*, Garrett. He had been my best friend, and he had been much more than that.

He never told me how he felt, and I didn't dare ask… but I had loved him.

My betrayal of him was absolute, I had turned my back on him as surely as I had turned on my own family.

I took in a sharp breath, on the verge of falling into thoughts that I should not reflect on. I moved away from the pot and went to observe a group of guards that were practicing sword manoeuvres together in a circle. I watched them for a while, and a few shot me curious glances, but I didn't introduce myself. Instead, I walked over to the forest, snapped a thick branch from the closest tree and made my way back again. I surveyed for a moment longer, learning their routine, and then, using the branch, I copied their manoeuvres. At this point I wanted them to see me as a threat, not someone to be bullied or picked off at the first sign of danger, because there would be danger. No doubt about that.

A few guards stopped to watch me, interested, but their teacher soon drew their attention back with a yell or a sharp tap of a blade on a shoulder.

After a time, a voice called out that the food was ready, and the guards were dismissed by their teacher. I threw my branch down and joined them at the fire. All received a cup full of the stew. I stood at the back and waited my turn, knowing from years of experience that the scrapings at the bottom had the most meat and vegetables.

The guard at the pot looked at me with distaste before wrenching my cup from my grip and scraping it along the pot until it was overflowing. I took it from her without complaint, my face impassive as I burnt my fingers on the painfully hot stew.

I found a spot on the floor, a little away from the others, and sipped at the broth. It was salty and rich and turned my breath to smoke. I drank it hungrily.

Vale came and sat down on the grassy floor beside me. She laid her sword out in front of us, and I recognised it as the same blade she had carried six years ago. What had she called it? Haze?

Wordlessly, she held out a roll of seeded bread for me to take. I nodded my thanks and accepted it without meeting her eyes. It was dense and a bit stale, but it mopped up the broth beautifully.

"You have been trained in swordsmanship?" she asked.

I shrugged as I used the bread to scrape out the very last dregs of stew.

"Trained from a young age at that." It was a statement, and I knew there was no use in denying it.

"Yes," I confirmed. "I had a good teacher."

"To what end?" she asked.

"To protect myself." I answered, not missing a beat. She sighed and took up her sword, shifting it between her hands and examining it for my benefit, as though it was the first time she had seen it.

"Protection is a worthy pursuit. However, I doubt any masters would spare the time to teach a no-name orphan girl-child how to fight. No. Not just for their own protection and betterment. Not without an end," Vale continued.

I remained silent.

"And you were taught by a master. It's easy enough to see," she continued. "I am a master myself, girl. I know how much coin, patience and time it takes to train someone." I stood silently and shook out my empty cup on the grass. Vale stood too and slipped Haze back into her belt. Its appearance had been a quiet threat, one that hadn't affected me.

"Why did you reveal yourself if you weren't willing to talk about it?" she asked, running a hand through her hair. She was referring to the practice. I knew she had been watching me. They had all watched.

"So you could take my measure," I said truthfully, meeting her eyes. "Now you know that I am skilled, so don't forget it." I made to walk away, but she placed a hand on my shoulder.

"My princess has expressed a want for you to stay and be her queen's knight," she said suddenly.

"Her knight?" I asked, caught off-guard. "Like the king's knight?"

"Yes. It is a very prestigious honour, to be chosen to give your life to protect the royal blood," she continued, with a sly look. I scoffed and spat a bit of gristle that had lodged in my tooth out onto the floor.

"I'm sure that's what you really think," I said. "I'm sure you think the blood guard is a great honour too." I wondered if I had gone too far then, and my eyes strayed to the faded scars along the brow of her head. If she was annoyed by my words, she didn't react.

"You do not have to be a member of the blood guard for this honour to be bestowed. It is freely given, which makes it all the more important."

"Nothing is given freely," I said. "There is a bargain or a trick in every exchange."

I didn't wait for her reaction before walking over to the fire. I tossed my cup into a bucket of water and soap and looked around, seeking out Kohl.

I spotted him relaxing and laughing with a group of men on the back of an open cart.

"Where is Odelia?" I asked, interrupting their banter.

"You mean Princess Odelia?" he corrected, as several sour faces turned towards me, annoyed with my perceived disrespect. Or maybe annoyed by my presence in general.

I couldn't force myself to reply tartly. "Yes," I said.

Kohl pointed down the line of carts.

"She is under protection, in one of the wagons," he said. The broad guard next to him nudged him roughly.

"Oh, like I wouldn't have found her without that very detailed piece of information," I snapped at Kohl, his smile dropped as I stormed off to the sound of laughter.

I searched down the line, ignoring the suspicious looks I received from other guards.

I found Odelia on a cart surrounded by guards. I was a little disappointed but unsurprised to find her dressed in the same combat gear as the other guards. Breeches, shirt and a leather vest all in shades of brown, green and black, with a linen cloak to keep her warm. I felt all the more uncomfortable in my own large gown and was keenly aware of how stupid I looked. She fitted in well with the guards around her. In fact, the only thing that could signal a difference was the bowl she was drinking from, it was much larger than the one I or anyone else had been given.

As I approached, her guards stood, obviously ready to strike the stranger down. With a lurch, I realised I recognised one of them, a girl named Maddie, who I had once had a close friendship with. My feet stalled a moment as I faltered, but I found the strength somewhere to carry on. I had to fight the urge to embrace her, to ask her all the questions I wanted to know about home and my family. She had been my confidant at the barracks. She alone knew of my feelings for Garrett. Her white-blonde hair was tied back in a ponytail, drawn close to her face, and her ice blue eyes stuck out brilliantly from her dark skin tone. Her face was hard and stern, and she stared at me like I was a threat. I remembered that look well, though I had never been on the receiving end of it. I took in a deep breath and focused instead on the man next to her, whom I wasn't acquainted with.

The princess noticed me last, and she jumped from the wagon when she did.

"Cera!" she cried, spilling half her bowl in her haste to get to me. The guards blocked her way.

"I'm no threat, and I have no weapon," I said, annoyed. "Search me if it makes you feel better."

They exchanged glances and then Maddie came forward and held me from behind, one hand on my shoulder, the other threaded through my arms behind my back. I let her grab me and didn't resist. My heart throbbed with the loss of our friendship, and an insane part of me wanted to face her and spill everything. I ached for the overwhelming relief that would undoubtably come from confiding in her.

I longed to hear another living being call me by my real name.

I bit down hard on my bottom lip to stop myself from acting foolishly, knowing that any relief would be short lived, because then I would have to answer to her. I would have to justify my actions.

I would have to explain why I had betrayed her.

"Oh, Cera, I am sorry!" cried Odelia. "The guards are under orders from my brother's knight, but once we get home, I will explain everything to my brother, and you will be free." She hesitated. "If that is still what you want?"

I said nothing, waiting for her to elaborate.

After a pause, she dropped her voice low. "Cera, can we make a new bargain?" she asked. That wasn't what I had expected.

"What kind of bargain?" I asked suspiciously.

"Well, this whole experience has made me realise how much I need someone who I can rely on, someone who will work just for me and be my creature. I trust you more than anyone I have ever known."

Part of me was acutely aware of the pain Kohl would feel at hearing that and felt for him. Odelia knew, as well as anyone did, that as a member of the blood guard, Kohl would do anything ordered of him, even hurt his beloved princess.

"I want you to be that person, Cera," she continued in hushed tones. "If you decide to be my knight, then I don't even need to ask my brother first. It's a lifelong contract between you and me." She looked at the guards around me and hesitated. "You would be a high rank, on par with the blood guard, higher even than that. So…" She raised her eyebrows at me knowingly.

Ah, I got it, if I accepted this lifelong commission, then I would have more freedom on this journey. No one here would be able to control me, other than the princess herself. As tempting as that was, I would rather endure one trip as a prisoner than a lifetime as one.

I'd had enough of that to last *ten* lifetimes. I shuddered as a chill ran down my back. I was scarred, physically and mentally from my time as a puppet to the king, a prisoner inside my own body. If being a knight was anything like that, then I would pass. I didn't want to crush Odelia's hopes right away, which in itself was frustrating. Harbouring any small affection for this girl would end up being a weakness that someone could exploit, and I didn't want that for myself or for her.

"I am honoured, Princess Odelia," I said because that was what she wanted me to say, and truthfully, a part of me was flattered. Some of that came from the way I had been raised to believe royalty was next to godliness. Years of being around feckless royals had almost quashed that from me, but sometimes nurture won over nature.

"I can't accept right away. I need more time to think about such an important role." I had to give it to her, she didn't seem surprised and only looked a little disappointed before resilience settled in.

"Of course," she said. "That's only natural. This is a big step. Take that time. We have to go over all the benefits, and a contract will be drawn out and agreed upon between us first in any case. These things do take time."

A contract? I couldn't help but immediately wonder what could be in the knight's contract between himself and the king. The only thing I could possibly imagine anyone from the guard wanting was freedom, but once in, there was no way out. Everyone knew that.

"I wish you would let her go," Odelia said frustratedly to Maddie. "She could have harmed me anytime at Riverna if she had wanted to. She saved my life, so what on earth would she gain from hurting me now?"

The grip on my arms didn't falter, and I half-wondered if this princess had any power at all, even in her own kingdom and with her own people.

If any other guard had been holding me, I would have protested, maybe even headbutted them as a show of strength. But all the fight had seeped out of me, leaving me deflated. Being this close to Maddie pacified me a little. She still smelt the same, like jasmine and vanilla. It was comforting and bittersweet.

"Let her go."

At the command, Maddie immediately released me. It was the knight. If Kohl had been good at creeping up on me, this man was an expert. I hadn't felt the vibrations under my feet.

"Thank you, Knight. I have been telling everyone that Cera is here as my companion," said Odelia. "I don't want her treated like a criminal."

"I understand, my princess, however, until we can be sure of what the king wants to do with her, we cannot allow her the chance of escape." He hesitated. "Also, we are under orders to bring only yourself and any valuable prisoners or traitors with us. A companion would not fall under that."

I almost laughed aloud at this. So, they wouldn't be able to bring me back with them unless I was a prisoner. Some orders were easier to get around than others, and when you were a member of the blood guard, you had to become good at reading between the lines and twisting words.

"I no longer want Cera as just my companion. I think she has proven her loyalty to me. Instead of running away, she came to defend me. I want her as my Knight."

The knight didn't look happy about this revelation, but to give him his credit, he said nothing of it.

"We will be travelling through the day and into the night now, my princess. Please finish your meal," he said, purposefully not voicing his opinion on Odelia's plans for my future.

"Surely there is no reason to think my husband would pursue us?" she asked. "He tried to kill me!"

"The King of Rivera would not want to risk a war. He is foolish and has been led by his own greed. But he has some clever advisors still, or the marriage between you both wouldn't have happened in the first place," the knight said. "He wanted your death to appear to be an accident. I wouldn't be surprised if he had dispatched men to search for you and finish the job before you got back to your brother. Recall, he does not realise we have come for you. He likely believes you have run away with a few betrayers."

The princess looked concerned and wrung her hands together in the way she always did when nervous.

"Besides, it is not the Riverians I am concerned with. There is civil unrest in the Mid-lands. Rogues are gathering numbers along the borders. They have been building forces for years."

"What would they want with us?" Odelia asked, her eyebrows furrowed in concern.

"Who could say. A horse? A sheep? A cart? Or a smarter rogue could find a bargaining tool in yourself or I. It matters not. The mid-lands are not safe now, but the southlands would have been more dangerous still."

I took this all in with fascination. I hadn't kept up with politics since I left Nordia. I knew nothing of the unrest or the dwindling friendship between nations.

"What must I do to help?" she asked.

"Nothing. Stay disguised, stay on the cart and we will guard you. If we are set upon, follow Maddie's instruction."

Odelia nodded.

He turned to me then. "What would you prefer, the cart or my horse?"

I rolled my eyes. "Is that really necessary?"

"You tell me?" he asked.

"I'll take the horse," I said. A horse was far superior to the hard wooden pallet.

"As you wish," he said before turning to a male guard.

"Marius, keep an eye on her while I brief the others." The guard named Marius didn't hesitate. He took up the space Maddie had just held, pulling my arms behind my back in the same way.

"This is just ridiculous," I protested. The Knight had let me walk around freely earlier, and I had a feeling he was just trying to piss me off.

I could hear Kohl somewhere behind me, loudly organising the food and equipment to be packed away The princess smiled weakly at me before she shuffled up onto her cart and pulled a blanket over her head. The day was bright, but there was a brisk chill in the air. Autumn would be coming soon.

Maddie stepped up onto the cart next to Odelia. I couldn't help but stare at her. She looked the same, but her features were sharper from age, her jaw more defined. I wondered if she was happy. When we were young, she was being trained as a spy, but she wanted to be a soldier. It looked like she might have gotten her wish.

I wondered if she ever thought of me. Did she hate me for leaving her behind, for not telling her my plans, or would she be happy that I had escaped? Not for the first time today, I felt myself wishing I could ask about my family. Maybe I could find a way to do it incon-

"Do I know you?"

The question pulled me from my thoughts and sent a bolt of excitement through me. Maddie was observing at me thoughtfully, no longer hostile.

"I have never been in the Westlands, so I don't think that is possible," I lied, my voice shaky.

"Then why are you staring at me?"

I felt my cheeks burn with embarrassment. Had I really believed she would recognise me? After six years apart, and in a completely glamoured body. Foolish.

"You are unique looking," I said quickly. It was true, she was, and always had been beautiful. She was probably gaped at quite frequently, so it was no wonder that she called me out.

She laughed in surprise at my open reply. It lit up her face.

"Well, I'm promised to someone already, so stop being so obvious." She smirked and pulled a cloak over her shoulders as she settled next to the princess. She unsheathed a longsword and hid it under the material. For all the world they looked like two tired travellers, wrapped up against the cold.

Promised already? What did that mean? Was she married? Or engaged? Had my best friend gotten married?

"Your ride, my lady." I jolted as the knight came up behind me, a stallion in tow.

"You are very jumpy. Have you noticed?" he asked.

"You have no idea," I mumbled as Marius unhanded me and I took hold of the reins the knight offered me. As I climbed up onto the large black horse, my foot missed the stirrup, and I slipped slightly. Quick as a flash, the knight had his hands on my hips and lifted me up into the seat effortlessly.

"I had it," I said as I grabbed hold of the seat.

"I didn't want you hurting Sayre," he replied.

"Sayre?"

"My horse."

I rolled my eyes.

"I wasn't going to hurt yo-" But my words died away as the knight mounted the horse behind me. His weight pushed up close against my back as he leaned forward to take hold of the leather reins. His arms encased me, penning me in on both sides.

"I am starting to regret my choice," I complained. "You didn't say anything about having to share."

"Do you want to go back on the wagon?" he asked. His chest rumbled as he spoke, sending a shiver down my spine. I would rather be alone on the wagon than with him on this horse, but I wouldn't give him the satisfaction.

"Just go," I said.

The Knight chuckled, and with a loud whistle and a gentle tap of the reins, we were off.

Chapter 16

Riding with the knight wasn't the most comfortable experience. His body was much larger than mine, and it was hard to not feel completely overshadowed by it as we trundled along. However, the horse was well broken and tottered over the uneven and unkept pathways with care.

The hours blurred into one another as the scenery around us changed from forest to hills, to hamlet and back to woodlands. At first I admired the beauty around us, but the monotony of rocking back and forth on the steady horse soon became mind-numbing, and a few times as the light began to fade behind the horizon, I had to stop myself from leaning into the Knight's warmth as I drifted into a light sleep. The Knight was silent the entire journey, which I was both thankful for and frustrated by. More than once I considered swapping my seat for the wagon, but pride wouldn't let me.

"What way are we going?" I asked eventually, after a sudden whinny from the horse had woken me to the realisation that I was resting in the Knight's arms *again*.

I couldn't help it. He was so damn comfortable, and my back still ached from lying in the damp dungeon and the wooden cart.

I sat up straight and rolled my shoulders in an attempt to wake myself up.

I blinked blurrily in the dying light and was surprised to see how much closer the mountains were.

"Do you know this area, renter girl?" the knight asked, seemingly ignoring my question.

"No," I replied, perhaps a little too quickly.

He grunted.

I could see a small, well-lit hamlet nestled deep in a valley ahead of us. The lamps glowed and flickered invitingly.

"Do we go around?" I asked, eyeing up the dark, dense forest that surrounded the valley.

"We go through." The knight urged Sayre on with a click of his tongue and steered us down the sloping hills towards the thatched-roof houses and fields full of cabbage and livestock. As we approached the village, people stopped in their various activities to stare at the large procession approaching them. A group of children who were playing by the side of a lake all rushed over to the weathered wooden gate that enclosed the entire hamlet. They greeted us enthusiastically.

"Get out of here and back to your mother's hearth!" A woman yelled at them crossly as she intercepted them at the gate. Her greying hair was pulled up out of her stern face in a tight bun. She placed her hands on her hips as we approached and rested her foot on a stile..

"What business?" she asked me as Sayre came to a stop in front of her. A few other folks gathered behind her, some wandering over from their houses, others stepping away from small stalls selling breads and buns.

"Just passing through," the Knight answered. The woman looked suspiciously at the convoy behind us.

"We are soldiers of the king, heading to the west," he continued, his voice pleasant. The woman looked him up and down and clicked her tongue disapprovingly.

"From the West, is it?" she said. "On your way to Nordia?"

The knight remained silent, neither confirming nor denying. "Where from?" she asked, uncowed.

I could feel Sayre getting impatient under my thighs. The knight's grip on the reins tightened, and he made a soothing noise deep in his throat.

"Well you had best hurry through then," said the village woman eventually when no answer was forthcoming. "If you get any trouble, just tell them Jinn let you through." She tilted her head up proudly. "They won't question that."

The knight smirked but inclined his head in acknowledgement.

"Also, a word of caution to your ears," she continued. "There are rebels and wildlings set up a few miles from here, along the south. They don't bother us, but I would wager they would make time to bother a band like you." She pulled up the wooden gate and dragged it over the muddy ground until the gap was wide enough for even our biggest wagons. "What with all these supplies your carting about," she said. "Swords, valuables and the like, and more women than men to guard them," she observed, craning her neck down the end of the line. I sighed and bunched my fists together at the remark, but before I could say anything, the knight chuckled behind me.

"Our women are more murderous than the men, Jinn, so I wouldn't disrespect them."

Jinn looked at me cautiously, and I tried to keep my face as passive and threatening as possible. She wasn't deterred though.

"Seems silly to me," she observed as the knight led Sayre off to the side, signalling for the others to go ahead of us and into the hamlet.

"What seems silly?" I asked when it became clear that the knight planned to ignore the comment. My curiosity got the better of me.

"That a party of kings-men should have so many resources to slow them down," she said, looking up at me with squinting eyes. "Soldiers ain't what they used to be in my day," she went on. "Don't no one live off the land anymore?" I got the feeling that she complained about this kind of thing often. She shot a harsh look at a group of children, playing with a wooden baby pram and eating sweet buns. "When I was their age, I was working on the farms from sunrise to sunset," she said, almost to herself. The knight let out a low, amused sound at this.

"Where was it you said you come from, again?" Jinn asked, casually enough.

The knight suddenly barked out a command to Sayre while pulling firmly on the reins. The silky black horse raised up onto his hind legs instantly. I gasped and held onto the saddle to keep my seat as Sayre slammed down, stomping his hooves threateningly. This surprised Jinn into stepping back a few feet, open-mouthed and wordless.

I brushed my hair from my face and elbowed the knight as hard as I could in the stomach, annoyed by the lack of warning. He didn't flinch.

"Why don't we all keep our own secrets?" he said to the now-flustered Jinn. "Mine being our route and yours being your trade with the wildlings. Then no one has to get involved, and we can be out of your village as quickly as we were in it."

Jinn looked affronted by this but said nothing. I had to wonder if the knight really knew that the people of this village were trading illegally or if it had been a guess. It didn't matter though, as it clearly got the reaction he was hoping for.

After the last wagon passed through the gate, the village woman shut it again and, with one last cold look, waved us away hastily. The knight smirked, and Sayre shot off to the front. I caught a glimpse of Odelia bundled up from the cold in the wagon. She looked pale and frail next to the more alert Maddie. I doubted Odelia was used to travelling like this. Her procession into the east when she first married King Henri would have been a celebrated event, with planned stops and comforts to make the journey easier on her.

The carts trundled through the small hamlet, and the villagers mostly ignored us, which seemed strange to me considering our large party. Children held their hands out as if waiting for sweets and gifts.

"They are used to this," I said aloud.

"Yes," the knight agreed, sounding as curious as I was. "Odd, considering this is not a common route."

I nodded in agreement.

The knight leaned over and beckoned a small child to come closer. The girl of about six or seven didn't hesitate. She broke from her doorway with her hands outstretched. The knight reached into a pouch from the back of Sayre's saddle and pulled out a roll of bread. The girl took it, looking a little disappointed. She ate a large mouthful regardless.

"You have plenty of bread here?" the knight asked her. She nodded. "The soldiers usually bring us sticky beans," she said. "Do you have any?"

"What do they look like?" he asked.

"Small and round." She made a shape with her fingers, about the size of a silver coin, "They are red, chewy, and they taste like sugar and jam." She smiled and smacked her lips at the thought of the sweets. "Do you have them?" she asked again.

The knight shook his head. "Maybe next time."

"What is it?" I asked as we pulled away, leaving the girl to rush to her friends and tell them the sad news.

The knight seemed to hesitate, making a low, pensive sound in the back of his throat. For a moment, I was sure he would ignore my question, but then he seemed to think better of it.

"Sticky beans…" he said, contemplative. "They sound like stoki."

"What's that?" I asked.

"A fruit. It lasts months without rotting. It's sweet and juicy and said to be a bit addictive."

"Oh, so those solders shouldn't be giving it to the kids?"

"That's not the concerning part," he answered quietly.

"What?" I prompted.

"It's native to the northlands," he said.

"Oh."

"So, the question would be why are soldiers from the northlands travelling through here in large companies?"

"The north and midlands aren't at war though," I said. "They could just be trading with them."

"This close to the border of Nordia?" he questioned. "And the child said they were soldiers." It was suspicious. There was no savoury reason for that many soldiers to be traveling through the mountain pass. They had to be going west, since there was no other place to go from here. There were only a few conclusions I could immediately reach. Either Nordia was enlisting help from the north, or the north was planning an ambush in Nordia. Neither of these possibilities made sense to me.

We drifted into silence, both lost in thought, until Kohl caught up to us.

"The princess wants to stop soon," he said, concerned.

"We aren't stopping here," the knight replied firmly, looking around suspiciously.

"She is very insistent." Kohl sighed.

The Knight growled in frustration and pulled his horse about. He swore under his breath and glanced around distractedly.

"Tell her an hour more," he said finally. "An hour more and we will set up a camp." Kohl nodded and went back to relay the news.

"You're anxious?" I asked.

The Knight looked at me.

"I have a bad feeling."

Chapter 17

An hour turned into two and then three. Kohl came to complain only once, but a sharp word from the Knight had silenced him. Four hours from the hamlet took us to the very base of the mountain pass. We set up camp finally, near a stream with a beautiful rocky waterfall.

Odelia jumped down from her cart the moment it stopped and raced over to me, Maddie in tow.

"Every part of me is aching," she complained. "These wagons are not made for human travel."

I smiled kindly. My legs were painful similarly from being on the horse with the Knight all this time.

"Shall we walk to the river? I'd like to bathe my feet," she said.

I turned to Maddie for confirmation, not wanting to get in her bad books right off the bat. She looked displeased but didn't forbid it. So, I hopped down off the back of the horse, ignoring the Knight's steading arm when he offered it.

"Stay in my line of sight" he commanded. "I will send some men to light lamps for you," he said to the princess. I smiled secretly, knowing he had no idea that I could see in the dark as well as he could.

Maddie and Odelia and I made our way off the path and to the river. Odelia stripped off her fleece-lined boots and pulled her stockings down. Maddie kept a weary watch over her as she sat down on the riverbank.

"Ah." Odelia let out a little yelp that had Maddie and I gripping our weapons in alarm.

"Sorry!" She giggled at our response. "It's just freezing."

"Of course it is," I said. "It isn't summer anymore."

The smell of burning meat drifted to us from the camp, and I squinted through the trees to try to see what they were cooking.

"Sausages," Maddie confirmed. "They are just searing them over a small flame." She looked from me to Odelia for a moment, unsure.

"I will fetch us one, but I need your word that you won't let my princess out of your sight."

"I will guard her with my life," I said, happy that Maddie even considered leaving her ward with me.

"I will be able to see you, so don't get any ideas," she continued.

"I'm not going to run" I said, firmly staring deep into her shockingly blue eyes, willing her to trust me. Secretly, stupidly wanting her to know me.

Maddie nodded curtly, then hurried off.

Odelia and I sat side by side at the river's edge while we waited for Maddie's return. Odelia sighed contentedly as she splashed her feet in the water and basked in the soft breeze. I, however, was taut and filled with confusion.

What was I doing here? I needed to come up with a plan of escape. it was imperative that I not end up in Nordia. Surely this was the perfect chance to flee? So why wouldn't my legs move? I felt the burden of my promise to Maddie weighing tightly on my pounding chest. If I ran away now, would Odelia be alright alone? Surely Maddie would be back any second now anyway. Yet as we sat waiting for her, the seconds turned to minuets, and the minuets stretched on.

I started to feel an uncomfortable anxiety gnawing at my stomach.

Maddie was taking a long time.

Odelia seemed unconcerned, but I stood and pulled my dagger lose from my gown anyway.

Something was wrong.

I heard the clash of steel on steel in the distance, and my body flooded with adrenaline. Then I heard the battle cries. I grabbed Odelia's arm roughly and picked up her shoes.

"Put them on now!" I hissed.

She did as she was told, her fingers fumbling with haste. I held my hand out for her to stay where she was and crept around a tree. I took a deep, steadying breath before peeking out from the cover of the tree. I saw what I had feared.

The wagons were being raided and upended, and the guards were fighting sword on sword with an unknown enemy. Some of the braziers had been knocked to the floor in the chaos, growing hungrily into a blaze that lit up the entire scene. I had no idea if it was the rogues or wildlings from the south, but either way our camp was under attack. I hesitated, not sure if I should take Odelia and run farther into the wood or hide her and help fight.

"What do we do?" she whispered. Her eyes widened with terror.

Just then, I heard footfalls approaching. I gripped my dagger tightly and signalled for Odelia to get as low and hidden as she could. I counted the steps, and when I knew that the unknown enemy was within my range, I sprang from the tree, my dagger finding its mark at the base of a long, elegant throat.

"It's me," Maddie gasped breathlessly. Her hands held up above her head in surrender. I dropped my hand shakily.

"Hurry," she said. "We need to get the princess away from here, before—"

An arrow landed in the tree with a heavy thunk, right where I had been hidden only moments before. We all darted down to the damp floor as it was followed by three more.

"Run!" I yelled. "I will hold them off!"

Maddie didn't falter, grabbing hold of Odelia's hand. They both ran farther down the river, using the trees as cover. Another arrow landed near my feet, and I picked it up and ran at the archer, who I clocked, hidden behind a tree to my right. Their eyes flared in surprise as I approached, and they hastily nocked another arrow but not quickly enough. I ran into the assailant with the full force of my body and knocked them down. I hesitated a breath before stabbing the arrow into the side of their neck. I let out an involuntary sob as warm, bright red blood rushed over my hand. An immediate wave of disgust hit my stomach, causing me to heave, and an onslaught of thoughts flooded my brain.

Had I needed to kill this person? Could I have disarmed them instead? Had I enjoyed the power of taking this person's life? My own voice in my head mocked and confused me.

I cried out in frustration and jumped up, refusing to be distracted. I couldn't afford a panic attack right now. I didn't stay to see the damage I had caused. Before I could waver again, I darted away through the trees to join the fight.

I gasped to see that the camp was overrun. Everyone with a blade was fighting, and the fire that had been burning was spreading now unchecked. Enemy and guard alike were getting caught up in the flames, and at least one wagon of supplied had been completely destroyed.

Almost as soon as I reached the road, a rogue was upon me, a man twice my size. Before I could assess the situation, he grabbed me by the collar of my dress, pulled me down into a chokehold and lunged his blade at my ribs. I bent forward with as much strength as I could, forcing his grip to weaken, then I stabbed my dagger through his side, under the thick animal hide lined clothing. It took two strikes to find a gap, but he thrust wildly, throwing off my aim. I swore as my dagger rebounded off his armour. I tried again, but he sank lower and wrapped his arms around me, trying to get a better grip . I wiggled away and lunged again. He let out a yelp as my dagger broke skin, not wanting to lose the upper hand. I threw my head back, connecting with his chin. He staggered away, cradling his bloody chin in his hands. Without a second thought, I attacked. My dagger found his heart in one quick, deep puncture.

The moment the man was downed, another enemy replaced him. A woman with blue pigment painted all over her face and green eyes that were wide with excitement. She carried a longsword while I only had my small dagger. I took a deep breath and braced myself for the attack. The woman laughed in my face and paced around me.

These fighters were dressed like rebels, but they fought like soldiers. I could see her assessing my stance, looking for wounds to exploit.

This was a planned attack. I was sure of it. They knew exactly what route we were on and our numbers.

Either they had been watching us for some time now, or someone had told them where we were.

"I have always wanted to fight the legendary blood guard." The woman spoke. Her accent was thick and not one I recognised. I wasn't about to waste my breath indulging my enemy in chit-chat. I struck first, running into her in hopes of throwing her off. She intercepted me, only staggering for a moment. She gripped my shoulders and smiled widely before attempting to run me through. I jumped back and out of the reach of her blade. Before she could swing again, I slid to the floor, knocking her feet out from under her. She hit the ground face first, and I slammed my boot down onto her sword hand. She refused to let go of the blade and tried to stand up, gripping my leg with her other hand and yanking. I went down, and in a blink, she was on top of me, her sword pointed at my throat.

"I thought you were supposed to be elite soldiers," she mocked. "I could best you in my sle—" My dagger found her heart, stopping her mid-sentence. I pushed it into her chest, down to the hilt, and she fell forward on top of me, dead instantly.

She had been trained well, but no hardened soldier would waste time gloating.

I swore loudly as I stabbed my blade into the eye of another attacker, kicking them dead in the chest with as much force as I could while they staggered, screaming and grabbing at their bloody socket.

I took a moment to look around then and spotted the Knight fighting against two enemies from horseback. He looked around wildly, no doubt searching for Odelia. His eyes alighted on me, and I mouthed the word "safe." I only hoped he could understand. I didn't have time to dwell on it though as an arrow whizzed past my head, catching me at my temple. It stung, and I felt blood well up. I looked around for the archer and instead spotted Vale, half hidden in the treeline, fighting off three attackers alone. She was bleeding heavily. My guts churned as I raced over to help her.

I got there just in time to see one of the attackers stab her clean through the stomach. I screamed in shock and ripped the sword from the hands of another attacker, stabbing their own sword right through their chest. They fell to the ground, dead and with wide eyes. The other two attackers turned away from the now mortally wounded Vale and faced me. I couldn't tell either of them from a woman or man. Their faces were painted with blood, and their smiling teeth were filed down to points. They both advanced on me together, swords raised. I turned my dagger in my hands.

It may have been a long time since I was in combat, but I knew the moves like I knew the steps to a dance.

One…two…three. The attackers lunged.

One…two…three. I leaned into their attacks, catching them off guard and sending them staggering. Both their swords drew blood, but only grazes.

One…two…three. I was behind them now, and as they wasted time turning to me, I stabbed my dagger into the base of the smaller one's neck. I swiped the head half off the other. They both fell in a grotesque heap at my feet. I didn't look at them as they died. Instead, I ran over to where Vale lay. I threw myself down at her side and watched as she clutched helplessly at her open wound.

Chapter 18

I felt hot tears falling down my face, and I didn't try to hide them. The fighting carried on around us, but no one approached us, gods help them if they did.

Vale gasped and choked on her own blood as she looked up at me in horror. I stroked her face reassuringly, then using my dagger, I cut and tore a thick panel of fabric from my dress. I pressed it to her wound to try to staunch some of the bleeding. It was saturated in blood within seconds. She was bleeding out and wouldn't last long.

My heart throbbed as I prepared myself for what I knew I had to do.

Now was my only chance, but fear and shame held me back.

There was no saving Vale now. She was gone.

There was something I needed to know, and only one way of finding out. But I knew it would break me to do it. I needed to know if Vale had orders to kill me or capture me on sight. Had the new king forgotten about me or were their guards out there actively looking to apprehend me? I needed to know.

"Vale," I whispered. Her dying eyes flared in confusion at the use of her name, and she looked at me afresh. "I'm so sorry for everything," I choked out. "I am so sorry that I let you down. You must have hated me." She searched my eyes, trying to understand, but they were unfocused from pain and blood loss. She didn't have long.

"You must have been so disappointed."

I held both her arms down and quickly checked for weapons. Haze was lying discarded in the blood-soaked dirt at my feet, and I could see no others.

I took a deep, shaky breath, very aware that I was running out of time.

"It's me, Vale. It's Celine."

The reaction was instantaneous, despite her weakened state. She used all of her remaining force to try to break free from me. I wept openly, knowing this must have been causing her immeasurable pain, to exert all the effort she had left. But while her body was desperately trying to fight me off, to get the upper hand, I could see she was battling against the compulsion mentally, and that was all the assurance I needed.

"Thank you for everything, Vale, I love you," I gasped. Her struggling grew weaker, until I could see it was almost over. She looked me in the eyes, and I expected venom but saw sadness and something like hope instead.

"My Celine," she breathed. "Run, dear heart. Run now." The kindness in her voice crumbled the last of my strength, and I grabbed her up, holding her close to my body as I sobbed. I knew she was gone. She didn't fight me. "I'm so sorry," I begged between sobs. "Forgive me please. I could have saved you!" The guilt and loss crashed into me like a wave. I went limp and sagged down on top of Vale's lifeless body, covered in tears and blood, and I let myself fall apart, struggling for every breath. I wasn't only crying for the teacher and mentor that I had lost, I was crying for my parents, for my brother, for every single child forced into the blood guard without knowing what it would be to give up their body to the whims of rich, stupid, power-hungry men.

"What happened?" It was the knight. I felt his arms grip my shoulders, and he pulled me up into the air away from Vale. I didn't fight as my feet left the ground, and I found myself staring into the darkness of his hood.

"What happened?" he asked again, his voice dark and threatening. I let out a weak sob in response. He squeezed me harder. "I won't ask again," he warned.

"I killed her!" I yelled into his face. He searched my eyes for a second, trying to read the truth, then threw me to the ground and went to Vale.

My whole body throbbed and hurt, and my heart was shattered. I didn't want to feel this, I wanted to be numb. Vale had been like a mother to me. Had encouraged and taught me, had picked me up when I faltered.

Could I have stopped this?

If I hadn't run six years ago, if I had stayed and carried through with my father's plan, would Vale have had the chance to taste freedom before she was killed here today?

Panic thrummed through me, and I stood involuntarily. I ran my bloody hands through my tangled hair and began pacing. This was my fault, all of this. Would the blood on my hands ever wash clean? How many deaths would be on my card before the end of my days?

I couldn't do this. I paced in a small circle, fighting the urge to run away, knowing the Knight would only chase me down if I did.

"I did this, I did this!" I breathed over and over. I forced myself to look at Vale's broken body, discarded in the dirt. She had been initiated when she was sixteen, and now she had to be in her early fifties, but she looked so small.

"Are you injured?" It was Maddie. I recognised her voice, but I couldn't focus on her whereabouts.

"I think you're having a panic attack," she said gently. "Ground yourself, it will help."

I shook my head and tried to move away from her, stumbling on my weak legs. Maddie had learnt that from me, from helping me in the past. The pain of old memories was too much to bear. I began to run but stopped abruptly as a large hand gripped my forearms and tugged me down onto the hard floor.

"Sit down!" the knight commanded, his voice a bark. I pushed away from him and stood. I needed to be alone. I needed to get away from Vale. I ran from the path and into the woods, forcing through branches and thorns. They cut my face, tangled and snagged on my gown, but I kept going.

I kept going until I felt water filling my boots. I could hardly breathe, so I let myself fall down into the ice-cold river. I lay on my back, looking up at the inky blue sky. I focused on breathing, on the rushing sound of my heartbeat in my ears, on the piercing water as it washed over me, on the twinkling of the stars above me. I kicked off my heavy boots and let them sink.

Was I always going to be weak to my emotions? It had been my constant failing. I had played the part of a heartless killer for so many years, pretending that nothing fazed me. So my father couldn't find fault, so my king couldn't exploit me. I had done a terrible job of it then, and it was even worse now.

I wonder if my father had been surprised when I betrayed him, when I showed myself to be the coward I was. I am sure he hadn't expected me to betray the guard at least. That must have shocked him.

Vale wasn't a coward, so why hadn't the curse released someone like her instead? Or Garrett or Maddie. They were so much stronger than me. They probably would have managed to unlock the secret and free the entire guard by now. Instead of hiding out like a terrified mouse.

They would have tried.

I didn't even try.

After a while, I dragged myself back to the bank of the river and pulled myself up through the mud back into the forest.

I collapsed against a tree trunk and took in deep calming breaths. I shuddered against the cold.

"I don't know what to do with you," the Knight said. I sighed, unsurprised by his presence, I was aware that he had followed me.

"What trouble you have been." His voice was soft, long-suffering.

He was leaning against a tree, and his bloodied sword was stuck into the ground near him, ready to be taken up in an instant to carry out my punishment.

His sharply chiselled face was smudged with black-red blood. I could see every inch of it clearly now, as his torn and bloodied cloak and mask were discarded on the riverbank by his feet.

I laughed humourlessly, hysterically as I met his unreadable gaze. It was fitting that *he* be the one to kill me.

It was almost a comfort.

My laughter died and morphed into wracking, heaving gasps. I wanted to throw myself into his arms, and I wanted to let myself sink into the feeling of utter relief that seeing him brought to me.

He looked at me with concern, his brow furrowed and lips parted. He pushed off from the tree but didn't approach, no doubt stilled by my madness.

Perhaps I was completely insane. I found that I wasn't surprised though.

Deep down I had already known that the knight had to be Garrett. Who else could he have been?

No one was as strong as him, and no one had as much reason to join hands with the king in the search for revenge.

I had murdered his only brother, after all.

No one else had those grey-blue eyes and that wide, playful smile.

He was more handsome than I remembered. The Garrett of my dreams was gentle, soft faced and reliable. The true Garrett before me was hardened, confident and very changed.

His thick silver-white hair fell past his ears in wet waves, and his face was scarred from past battles. The thin, raised lines ran over the sharp planes of his face and through his eyebrows. It didn't detract from his beauty.

I was responsible for one of those scars, the one that ran down from the curve of his high cheekbone to the tip of his chiselled chin. I had misjudged my lunge during a practice, back before I even knew his name. We had been paired against one another, the smallest recruit and the biggest. I suppressed a smile, thinking about how shocked everyone had been when the stroke landed, none more than I.

I took in a deep lungful of air and let myself fall back onto the dirt. The autumn breeze caressed my face and made me shiver.

"Just make it quick, knight," I breathed, my throat raw. "I'm more than ready." A warm tear trailed its way down my cheek. It was salty on my dry, cracked lips.

Garrett was unresponsive and still. The silence between us stretched until the sun disappeared behind the trees, plunging us into almost complete darkness.

I sat up slowly, my body aching and shivering uncontrollably now. My teeth chattered together loudly, and I realised my bare toes had gone numb.

Dancing light from the camp behind us touched the edges of the riverbank, and I could hear the sound of voices carrying on the wind. They were closer than I had realised.

"Don't run," Garrett said as I shuffled into a crouch. His voice was surprisingly soft. It made my heart ache longingly.

"I wasn't going to," I said honestly. I crawled until my back met a tree, and I let my body relax into it. I was stiff and bruised and emotionally exhausted. The silence extended again, until I could hear the voices from the camp calling my name.

I wondered what Garrett was thinking, why he hadn't raised his sword to me or forced me back to camp yet.

"I don't believe that you killed Vale," he said suddenly.

"I can assure you that I did." I laughed bitterly.

"To spare her, then?" he asked. "You had no reason to kill Vale. I have seen cold-blooded killers at their work, Cera, and they don't cry like that."

"I find that hard to believe," I mumbled.

"Cold-blooded killers, those that kill for no reason but the joy of killing, do not feel remorse. And there was no reason for you to kill Vale."

"What does it matter?" I exploded, frustrated by his calmness. "I did it, and it's done. Your friend is dead by my hand, and now it's time to get your revenge. Don't drag it out." I goaded him. I don't know what I wanted, for him to comfort me? For him to strike me down? Every time I looked at his face, I had to force myself to look away again.

If only I could turn back time.

"I was never a fan of revenge," he said quietly. "I prefer to understand the reason. No one acts without *reason*." His word felt like a threat, and I tensed up, afraid that those sharp eyes would be able to read my every secret if they looked hard enough.

"So, what was yours?" he asked. I sat silent, not trusting myself to talk, not wanting to hope that this situation would play out in a way that saw me still alive and somehow forgiven.

Garrett pushed away from the tree, leaned down and grabbed my arm forcefully. I let him pull me up so that I stood face to face with him.

My heart hammered in my chest in response to his proximity. His eyes were lit by the distant blazing torches, the scarce glow dancing over his familiar features.

I looked hungrily, my eyes trailing each flicker of light across his face. He and I had once been so close. I had sought my comfort from him, shared my joys and successes with him. I had loved him without ever knowing if he loved me too.

"I don't understand you," he said, stepping back slightly and dropping my arm. He looked confused and almost afraid. "I can't comprehend your motive or your reasonings," he continued "Why are you here? It couldn't possibly be from loyalty to Odelia? Why have you not run when it is clear that you could escape with ease?" I said nothing, but he didn't seem to have expected a reply. "The money?" He appeared to be asking himself now. "Only a fool would go to such lengths for money not yet in their pocket." He looked at me intensely then, his eyes searching mine. "I don't understand now, but I will. You would be mistaken to think you can hide your plans from me, *Cera*." He spat my name mockingly. As though he knew it was fake.

"And I will—" He stopped dead then, suddenly alert to the woodland around us. He looked off into the distance, over the other side of the river. I followed his gaze but saw nothing out of the ordinary.

"Come here," he hissed as he pulled me in closer. I stumbled slightly, but he steadied me, all the while searching the treeline.

"What is—" I began, but he silenced me with a finger to his lips.

Just then the riverbank was illuminated by a blinding blue-white light. I gasped and turned my head away into the darkness of Garrett's shoulder. My eyes stung and watered from the abrupt burst of light.

When the surprise wore off, I pulled away and tried to escape out of his hold, but Garrett gripped my waist tighter and raised his sword out in front of us. I pushed against him again in panic. I didn't want to be this close to him.

"Stop," he whispered, irritated. "This is witch-light."

I paused in my struggle and looked around. He was right, the light wasn't natural.

"Who goes there?" he demanded, his voice like venom. He moved me so that I was behind him. I bristled at the treatment, but the rational part of my brain knew that I was a liability. If faced with another assault I wasn't sure how long I would hold out. My legs were barely supporting me, and I was still shivering violently from the icy river water.

He spun us both around suddenly, swapping our positions like I weighed nothing. He widened his stance, and I knew he had spotted the threat. I followed his gaze, but my eyes were still struggling against the light. I could see a hazy, dark silhouette between the trees, separating us from the camp.

"Stay behind me," he hissed, holding an arm out protectively as he rolled his sword in his hand. I drew my own dagger from my hip, frustrated that he felt I wasn't able to help, I could still be useful.

My eyes finally began to adjust to the too-bright light, and I recognised the silhouette standing above us in the trees.

I instantly relaxed in relief. I felt an overwhelming sense of comfort that brought tears to my eyes.

"Mags!" I yelled into the quiet, my voice cracking. I tried to make my way past Garrett to get to the witch. But he stilled me with an outstretched arm, pulling me back easily.

"Let go. She is with me," I snapped. "She's safe."

"Safe?" spat Garrett. "The Poison Witch has been called many things in her time, but "safe" is not a common one," he said darkly. I faltered at the name, both because it wasn't one Mags had shared with me before and because it was a name I was familiar with from childhood. It was a horror story, a tale told to the children of the Westlands, to make sure they behaved. The witch who poisoned sweet treats and fed them to naughty children before luring them through the forest to her hut. The poison witch, who kings and men feared for her ruthlessness.

"No," I said, laughing uncomfortably. "This is Mags."

He pulled me around and looked into my eyes, trying to read the truth there. "This is the poison witch standing before us now," he said. "I would know her anywhere."

I turned back again. All I saw was Mags in her familiar dress, looking young, beautiful and happy to see me.

"Mags?" I asked, unsure.

"One in the same." She smiled and lowered her staff, dimming the light so that we could see her better.

"Stay back, you poison bitch," spat Garrett. I gasped and slapped him hard across the face without even thinking. His jaw tightened, but he showed no other reaction to my attack. Mags laughed heartily at this.

"Oh, I am that too though," she said.

I felt my stomach drop.

"What?" I spluttered. Mags met my gaze unwaveringly as she stepped closer.

"I am both. You could call me Mags, the poison bitch, if you like, Knight."

The poison witch, who stole children from their beds and murdered the Black King's heirs?

The Black King had been the king of Nordia and all the Westlands centuries ago. Back when witches still tried to claim the rights to the Westlands. He'd outlived all his children, and the rumour was that the poison witch had killed them. It caused a short-lived war between the old bloods and the new, with the king's brother eventually taking the crown. Any whisper of witches once having ruled Nordia was supressed, and the crown passed peacefully from parent to child ever since then.

"Don't start fretting over a name," Mags said softly. "You know me Cera, and the rumours are mostly exaggerated anyway."

"How are you here?" I asked.

"I came, as I always do."

I smiled. I couldn't help it. I had hoped she would come.

"You can let her go, brave knight. I won't hurt her nor you."

Garrett didn't let me go nor did he lower his sword.

"You need to go," he said to Mags.

"I can't. I am bound to Cera, so where she goes, I follow."

"I won't have the poison witch joining our party," he warned through gritted teeth.

"I'm not sure how you would stop her?" I said, truthfully.

He looked at me then, his face calm, despite his anger.

"Then you are underestimating my power," he said, simply.

I shrugged and pulled away from him to meet Mags. "Cera, this is my one and only warning to you," Garrett growled "Get away from the Poison witch."

I hesitated. I knew in my heart that Mags was safe, whatever name she used. However, Garrett was clearly filled with some kind of ingrained prejudice against her. "She is harmless, knight," I said firmly. I held my arms out to Mags in welcome, only to find them forcibly snapped back into place by my side.

I looked down, wide-eyed and saw red-black witch-light crackling over my arms and torso. I gasped and looked up at Mags, questioningly. She seemed shocked herself, an expression I then realised that I had never seen on her face before.

"How?" I asked, because surely this could have only come from one place, if not Mags… then?

"You aren't a witch," I said confidently. Turning my head to look at Garrett. "You aren't a witch," I repeated.

Witches were initiated and came into their powers at fourteen. Garrett had been nineteen when I left Nordia, and he couldn't have hidden it from me.

I tried to move but found that my legs were rooted to the floor with the same magic that held my arms. Another glance at Mags showed that she was in the same position as me, bound by some kind of magic.

I could hear Garrett's sure footfalls, and he came to a stop in front of me with his back to Mags, confident in his power over us both.

"You know nothing of me," he said with a sigh. His blue-grey eyes searched my face, no doubt taking in my chattering teeth, blue lips and bloodied appearance. For a moment, his face softened, and his lips parted, as though he wanted to say more. Then his face hardened again. "You know nothing of my power, or the power of the blood crown," he continued. "You are here as my prisoner, and it is in your best interests to remember that." I looked up at this stranger. How could he have hidden this from me? When I had confided everything to him...almost everything.

I felt betrayed, which I realised was hypocritical of me, but I couldn't help it, it stung. The urge to know more was almost overwhelming.

What had I got myself into here?

"So, what happens now?" I asked him. "Where do we go from here?"

"Your friend leaves. She cannot join us. If I sense her following, then I will come for her. The poison witch is no longer welcome in the Westlands."

"What if I come as a willing prisoner?" Mags asked calmly.

Garrett scoffed.

"Why would you do that, witch?" he asked, without even turning to look at her.

"The king used my services often in the old days. He might be happier to see me than you think."

I didn't remind Mags that there was a new king now, who was younger than me and no doubt had grown up listening to the old tales as much as I had.

"And if not," she continued, "then you will no doubt be very popular for bringing in the notorious witch, who poisoned the Black King's own family."

If I could move, I would have probably been bowled over. Was that a confession? Or Mags being flippant and playing on the rumours?

I felt frustrated. Two people I trusted had purposefully withheld information about themselves from me. I knew it was ridiculous of me to feel that way as I stood here in a glamour with a false name and a plan to abandon the princess at first chance.

Garrett and Mags were staring one another down now in silence. It was almost as if they were communicating without words, which perhaps they were.

"Your reason for wanting to come?" Garrett asked eventually. Mags laughed.

"You know as well as any that if I were to say it aloud, you would be compelled by your curse to kill me. It's best I say nothing." She raised her eyebrows meaningfully. "Perhaps then we can both get what we want?" Her words seemed to hold a deeper meaning, and Garrett's eyes widened.

"Don't promise things you cannot fulfil. You would regret making an enemy of me."

"I am fulfilling it as we speak," Mags said with a friendly smile.

Garrett was silent for a moment longer, then I felt the power go from my body, and I sagged in the dirt. He gripped my upper arm and held me up before I could fall.

"We will see" was all he said before pulling me away. I watched as the pulsing firelight moved over Mags's body to surround her legs and arms in thick, flame-engulfed chains. She could shuffle behind us, but no more than that. Her witch-light dimmed and tapered out completely, leaving us once again in the almost dark state. I turned back to Mags in concern. In all the time I had known her, I had never seen her vulnerable like this. It made my heart twist in discomfort.

Garrett led us back to the camp, where we were quickly enclosed by frantic guards.

"Send word ahead to the king," Garrett said. "I have a gift for him."

Chapter 19

It was a bleak evening for the guards. Bodies were buried and mourned. Everything was hurriedly packed away, and Mags let herself be tied onto a cart, with Kohl, Marius and Greta ordered to watch her.

Garrett and I sat upon Sayre at the front of the procession. It was dark, with only a little moonlight to guide the way. After the ambush, everyone was more cautious, and the lamps were minimal and burning low. As guards we had been trained extensively to find our way in the dark and to follow natural trails. But it had been a long time since I last used that particular skill, and I found myself losing sight of the pathway again and again. Garrett would silently take the reins from my hands and redirect.

"I have it," I said, pulling the reins back for the third time, frustrated by my failure.

"I know," he said, his voice soft above my ear. I repressed a shiver. I was exhausted from the night's events and revelations and fighting against the urge to completely give in and let myself fall asleep in Garrett's arms.

I should be trying to keep my distance from him, as hard and unnatural as that felt. If Garrett knew my real identity, then he would want me dead, and there was something unbearably dishonest about being around him, knowing that. I was overly aware that I had destroyed his life,

"Do I have to share a horse with you?" I asked, flustered. I heard his soft chuckle from behind me, and he leaned down closer.

"Am I bothering you?" he asked, his voice so quiet that it was almost lost in the wind. I didn't trust myself to answer and focused instead on the road. My heart fluttered excitedly in my chest. I shimmied forward in the seat to try to put as much space between us on this horse as was possible.

Garrett took the reins from my hands then and pulled on them hard. Sayre stopped dead, obediently. In one fluid motion, Garrett was off the horse and halting the procession. I turned in my seat to watch him walk down the line, holding a hand up to any questioning guards. He disappeared out of my eyeline.

I turned to Kohl behind me. He shrugged and steadied his own mount. I was beginning to think that the guards were used to Garrett doing whatever he wanted.

When the knight retuned, he was on horseback. He cantered over to meet me.

"Go," he said.

"What?" I asked, dumfounded.

"Go," he said again, inclining his head forward. He leaned over and rubbed Sayre's neck gently. "There are too many riderless horses now. It was slowing us down. You take Sayre. He won't steer you wrong."

I met Garrett's blue-grey eyes in confusion.

"Sayre is your horse," I said simply.

"And Fax was Vale's," he said.

I looked at the beautiful tawny-brown horse. Its white mane was braided carefully with red ribbons and its reins were adorned with hand-stitched ward-evil signals. Vale had taken good care of this horse.

"Are you sure you can trust me?" I said, half-joking.

"No, but I trust Sayre. You wouldn't get far if you ran, Cera." He voice was a low threat, but he didn't look angry. He looked a little sad. He had purple smudges under his eyes from lack of sleep. I wondered if he had also spent the years apart abusing himself and pushing too hard, like I had.

"You aren't going to run, Cera," he continued. "Not because you couldn't but because you want something.

It's clear for anyone to see. I don't know what your reasons are, but I wish you would give them up and go back to wherever you came from." I jolted at the sudden sincerity in his voice, rough and a little resentful. He stared at me meaningfully before urging Fax forward. "There is nothing good in the west."

Was he warning me? Did this mean he would let me go if I tried to escape?

I recalled the night in the dungeons when he and Kohl had liberated me from my cell. Garrett hadn't wanted to bring me along, but Kohl insisted.

I stared ahead unabashedly at the man I had loved so childishly in my teen years, knowing that he couldn't see me. He had always been so full of goodness, to his very core. Stubborn, with an unwavering sense of justice and a formidable sword hand, but good.

I ached to know him as I had known him back then.

It was folly though. Our relationship would never be the same as it had once been. Not after what I had done. The time apart had changed us both, and our actions and experiences had estranged us from one another irreconcilably.

Time passed slowly as we progressed up through the mountain pass, and Garrett led the way on Fax. I purposefully put two wagons of distance between us before the twisting pathways became too narrow. I had tried to pull Sayre alongside the wagon Mags was traveling in, but Marius and Greta had both forbidden it. So, I was behind Maddie and Odelia. The princess was fast asleep, buried under a large pile of blankets and cloaks. Maddie sat alert at the edge of the cart, her blade in one hand and a skin flask of water in the other.

The air around us became intolerably crisp and sharp as we ascended, and by the time the sun was beginning to crest the horizon, I was thoroughly uncomfortable. My dress hadn't dried from the river, and the weight of it was heavy on my shoulders. I could only imagine how hideous I looked. I had no shoes to cover my numb feet, and my wounds weren't healed, and I was drenched in blood from the battle the night before. A common mortal wouldn't have survived a journey this way, but I had been conditioned from childhood to withstand almost any climate.

Still, my grip on Sayre's reins faltered more than once, but the horse carried on regardless. The biting chill air of the mountains seemed to blow into my very bones. I could see lights twinkling below us from distant hamlets, encampments and villages tucked away in the forests and valleys below. I longed for their fire pits.

"Here, you look like you need this."

I faltered at Maddie's words, dropping my reigns again. Maddie held her canteen outstretched towards me, without hesitation I leaned over and took it from her. I downed a large sip and felt the burn instantly as it rolled down my tongue and lit a fit in my chest. It wasn't water—it was some kind of spiced spirit. A strong one at that.

"Thank you," I croaked. Maddie laughed, and the familiar sound warmed me more than the alcohol had.

I took another sip before handing it back.

"You should take that thing off or it will never dry," she continued, waving her hand at my gown.

"It's silk and taffeta. You're better off in your stays."

"It keeps most of the wind out," I countered. Maddie frowned and looked around, unsure. Then she put her lips to her mouth and whistled loudly. The sound echoed, bounding off the mountain valleys and through unseen caverns. The procession came to a slow stop, and she hopped down, signalling for me to follow. I dithered.

"What's happening?" Kohl called from somewhere behind me.

"She's going to die frozen to this horse if she doesn't change her clothes," Maddie replied. "Give me your boots!" I scoffed at the command, but surely enough Kohl hopped down from his cart and yanked his boots off, one after the other, revealing that his feet were covered in leather and linen, bound with string.

"Keeps the water out," he explained. Maddie rubbed my feet to get some of the blood back into them and then pushed the boots on for me. They were too big, but I didn't care. I felt in awe of her kind actions. I stared down at her in wonder as she began to untie the laces of my outer dress. I climbed down from Sayre's saddle and let the dress fall away to the floor with a heavy thud. The cold hit me like a kick to the chest, and my teeth chattered together uncontrollably.

Unbidden, Kohl pulled off his top shirt and reached to place it over my head. Maddie did the same.

"Your dagger," Kohl reminded me. He pulled it out of the layers of my discarded gown and slotted it into my right boot. I thanked him, mortified that I hadn't remembered to retrieve it myself. I felt slow and groggy from the bitter cold and the pain. A cloak was placed around my shoulders, and I pulled the hood up over my face, my ears immediately began to burn from the change in temperature.

"All clear?" came the low growl of Garrett's voice from up ahead.

"Thank you." I breathed again as Maddie and Kohl rushed back to their posts.

Maddie took a large draft from her canteen and offered it to me again.

We shared it until the last dregs were gone, and I felt a flush in my cheeks. It was potent stuff. I had to wrap Sayre's reins tightly around my hands and bloodied wrists to stop them from dropping.

The grogginess fell away from me like a slap to the face, however, when I realised that we were following a small trickling stream of water that I remembered clearly from my childhood on these mountains.

It ran slowly along the rock face, gathering into thicker pools at the edge of the pathway. It seeped down the mountain side like water from an overflowing flagon, feeding the large winter blooms that I'd memorised so fondly. In a daze, I reached out and plucked a flower from its vine, turning it over in my hand. The rough faded-pink petals were coated in tiny intertwining hairs. I couldn't remember what the flower was called, but I recollected that my father had been a fan of its resilience.

I placed the flower at my breast, hidden under my stays, next to my mother's talisman that sat warm against my heart at all times.

We were close now to the road that, if followed, would lead to my family's winter home. I knew we wouldn't go down that way, yet my heart palpitated wildly as we came closer and closer.

"Are you alright?" Maddie asked me. I realised I was staring wide-eyed at the tips of the mountain, secretly hoping for a glimpse of the towers that carried my father's flag. What would it mean if the flags were still hoisted?

"My family owns a home near here," Maddie continued, "Kohl's family too." I had almost forgotten that Maddie also came from an aristocratic family, many of the guard did. She had been enlisted much younger than me, at only five years of age. So, it was likely she had never even stayed in these mountains.

"It's beautiful," I said, then I worried that I had sounded too romantic. Maddie simply shrugged, however.

"Its bloody cold, I don't know about beautiful."

We made it to the fork in the road, and I found myself staring longingly down the frozen pathway. Irrationally, as we passed by, I contemplated leading Sayre back there, riding to the lake, and then on to the manor.

But where next?

Back to the East?

I think not.

"It's Lanchel," Maddie said in a breath, almost to herself.

Lanchel.

A small town built into the mountains, the last stop before crossing the border to the west. I took a deep lungful of air to steel myself.

It would be time to make my escape soon.

I had to go.

BOUND TO THE CROWN

Things weren't quiet as simple anymore though, not now that Mags was a captive. A willing one at that. It confused me. I couldn't understand her actions, and I had no chance to talk to her openly while she was heavily under guard.

I knew Mags could look after herself, but why had she come here and insisted on joining our party anyway? When she knew that I wouldn't want to stay?

The sunrise over Lanchel was breath-taking, the snow topped homes sparkled dazzlingly, and flags and banners of sky blue and moss green danced playfully in the breeze. Bells chimed out a five-note tune that I remembered hearing as a child. The familiarity brought a genuine smile to my face. When I was younger, I had wanted to live in this town, and I had often wondered what it would be like to grow up here in the open, to play with children my own age instead of learning how to kill them. To attend the little school and worry about nothing but crops and cattle and who I would marry.

As we progressed through the stirring town, I noticed that a fayre of some kind was being set up in the sparkling market square. Blue-and-green bunting hung from the rafters of every home, wooden stalls overflowed with various types of flowers and a large bonfire was erected, ready to be lit.

They must've been preparing for their harvest festivals.

Without meaning to, I began to lead Sayre over to the stalls, away from the pathway. I didn't comprehend what I had done until Garrett rose up beside me on Fax. He placed his hand over mine and took the reins from me firmly while clicking his tongue.

Sayre instantly obeyed, trotting back over to the wagons.

"We don't have time for sightseeing, Cera. Maybe another time," Garrett said. He sounded so earnest that for a moment I believed that there would be another time and felt myself smiling. Garrett blinked at me, his face unreadable. His gaze flicked quickly to my mouth and then away.

I quickly snapped out of it, internally scolding myself for being so stupid, and hoping my hot cheeks weren't turning red.

"There is no cover here," I said with a throat-clearing cough. "We need to hurry back down the mountain.'"" I pulled the reins back from Garrett, harder than I meant to, and Sayre whinnied loudly in annoyance. I rubbed behind his ear in apology before driving him onwards towards the path out of town.

Garrett caught up to me again as I found myself leading the procession of carts.

"You have been here before," Garrett stated calmly. "I can tell."

"What?" I snapped, suddenly frightened for what I might have given away.

"You know your way around these lands," he continued.

"I know how to follow a path, Knight," I countered.

He reached for my reins again, forcing us both to a stop.

"I saw you the other day, staring at the mountains. Is this your homeland?" he pressed.

"Who goes there?" cried a voice from one of the log houses nearby, distracting Garrett. I let out a shaky breath, not aware I had been holding it. I was starting to question my ability to lie to this man.

A large figure stepped from the doorway, lit by the light of a roaring fire.

"Friend or foe?" he asked.

"Friend, passing through into the Westlands, good man. Go about your morning," Garrett called in reply.

"Impossible, sir!" the voice boomed suddenly.

"I have been waiting patiently for you. It's the morning of our harvest festival of Garn! Travelers are a good omen! Won't you stay here with us and sup at the festival tomorrow?"

My hands tightened on the reins. Some childish, weak part of me wanted to turn to Garrett and implore him to agree, like I had in our childhood, convincing him to sneak into a party or steal food from the kitchens.

However, there was a gap between us now that stretched out over the passing of time. To him, I was a complete stranger, and a dangerous one at that.

Garrett dismounted and greeted the townsman, who was busying himself lighting a large wooden torch. They spoke for a while in hushed tones, and Garrett took the torch. I stared at him, bemused.

The townsman disappeared into his home and reappeared with a wicker basket in hand. I could see it was brimming with jars of jam and chutney, bundles of cheese sealed in wax and a large loaf of thick, seeded bread.

"Greetings," he said, "and may the gods of winter cherish you." He handed the parcel to me, which I took thankfully.

"And you," I returned warmly.

. The bread was still hot, and it smelt divine.

"Eat," implored the villager. "There is much more where that came from!"

Garn was a day of gifting, of being abundant and thankful to the gods for the harvest before winter. Villages like this were self-sufficient but surely not able to fill every guard's belly with a loaf of bread. However, to refuse would be an insult. I tore a large piece and ate it plain. It was delicious, bursting with seeds and dried fruits. I ripped another bit and handed it to Garrett. I passed the remainder of the loaf off to a guard in the cart behind me.

"We cannot stay," Garrett reiterated. "I thank you for your hospitality though," he said. "We would happily return the favour at the king's table."

The villager looked touched.

"Thank you," he said. "I beg the gods for your safe journey." He motioned to Garrett, who still held the large torch in his arms.

"You must light the fire. We have had no other guests for days, so it must be you." Garrett followed the man back into the square and threw the entire brazier down. It set ablaze instantly, and several people came to their doors, clapping merrily.

"I hope to see you all back here!" the townsman declared jovially.

I doubted very much that I would be back, but the idea was a comforting one.

Garrett clapped the man on the shoulder in a friendly manner before mounting Fax once more. On her cart, wide awake now, Odelia was dipping bread into some kind of flavoured oil. She looked up at me with a thankful smile. If this villager was aware that he had just fed the princess of Nordia and the queen of Riverna, he probably would have been overjoyed with pride, but, of course, we couldn't tell him that.

SIMONE NATALIE

The procession continued along the pathway, I couldn't help but look back to see the villager waving widely back and forth in farewell to us.

I hoped I would be back one day.

Chapter 20

Our horses whinnied nervously as we made our way down the other side of the mountain. The path was steep, and the wagons had to be guided around the bends carefully.

The party itself was silent and on edge, as if waiting for an enemy to strike from an unseen vantage. It was a stark contrast to the welcome break in Lanchel.

As the day wore on and the mountains made way to more woodland, I found myself imagining that I could see faces in the trees, but if anything was watching us, it was keeping its distance.

The closer we got to Nordia, the more anxious I felt. I searched the treeline obsessively in anticipation of an attack. Though no one had announced it, I knew we had entered into the western territory now. I felt adrenaline pulsing faster through my body with every advance towards Nordia and the Black Gates.

I had missed my time to act.

I had purposefully missed it. Several times I had tried to speak with Mags, but it was impossible with Kohl, Greta and Marius huddled around her. She shot me reassuring glances from behind their tall frames, but no other communication had passed between us since the night at the river.

I had to trust that this was all part of some plan.

Trust was hard for me.

When had my trust in Mags grown so strong that I would willingly ride back through those gates?

I could no longer focus on scenery or keep up with conversation as the feeling of pure panic built up inside. Flashes of scenes from the past scorched my vision.

I found myself struggling for air as my breaths came fast and shallow.

Sayre trotted on, unaware that I was lost in panic and blind to the familiar forests where I had roamed as a child. Blind to the rivers and lakes where I had spent my summers swimming. I kept my head down as we rolled through the villages on the edge of Nordia.

I knew that if I dared to look beyond the thatched roofs and billowing chimney smoke, then I would see Tharnham Hold, fortress of the king of Nordia rising up into the clouds. Looming over the hamlets below like a beacon of death.

Panic seized me, and I jumped down from Sayre's back, staggering as the poor creature juddered to a surprised stop.

The moment my feet hit the ground I was off, walking back down the line of carts and away from Nordia. Greta ordered her horses to halt and leapt down from her cart, her arms in the air as she stared after me.

"Cera?" She called, confused.

Maddie and Odelia both cried out as my fast-paced walk morphed into a full-speed sprint.

Embarrassment and fear warred for dominance inside of my chest as my feet pounded on the hard dirt path, so fast that I stumbled. Fax and Garrett caught up to me, stopping dead in my path. I didn't hesitate as I swerved around them. "Hey!" Garrett exclaimed, as he reached out for me. "What's going on?"

"I'm leaving." I panted. "Changed my mind."

"It's not as simple as that," he said. "You can't just run away."

I spun about to face him. He had discarded his torn mask, but his face was still shrouded by his hood.

"Why not?" I wondered. "I'm good at running away."

Was I? If I was good at it, then I never would have ended back here.

Garrett observed me silently for a moment, as if to ponder his next move.

"What will I do with you?" he asked himself, shaking his head and smiling slightly. My heart fluttered.

"I can't let you go," he admitted, and I felt dread rise up in my throat like bile. "Not yet," he continued. "However, as soon as we have met with the crowned king, you are free to walk."

"As long as he agrees?" I prompted.

Garrett chewed on the side of his bottom lip and looked away, surveying the wagons, lost in thought for a moment. Eventually he inclined his head, facing me once more.

"Yeah, as long as he agrees," he admitted.

The decision was out of my hands now. I knew that in a fight, right now, he would best me.

It was almost a relief to know that I couldn't turn back, despite how much I wanted too,

Was this a story that needed to be played out? Or was I a complete fool, about to walk into her own cage?

"Come on," Garrett pushed. "We will enter the city together through the Black Gates."

I shuddered.

I remembered the Black Gates all too well, as well as the city that lay behind them. The last time I had seen them, I was covered in blood and fleeing for my life.

"Remember, Cera," Garrett continued. "Just stay with me."

I was too lost in ghosts and the past to reply. I merely followed as he led us back to the horses. Odelia was standing on her wagon, looking for me worriedly.

I smiled reassuringly at her as Garrett directed me to Sayre.

"I'm fine," I stammered when he attempted to help me on.

The Black Gates loomed above us menacingly. It was a stark contrast to the pretty little flint houses and simple village life that thrived in its shadow. The gate consisted of three obelisks of blackest, sharpest obsidian, extending towards the sky, reaching out of the earth like a broken blade. The gates were as beautiful as they were haunting.

They were ancient, from before recorded time, back when Nordia, and all the west, was overrun with witches.

When the lands were wild and crackling with untamed magic.

I shut my eyes tightly as Sayre carried me under the gates.

I could feel vibrations thrumming from around me. The air was dense and warm. I could almost taste the static.

I kept my eyes shut, even when I knew we had left the gates far behind us. Steady Sayre didn't stumble without my guiding hands, following her master loyally and unfalteringly.

"They can look a little scary, when you first see them."

I blinked my hazy eyes open at Odelia's calming voice. She was sitting astride Fax, behind Garrett, her arms wrapped around his waist tightly.

"I'm fine." I reassured her. The princess opened her mouth to say more, but I looked away, and she swallowed the words.

I needed to get a grip of my emotions. I needed to put on a mask. There was still every chance that I would be able to help Odelia and leave here with my freedom intact.

In silence we made our way past pig farms and market stalls, up to the inner gates of the city, where Garrett exchanged some pleasantries with the guards stationed there.

A page was ordered ahead to announce the princess's arrival, and I tensed up further, thinking of the familiar faces I would meet there.

Relax, I cautioned myself. Mags's enchantment had never failed me, not in all the years I had been free.

The streets echoed with memories as we trotted down them. Phantoms walked the streets in place of the actual townsfolk, and sounds and smells long since forgotten came back to my senses in full force.

I hid behind a mask of indifference and focused on the princess, who was anxiously looking about from the back of Fax, equal parts excited and scared.

She locked eyes with me and gave a little smile, forced though it was.

I returned a smile in kind and nodded to offer some form of encouragement.

We approached Tharnham Hold as the sun began to dip below the city walls, painting the sky with its intimidating silhouette. I could hear the chattering of people inside its walls.

"The princess is here!" a soldier managed to yell before his voice was drowned in a sea of cheers and adulation.

All at once, we were at the gatehouse of the castle and beset with people gathering on all sides to catch a glimpse of the convoy and their returning princess. Panic caused by the sudden excessive crowds threatened to overwhelm me. I slowed Sayre and focused on breathing calmly while the wagons, Garrett and Odelia continued on through the crush of onlookers. I searched for a glance of Mags, desperate to speak with her before we were separated. But there was no pushing through. We entered the inner bailey of the castle, and attendants met us in a flurry of activity.

Odelia was helped down from Fax by Maddie. I saw the princess search for me, her face lined with worry. She whipped around frantically. Then she was out of my view, as a group of ladies-in-waiting bustled her into the fortress while Garrett, still on horseback, conferred with Kohl about something imperceptible.

All of the sudden, another shout rang out.

"Bow for the king!"

He had appeared. The king. Odelia had already been hurried inside, so he was here to see Garrett. Everything was happening so fast, and I was beginning to feel a quiet sort of numbness.

I dismounted Sayre and pushed my way through the courtyard.

I couldn't get a good look at the king through the crowd of people. It was complete bedlam, and I had to fight the urge to spirit away somewhere quiet. I looked around in search of Mags again, but the wagons were all empty. The attendants had been quick at their work.

I needed to get higher, so I could make out what was happening and where everyone had gone. I shoved my way to the back of the courtyard and with a running jump, scaled the curtain wall. I gripped the edge of the battlements tightly and pulled my body up and over.

A sentry on parole stared at me in astonishment as I crouched at his feet. He hesitated, raising his bayonet at me.

"I'm in the guard," I explained. Those words tasted like poison in my mouth. I was more thankful than ever that Maddie and Kohl had gifted me their shirts.

The sentry inclined his head, lowered his weapon and continued on. I'm sure if I had been scaling the other side of the wall, that excuse wouldn't have been so easily accepted. I could see the courtyard clearly now. Mags was with Garrett on the steps into the main entrance, and he was handing her off to a large unit of guards.

Shit.

I rolled to my feet and ran along the battlements, hoping no other sentries would question me as I pushed past them. I dropped down to the courtyard floor when I was close enough to hear what was occurring.

"You have brought me the poison witch?" That must have been the king's voice. He didn't sound overly impressed with the news.

I had met Prince Leander several times during my work with the guard, yet I had never been able to make out his temperament. I had a feeling this would hold true now also. "Send her to the tower, Garrett," he continued flippantly. "We have much to discuss, and we can deal with the little witch later."

"There is also a guard that the queen has—" Garrett began.

"Yes, yes. I want to know everything," the young king interrupted. "I will hear it at the council meeting. For now, I have a feast prepared, the likes of which you have never seen!" The king clapped a hand on Garrett's back and led him inside.

I realised that I was going to be left to my own devices, and that stirred an odd sort of fear in me.

I went back to where I had left Sayre, only to realise that some stable hand had already claimed him. The courtyard around me was beginning to empty as quickly as it had filled, and my emotions felt the same way.

Like all the pent-up fear of how terrible this homecoming would be was seeping away with the crowds.

Almost in a daze, I slipped inside one of the servants' doors, as I had done many times in my youth.

I wondered with a feeling of sudden clarity if I might be in some kind of shock. Maybe the adrenalin from the fight with the rebels was finally wearing off and that, mixed with the apprehension of being back here, had left me numb.

I ambled through the hallways, slipping past various servants and attendants as they went about their work.

I found myself at the base of a staircase, one I knew well.

Reaching out, I rubbed my hand over the polished wood of the banister. If I followed the steps up, I would be in the palace quarters my family once held. Someone would apprehend me or come searching for me soon. I'd managed to pass through undetected in the rush of the princess's arrival, but I clearly didn't belong here, and several courtiers were gossiping suspiciously, affronted by my appearance.

Unsurprisingly, a pair of guards appeared to apprehend me. I smiled warmly at them from across the hallway before spinning and ducking into the hidey-hole under the stairs. It was a common passageway the guard used to get around quicker. More fool to them for not having used it today.

I crouched down in the dark, shuffling forward through the tunnels, staying low in hopes of not being seen should I come across any other guards.

I pushed against a door and fell out onto the cold, damp grass. I laid there, staring up at the stars and giving in to the urge to laugh while squinting up at the chalky moon through tears.

Out of habit, I reached for my mother's talisman. It tangled in my hair, and I laughed all the more as I worked the knot free.

It was all I had from home now. I turned the metal around in my hands, and it flashed in the moonlight, raven, dagger, raven, dagger.

I rolled over and up while lifting the pendant back over my head and tucking it safely under my shirt.

My feet carried me aimlessly over the grounds.

I stumbled as my ankle knocked against a stone block, and I realised I was in my old training grounds. I had spent some of my happiest moments here, training with Garrett and Maddie.

Squinting into the distance, I thought I could make out a shape. I crept closer, cautiously, then stopped in my tracks as I realised someone was in the target range, staring up at the night sky.

No, not just someone.

Garrett.

Damn it. I willed my feet to turn around, but I faltered. My heart fluttered as I scanned him in the darkness.

There had been a time I thought I would never see him again. It felt like an indulgence to stand here and stare openly.

I hesitated, trying to decide if I should leave him to it. But he turned to me just as I was about to leave, and his eyes narrowed in suspicion.

"Who's there?" he demanded.

"Only me," I said. My voice sounded wrong, shaky and hoarse.

"Gods, I thought…" He trailed off. "You looked like someone else for a moment there."

"Who?" I prompted, heart pounding.

"An old friend."

I didn't press further, both hoping and fearing to hear my true name from his lips. Though I was sure it would only confirm his hatred of me.

Had he been thinking of me?

No…I had no doubt he hated me.

He closed some of the distance between us and I was reminded again of how much taller he was than I remembered, it wasn't the only way he was changed. My mind flew back to the night at the riverbank, and how he revealed he was a witch. It felt like having the rug pulled out from under me.

How could there be so much I didn't know.

"What was Mags hinting about, Garrett?" I asked boldly. "When we were in the forest after the fight with the wildlings? She said she could help you?"

Garrett's face darkened, and I wondered if I had overstepped.

"I never told you my name," he said. My mind scrambled as I tried to come up with an excuse for knowing, abd my heart pounded all the more when I realised he was carrying one of the throwing axes. He lifted it up into the air, and I held my breath.

He threw his axe at the target, hitting the ring in the dead centre.

I let me breath out, feeling foolish.

I didn't need to think up a false excuse at all, I realised, I had a real one.

"I overheard the King speaking to you," I admitted. "I was hiding along the battlements. He called you Garrett."

The Knight nodded as he pulled his axe free from the cork board.

"I see," he said as he approached me again. "You can call me Knight." He held the axe out to me. I took it and balanced it in my hands, testing the weight before launching it at the target. It landed in the exact spot Garrett's throw had. He whistled with appreciation.

"You have done this before?"

I nodded. I had done this before, many times in this very spot.

"Mags is trying to promise me things she cannot fulfil," Garrett said, going back to my earlier question. "I don't trust her and neither should you."

I frowned at this. "You don't know her," I said firmly.

"And you do? Tell me everything you know of the poison witch, and I will see if it changes my mind." It stung to be reminded that Mags had a whole other identity that I hadn't been aware of. Yet, she had lived a long time, and wouldn't it have been stranger for her not to have used aliases?

"I know who she is," I said. "I don't understand all her past, and I can't show you a list of all her names, but those things are meaningless. Who a person actually *is* cannot change."

He laughed bitterly at that.

"Don't be so sure," he said, throwing the axe again. It landed a little to the left of the board, and he frowned.

"She let herself into my mind," he continued. "She saw what I desire most in this world and used it to try to manipulate me. I should have left her stuck on that riverbank for a thousand years."

I had so many questions. What was it Mags had seen? Was Garrett really a witch with that kind of power to spell a person for a thousand years? I shivered at the thought.

Garrett pulled the axe free again and tossed it down to the ground where it stuck upright in the soft grass. Then he walked over to me and reached out, as if to brush the hair out of my eyes, but stopped himself, clenched his fist, and let his hand drop. He looked into my eyes, and I felt myself flush. I wanted to pull away, but something in me felt awed and rooted to the spot.

"Go to bed, Cera," he breathed. "Calm your curious nature. Nothing good will come from skulking around this palace at night."

"I wasn't skulking. I just couldn't sleep."

His brow furrowed then, and he seemed to look at me anew, his gaze flicking over my features. He rubbed his thumb over my cheek. I shivered, feeling weary.

"I haven't seen you sleep," he said, darkly.

I stepped back and out of his grip.

"How is that possible?" he continued. "Only on the wagon, after I administered the green-lock thistle. It has been days, and I watched you before that at the Blackmoore castle and at the cemetery. You barely slept there."

"That was you?" I gasped, remembering the reflection in the glass. I had presumed it was Kohl.

"Why did you follow me?" I asked.

"Kohl was trailing you. He thought you were… unique, so I investigated." He stepped closer again, bridging the gap between us. I was suddenly very aware of how isolated we were here out on the field. I knew Garrett was stronger than me. I would put up a good fight, but I couldn't go against his magic. If he turned on me now, I would lose. I held my ground as he stood before me, his tall frame towering over mine.

"Stop it," he said suddenly, voice low as thunder. "I'm not going to hurt you," he said gentler. The air between us crackled and my heart hammered in my chest as he seemed to lean in closer. His mouth was so beautiful, thin and playful, with a fuller top lip "I can see everything behind those eyes," he breathed "You need to learn how to mask your thoughts."

I blushed fiercely, hoping that he couldn't really imagine what I was thinking.

"I won't ask for your secrets, Cera. I already know there is something less than human about you," he said. "When my plans come to their end though, make sure you aren't in my way." His gaze flicked ever so quickly to my mouth before he turned on his heel and walked away. I let out a long, shaky breath.

"Also," he called back. "Greta has been assigned to tail you. So, stay out of trouble." He pointed over my head into the darkness, and I spun about. Sure enough, Greta slipped into view, I couldn't work out where she had come from, as if she had materialized from the shadows themselves. Her face was stony, annoyed.

I'd had no idea she was following me.

But that wasn't what alarmed me.

Why had Garrett revealed my stalker? Either he wanted to lure me into trusting him, or he was genuinely helping me.

A rush of panic darted through me then. Had Greta seen me use the passageway? Had she seen my mother's talisman? What were the chances that I could convince her it was just luck that led me out here tonight?

I ran my hands through my hair and turned to find Garrett gone. I spun around, and Greta had also slipped away, though I doubt she had gone far at all. I did need to sleep, but there was one little problem. I hadn't been assigned a room. There were plenty of places I could crash, but with Greta trailing me, I was wary of giving away my familiarity of the Hold.

Urgh. I needed to find Mags.

Chapter 21

Mags had made a comfortable seat of her confinement. She had already managed to talk her way out of a damp cell and into a tower room. Though it had only one small window that looked out towards the gatehouse, it was nicely furnished with chairs, cushions, a small daybed and a table laden with needlework. I found her sitting cross-legged on the floor, knitting with a large ball of tawny wool.

"I'm surprised they let you have them," I said, gesturing at the long wooden needles.

"It was a mistake on their part, but I am sure they are all too scared to attempt to take them now." She laughed, not looking up from her work. The tower guard behind me muttered something about "idle hands" before hastily closing the door behind us.

"Do you have them spelled?" I asked, half-joking. "I didn't think they would allow me to see you, but the first assistant I found brought me to you as soon as I asked, and now they have let us alone." I sat down next to the witch. She lifted her knitting wordlessly, and I lay back with my head in her lap.

"I didn't need to do a thing. They are all in awe of me, I think."

"The stories preceded you," I said with a frown, feeling suddenly nervous. I had to ask her about the poison witch, but I was afraid of what I would hear.

"Stop fretting," she scolded. I looked up at her face, but she didn't meet my eyes, focusing intently on the click-clacking of her needles.

"Why did you keep it from me?" I breathed.

"I kept nothing from you. Had you asked, I wouldn't have hidden it," she replied. "I have had so many names over the years. They matter little to me."

"And the stories?" I asked. Mags placed down her needles then and looked at me solemnly. Purple eyes twinkling in the low candlelight, her mouth turned down a little. "We have all made mistakes in our past that we wish we could take back," she breathed as she stroked my hair off my forehead. "Most tales have some truth in them."

My stomach sank, and I felt ashamed of the disappointment her words incited in me. It was naïve and hypocritical of me to imagine Mags as a faultless creature. What she said was right. I had yet to meet a person who had made good decisions only.

"Take heart, Cera, I have never done anything needlessly. I have never been thoughtlessly cruel." This didn't reassure me, and I couldn't place why. I sat up and shifted so that my back was against the wooden day bed. Mags watched me, silently, and I smiled weakly at her. She went back to her knitting.

"Why are you here?" I asked, genuinely curious.

"I came to be here with you," she said simply. I sat in silence for a moment, biting my lip. Something seemed off between us all of a sudden, and I didn't know how to address it. In the five years that I had known Mags, she had been a constant for me, a person who was almost always available to me when I needed support. Yet I couldn't shake the feeling that there was another reason for her to be here.

"Tell me what is on your mind. I can feel clouds of confusion gathering around you."

I laughed and met Mags smiling eyes.

"I hate to see you locked away here," I said truthfully. "You didn't need to come with me."

"I did," she said simply. "You need me to guide you."

"Guide me?"

"Yes, don't you think the time for redemption is upon you. I think it has been five years too long in its coming." What do you mean?" I asked wearily, trying to taper the flare of anger that rose up in me at the mention of redemption.

"I know you well, Cera. You have toiled and repeated in your mind that terrible day six years ago, and though you have run from it, here you are, right back where you started from." I looked at the door in panic and jumped up to make sure it wasn't open.

"Still your tongue Mags, anyone could hear," I hissed, thinking of Greta.

"No one can hear but us," she said, clacking away with her needles, unconcerned.

"I have to guide you, as you will not guide yourself," she continued. "There is a reason you are no longer bound to the blood crown, Cera, and I know it has occurred to you, that you could work it out and free your fellow guards."

I walked back over to Mags at sat down by her side. I pulled the yarn from her hands and placed it down at her feet. She stared at me, like she could see through into my soul. This was a subject neither her nor I had brought up in years, and to hear her now speaking as though this had been the plan all along sent shivers of cold fear through me.

"You are right. I have replayed those last days in my mind until they were scorched into my memory, and I still have no clue as to what freed me," I whispered. "I didn't come back to Nordia to become some kind of saviour. I didn't mean to come back here at all!"

"Then, dear one, why are we here?" She looked at me steadily. I couldn't answer. Why had I come here, really? I shouldn't have. At first I had been a prisoner, but I could have escaped if I wanted to. I could have turned around and walked out of the gates this afternoon if I had wanted.

There was something magnetic and irresistible about being back among the people I loved and missed and having them not despise me. Plus, there was the chance to find out what really happened to my family.

Was I kidding myself that I could get a little of what I wanted before slipping away unscathed? Was I relying too heavily on my disguise?

After a while of silence, Mags sighed and picked up her yarn and needles from the floor.

"Here, a scarf. The nights are growing cold." She unpicked the scarf and tied the fringed edges. I took it and wrapped it around my neck.

"Where would I even begin?" I asked, my voice barely more than a whisper.

"If I were you, I would start at the beginning," she answered. I looked at her questioningly.

"And that would be?" I pressed.

"The crown."

A shiver ran down my spine. I was completely taken aback.

"The crown? Do you mean the blood crown?"

"It has an inscription upon it," she said, smiling knowingly. "A spell."

"An inscription?" I repeated, dumbfounded. I knew the silver crowns had words of magic carved into them but had never seen those words with my own eyes.

"Yes, with instructions on how to break the bond."

"Instructions… to break… the bond?" I repeated, completely astounded by this bombshell. "That's impossible."

"Why?" Mags asked. "The bond is created with magic and words and blood. I see no reason why it cannot be destroyed the same way."

Destroyed.

Could the bond really be destroyed?

"It won't be as easy as that," I said.

"Why not?" Mags laughed. "It's as easy as that to bind one person to another for life. The king said some words and placed the cursed crown on your head, and that was all he need do."

I hesitated. It *had* been that simple at the time yes, but I had always presumed more went on behind the scenes, spell work and enchantment that I was too young to understand.

"Trust me," Mags said with a knowing smile. "Find the crowns, bring them to me, and together we will fix this."

Simple indeed.

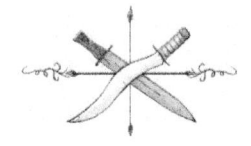

I walked down from the tower room in a daze, and that was how Kohl found me.

Mags had made it all seem so simple… like everything I wanted was within my grasp now.

"I have been looking for you everywhere," Kohl said. He was flanked by two other members of the blood guard, all three looked frazzled.

"What's going on?" I asked, suddenly alert. He ran a hand through his golden hair and sighed. "There is a meeting in the king's rooms. My princess has asked for you to be there and is refusing to speak until you are found."

"Then let's go" I said, breaking into a fast-paced walk. It took me too long to remember that I shouldn't know the way to the king's council rooms. I slowed down abruptly with the realisation and signalled for him to go ahead.

"It's this way?" I asked. He nodded and continued, too busy with thoughts of the meeting to worry about my odd behaviour.

"What happened then?" I asked.

"There is a letter from King Henri." He stopped and faced me, looking concerned.

"I think…" He broke off hesitantly and chewed at his bottom lip, obviously debating whether to share his concerns or not. "I think the king has been planning something," he admitted. "I have a bad feeling."

I reached out and squeezed his shoulder reassuringly. "We won't know until we get in there," I said. He nodded, and we continued down the corridor.

When we reached the outer doors of the council chambers, I stopped, suddenly flooded by the unpleasant memories of those ornate wooden doors and the meetings and orders I had endured behind them. The arched doorway was carved from oak and stained a ruddy dark brown. I was taller than the last time I had stood here, but those foreboding doors made me feel small, even now.

Two guards were stationed, unmoving at either side of the meeting room at all hours of the day and night. I had been called in there more times than I could recollect in my childhood, often still dressed in my nightgown and cap.

The frame was decorated with detailed intricate carvings, of skulls, scrolls, crowns and swords. I had spent hours staring at them as I fought against the blood bond, willing more time before I had to walk into the room and be given another dreadful order or assignment.

Kohl seemed to have no such hang-up though, and he moved to push the doors open without hesitation. I grabbed his arm to stop him.

"Kohl," I said, seriously. "Kohl, I cannot go in there like this."

He turned to face me quizzically.

"What do you mean?"

"I mean, I cannot go into the king's chambers dressed in rags and covered in blood," I elaborated.

Kohl sighed but didn't disagree.

"We don't have time for this, Cera. No one is going to care."

"We must make time," I insisted, pained. I knew I was right. If Odelia needed me, no one would listen.

"Fine," he consented. "But we have to make haste, they are waiting for us."

He led me down the corridors and into a washroom. The maids looked at me in disgust as I carefully riffled through their boxes of clean linen.

"Wash your face, Cera. I will find you some armour," Kohl ordered. I took up a clean white cloth and dunked it into a barrel of steaming hot water. A washer woman yelped in protest, but I didn't have time to appease her. The hot flannel felt refreshing on my dry face, and I scrubbed until I was raw.

"All good?" I asked Kohl.

"Good enough. Here." He handed me a set of full armour, the same kind that the sentry from the battlements had worn. Heavy and old-fashioned. It was silver with navy-blue detailing. Kohl turned around as I pulled it on over the stained shirts he and Maddie had given me. I strapped the leather braces around my back, fumbling clumsily in my haste.

"Done?" Kohl urged.

"Done."

"Oh wait!" Kohl cried suddenly, stopping me at the door.

"Here." He rooted around in his inner cloak pockets for a moment. "I keep forgetting to give you this." He mumbled to himself as he struggled. Eventually he pulled his hand free, and in it was a pouch, the gift that the hedge witch had passed on to me through Mags. I reached out and took it, open-mouthed.

"I tried to find your other things, but you hid them well."

"I did," I agreed. "When did you do this?" I asked, touched.

"Before I sprang you from the cell. I know you had more. I think I saw a book?"

I didn't agree or deny.

"Well, either way, I don't think anyone else will be able to find them." We both stood silent for a moment, me in surprised, uncomfortable gratitude, and he in amusement.

"Thank you," I said eventually. I tucked the pouch into my pocket.

"I'm only sorry I couldn't find the rest. Now can we go?"

I nodded silently.

We flew back to the king's meeting room and this time I didn't spare a moment to reminisce at the doors.

The chambers were beautifully decorated, with tall bookcases along the walls. Tapestries and maps of the entire island were hanging up above fireplaces and spread over side tables. At the centre of the room was a long table, and gathered around it looked like the entirety of the king's council and more. Attendants and maidservants strolled around the room, carrying large jugs of wine and water or platters of bread and meats. I picked a lump of cheese from one of the trays as it passed and tossed the entire thing in my mouth. It was salty and creamy with a burst of floral sweetness. My stomach growled uncomfortably.

Kohl looked at me, his face marked with worry. The princess stood near the end of the table. Maddie was behind her, and she raised her eyes and let out a low sigh of relief when she spotted us.

"Not good," Maddie mouthed.

I found Garrett, standing alone in the shadows of the room, rested against the papered wall and surveying the chambers with crossed arms, still half hidden under his cloak. His eyes alighted on mine for only a moment before we both looked away.

At the head of the table sat the king. He had only been a boy of fourteen years when I left Nordia. I had spoken with him many times and found him arrogant and obsessed with his own fame. He used to take great delight in reminding the guard members that they would be under his control one day. And now that they were, I wondered what kind of king he was. I already knew he was the type of brother to sell his sister off to a hostile land.

He looked very similar to Odelia, but he had more of his father's features. Olive skin with a soft chin, full cheeks and a pointed nose. His eyes were large under dark eyelashes as he surveyed the room, and his hair hung down his back in dark cedar waves.

He sat back in a chair that completely overshadowed his slim frame. Standing to his left was a commander of some kind, dressed in the ornate blue and silver armour of Nordia with medals pinned to his shoulders. He leaned to whisper solemnly into the king's ear.

I chanced a glance around the table. I could see many of the old king's favourites still in attendance. The war general, Paine, who had once stabbed me right through the hand as punishment for embarrassing one of his sons in a fight. That son sat next to him, and he looked very much the same as he had then, perhaps a little smugger as he displayed the medals along his collar. The old king's seneschal, Amon, was also there, on the king's right. I was surprised to see him alive and more surprised still to see him on the council. He had been old and unwell when I left six years ago, but here he sat, hunched over and ever watchful. My eyes alighted on several other men and women that had played the various part of villain or comforter in my youth. There were no more than five new faces that I could count. I didn't like the confused feelings of nostalgia and comfort that came unbidden to me as I stood in this room. I had no good memories from my time in the Kings council chambers. Yet, there was a discomforting sensation of home that kindled in my chest just from being here around so many familiar people. It was a home that had felt like a caged nightmare more often than not, but it was my home, nonetheless.

A place I had never thought I would see again.

Faces that had become distorted in my memory by time and wakeful dreams were now right before me, in all their realness. Some had barely aged in the long six years that I had been gone. So many chairs filled with the same old people, like nothing had really changed and no time had passed.

There *were* several empty chairs, however.

My eyes were drawn to one in particular, half hidden from my view by Maddie. I stepped around the guard, unable to stop myself from seeking a look at what had once been my father's seat. My family's pride and what would have been my brother's birth right.

As I moved, an arm came into view. Long and slender, with a hand covered in rings that gripped tightly to the back of my family's seat.

I flinched as I realised the seat had been passed to another man. My brow furrowed in confusion though. He was dressed in the forest-green colours of my family. He leaned over the chair, looking down at something on the table so that I couldn't see his face.

He shifted an inch, and I gasped aloud when I recognised my father's crest of dagger and hare emblazoned on the arm of his cloak.

My heart leapt up into my throat, and a flame of hope burst into life in my chest.

I had no other family, no grandparents, uncles or cousins on my father's side, none that carried the name Flint. None that would wear the colour and crest of my family so boldly at the king's side. None that could sit in my father's place.

Save for my myself… or my brother. Had he escaped execution? Had they pardoned him?

In my heart I knew it couldn't be him, for even if he had somehow evaded the axe, he would never have been granted that seat on the council. Not after I turned traitor and ran away. The old king was vengeful, spiteful and wicked. He delighted in revenge.

Still, I had to know. I pushed past Maddie in my haste, who stopped her whispering to Kohl and looked at me questioningly. Luckily, Odelia had not noticed me yet, standing as she was at the opposite end of the table to the king with her back to the room.

"Flint!" cried the king suddenly, causing me to jump almost out of my skin. Both Maddie and Kohl were watching me with concern now, but I couldn't bring myself to care, so great was my desire to see if this stranger was the brother I had long thought to be dead.

"Bring me the letter," the king demanded.

Finally, the man looked up, and I felt my heart judder. All the air in my lungs escaped in one quick exhale, like they would never fill up again.

It was not my brother.

It was my *father*.

Chapter 22

My father approached the king with his familiar slow swaying walk, so full of confidence and self-importance. He placed a scroll of paper down in front of the king, bowed slightly and headed back to his chair. I watched all of this with anger and disappointment threatening to boil up and over inside of me. I chewed on my lip aggressively and bunched my hands into white-knuckle fists. Blood rushed loudly in my ears as my mind raced.

Of course he was alive.

Of *course* he had talked, manipulated and weaselled his way back into the king's council.

BOUND TO THE CROWN

It was all I could do not to walk up to him and bash my fists against his breast. I wanted to free his head from his shoulders myself!

When I'd left, he was all but executed, imprisoned in the cells yet still sending messages to me through his supporters, begging me to save him without a care for what it would do to me, without any thought for how broken I was already.

There were many things I regretted about that day, but leaving him to his fate was not one of them. He had played the game and lost, all while using myself, my mother and brother as his disposable collateral again and again.

And here he was, alive, unharmed in any physical or political way.

And what of my brother and mother, where were they?

Were they alive, or dead? I looked around the room again, searching the faces of the men and women of the council, even those of the cup and plate bearers, just in case I had missed them. I had left the day my brother and mother were set to be executed. I had abandoned them. Guilt burned up in me, always at the edge of my mind, ready to send me mad with the shame. I couldn't face it. But that was what I had done.

I had never dared let myself believe that they were pardoned.

I still couldn't. My father had a way of twisting people's minds to his will, and I doubt he would have spared a thought for Cian or my mother.

"Cera!" Odelia called, noticing me at last. I flinched at my name but quickly steadied myself and forced my face to appear calm, keeping my features passive. Garrett, who stood behind the king's chair, stared at me, his face as impassive as my own, yet I couldn't help but wonder of he noticed some of the anger burning behind my eyes.

"You're here," Odelia continued, approaching me with an open smile and taking my hands in hers.

"I'm glad you have come," she said, leaning in and dropping her voice so only I could hear. "Kohl is worried that my brother might have a trick or two up his sleeve." Then to the room, she announced loudly in a commanding voice I hadn't yet heard from her, "My personal guard is here, so we can start now." Still gripping my hand tightly, the princess turned to face her brother. I noticed a few meaningful glances between councilmen and more than one patronising smile.

I made a mental note of those people to remind myself that they probably wouldn't take the princess seriously or respect her should we need any allies in the future.

"It is a happy day, sister," said the king. He picked up the scroll and waved it slightly in the air. "Happy for more than one reason," he continued. "You have come home to visit us, and we have all missed you terribly."

The use of the word "visit" was an alarm bell in my ears. Kohl looked back at me, his eyebrows raised. I nodded to him calmly. His instinct had been right. Something was happening.

"And before you even reached us here, your husband has sent a letter, begging me to keep you safe and hasten you back to him." The King winked at her conspiratorially. "Is it to be this way your entire visit? Will I be receiving a letter upon every hour from your sweetheart?" I felt sick. King Leander couldn't be that foolish. Either he had a remarkable ability to lie to himself, or he genuinely knew nothing of Odelia's troubles in the East. Could someone close to him have intercepted the letters? Possible but doubtful. He spoke with conviction, as if he really believed what he was saying. Odelia, however, was completely silent in her bewilderment.

I couldn't blame her. I squeezed her hand in reassurance, and she looked at me, mouth agape. I could already guess what would come next.

"My sweetheart?" she breathed, her eyebrows drawn together in wary confusion. I nodded and stood straighter, willing the princess to do the same and to brace herself for what might be next.

"King of the West," I dared, speaking loudly, with the exaggerated authority that someone in a high position might use to address royalty. "Perhaps your council has misrepresented the letter to you. May I have it for my queen to read over?" I asked, being sure to place no blame with the king while still making it clear that we would not go along with a falsehood. Kohl reached out and gripped my elbow in warning as all eyes in the chamber settled on me. I was careful to stare directly at the king, afraid that my eyes would seek those of my father's. What would his impression of me be?

"Who are you?" asked the man that had been whispering into the king's ear. He stood up taller and rolled his broad shoulders as he rested his hand on the hilt of a bejewelled sword that jutted out at his left hip. He obviously thought himself very important. A fighter or commander of some kind then? He didn't look the part of advisor or Hand. I met the man's gaze steadily and smirked.

"I am the queen's knight," I informed him. The moment I said those words I heard an excited squeak escape from Odelia.

I didn't falter or look her way, but my heart was pounding.

Later I would have to think of some way to scramble out of this commitment, but for now, I needed to command attention, and which of these self-important fools would listen to the opinion of a lady-in-waiting or a personal guard? Few to none.

"And this gives you the right to speak for her?" he asked. I inclined my head and looked away from him, as though his question was below my station to answer.

"King of the West," I repeated. "May I show my queen her husband's letter?" The king shrugged, seemingly unconcerned, if a little confused, and held the letter out between two fingers. Kohl went to collect it and bowed low. I saw him discreetly open and attempt to read some. His face turned white.

He handed the letter to the queen, who read it aloud without hesitation.

"Dear Brother-King," it began, *"I beg this letter reaches your hands quickly. I have received your last correspondence, and I am deeply chastened by the misunderstandings that have occurred between my wife and myself. I regret her unhappiness deeply and wish to rectify any mistakes on mine own part that could have caused it.*

Perhaps I was too busy with our harvest celebrations to give her the proper comfort and reassurance that any woman in her condition would need? I can only blame myself, as you are aware the lot of a king is all-consuming.

All this talk of imprisonment and bastards has left a poisonous taste on my tongue. I can assure you that the offending rumour-mongers have been found and disposed of in the most thorough manner.

With such distance between our lands, it is not unprecedented that such lies should occasionally reach you. Lies they must always be understood to be though. You are welcome at the hearth of Blackmoore or Gathe Castle to see for yourself how our family is thriving.

I am happy that my dear queen has found comfort in her brother's home, where I know I am also very welcome. I am anxious for our lands to continue in family harmony, but I beg you to send our queen and unborn prince back to my side as soon as she is ready and rested. I miss her terribly, and we have many preparations to make for the birth of my heir.

I will write again shortly and await more news of my wife.
His Royal Highness, King Henri Bastillion Riverna III."

Chapter 23

The room was silent a moment as the princess appeared to read and reread the letter.

"Leander, what is this?" she asked eventually.

"My princess, please understand—" the Seneschal began to implore.

"Are you my brother?" snapped Odelia, cutting him off. I grinned at the aging seneschal, who raised his eyebrows at me but nodded his head in concession to his princess.

"Dear sister, this is the way of things. You are married to the King of the East, and you cannot just run away from your lover."

"But I am not pregnant," she spluttered, throwing the letter to the floor in disgust. "What lies are these!"

"King Henri is incapable of having children. Everyone knows this," her brother continued.

I looked at the queen, but she didn't contradict what was being said.

"Everyone knows now?" she said, waving her hand around the crowded room. "As everyone knows you are trying to send me back to a man who wanted me dead!" I had to admit, I hadn't expected Odelia to be capable of an outburst like this. In Henri's court, she was meek, but here, among her own people, she certainly had no qualms speaking her mind.

"Leave!" The king erupted suddenly. "Leave, leave, all leave!" He waved his arm, and Garrett began ushering people out. He approached the seneschal with a humorous smirk on his face

"Not me, obviously!" the man complained, annoyed. Garrett shrugged and made a show of looking to the king for confirmation, who shot Garrett an unamused look.

"All but my council and the blood guard," he clarified.

"Cera stays too, Leander," the princess insisted. "She is to be my knight, so she goes where I go." Garrett furrowed his brow at this but said nothing.

"Sister, Henri is desperate for an heir," the king continued when the room was cleared of all except the council members, Garrett and myself. "So desperate that he has named a bastard that could not be his own," he said. "It's madness. He is weakened, old and frustrated."

"And what does this have to do with me?" Odelia asked. "He is my husband in name only, and he tried to have me replaced. There certainly wasn't any time for me to get pregnant, even if I could."

"He is a fool with disloyal, grasping, social climbing advisors who are frantically trying to keep the crown out of our hands," said the seneschal.

"It doesn't matter that you are not pregnant with his child. You are his wife, legally," the king said, leaning forward in his chair imploringly.

Odelia's eyes flicked from the seneschal to the king, confusion and irritation clear on her face.

"They are saying that the king does not care if your baby is his, or no. He cannot have biological children and is at the point where any child will do, my queen," I explained to her as the silence stretched. She stared at me, open-mouthed and indignant, then back at her brother.

"You want me to get pregnant and claim it as the king's?"

"It happens often, sister. It's not the blood that matters, but the name. You read his letter. He will accept the child as his heir and son."

"And this is your plan?" she asked.

"We could not risk it in writing," the king confirmed as the queen's face flushed pink with embarrassment or anger.

"So, I am to be sent back, after all of this. You are sending me back!"

"Not right now. You have a few months," the king said reassuringly

"About nine," added my father sneeringly from his seat. He had been watching the proceedings with quiet disinterest up until now, as though being here was beneath him. It was a tactic of his that I remembered well.

Odelia looked for a moment like a bird trapped in a cage. Her eyes darted about the room in panic, and I saw them alight on the window. I genuinely worried that she would have a moment of pure insanity and launch herself out of it. I faced her, gripping both hands tightly in mine and quickly led her to a chair.

"He is old, Odelia," I whispered, knowing that this fact didn't really help her now but wanting to say something to alleviate her fear. "He will die soon, and you and your son will have absolute power and position." I couldn't add freedom or safety to that list.

"My son?" she whispered, looking faint. "What if it's a girl?" I looked at her sympathetically as a fierce sense of protectiveness came over me. She was not built for this life that she was being forced to lead. Maybe we had more in common than I had thought.

"They will make sure, dearheart," I explained. She gazed up at me, confused. Still unable to figure out the plan that was being set in motion around her.

I stood, suddenly angry. I wasn't foolish enough to aim my ire at the king himself, so instead I turned to the seneschal.

"I presume the preparations are already underway?" I asked. "Is this all being left to chance with an infant being procured randomly? Or is there a group of mothers chosen for their attributes?"

The seneschal hesitated, obviously unsure of what to share with me. He looked to my father for a moment, and I smiled without humour. It was clear who the true puppet master was.

"Well?" I demanded.

"The mothers are all ladies of the blood, cousins of the princess, and with similar looks," he said when no one bid him to stay silent. "The child will have the Trine features," he continued.

"I daresay it wouldn't matter anyway," I muttered. If the king really was that desperate for a legitimate child, he would probably take any.

"Who is this?" My Father spoke up. "Who are you?" he asked. I snorted at his arrogance and entitlement. He stood tall, as though he had no fear of being knocked down, and he demanded my identity as though it was his right to know "Who are you?" he repeated, waving a hand in my general direction.

"I am the queen's knight," I said to him, meeting his gaze unwaveringly. It was somewhat liberating to face him, knowing that he had no idea of my identity.

He frowned at me, clearly trying to work me out. He liked to figure out people's motives, but more importantly, he was only interested in those who could be swayed to his side with either fear, promises of money or power. Everyone else could be a potential threat. I wanted to make sure he saw that threat in me.

"Yes, you already said that," he replied derisively. "Only, we do not have a queen. I think you mean *Princess* Odelia," he corrected, his left eye twitching slightly.

"My lady is a queen," I reminded him, stepping closer, refusing to back down or be made timid by him. I felt a petty sort of superiority as I realised that I was almost a whole head taller than him now. As a child, he had always seemed so large, and in my memories still, he was a stern giant of a man.

"Not within these walls," he said. "There cannot be two royals of the blood."

"Oh, stop this," the king interrupted suddenly. "She is a queen. Did we not scheme for that very outcome? Leave it be." He slammed his fist onto the oak table. I looked at the young prince seated at the head of the table and began to think that I had underestimated him. His face was lined and drawn, and he appeared older than his twenty years. King Leander was hunched over slightly and rubbing at his temples where strands of his brown hair had already given way to streaks of shocking white. Perhaps the crown had sat heavy on his young head these last six years.

"Let's end this meeting." He sighed. "Lord Flint, see that the queen's knight has a room and a situation."

"My King." My father nodded, but his voice was hard, and I could tell he resented the order.

"My own knight will see that she is up to the job, before we perform any official ceremony." The king gestured to Garrett. "Watch her like a hawk, and see she passes all the common challenges. I entrust this to you."

"My King." Garrett inclined his head. I didn't want to be "watched" by Garrett. I wanted to stay as far away from him as I could, but if I was to figure out a way to fix this damned bond like Mags wanted me to, then I would probably need his help. I had little faith in the plan, but getting Garrett on my side wasn't the worst idea, and as I knew a lot of his character already, it shouldn't be too hard.

"She is up to the challenge, brother. She has—" Odelia began.

"Stop," the king interrupted. "I know you well enough to be used to the fancies that take you. Binding yourself to a knight is no small thing, and it is my duty as your king and your brother to make sure she can work at the same level as an elite soldier." For a moment, I thought Odelia would argue more, but she looked as though all the fight had gone out of her today.

"Sister, you are dismissed from the events tonight," the king continued. "Sup in your rooms instead and take this time to rest. Leave your fate in my hands and the hands of my men. Trust that I have the best intentions." He sounded sincere in his words, which made me wonder if he truly believed that this was all for his sister's good. And if so, what sharp-minded council member had managed to convince him of it.

Odelia stood shakily, and I gripped her forearm to steady her. She glared across the room at her brother, the king.

"I may not be as clever as you all," she said suddenly, her voice shaking. "But I can see clearly what is coming. if you think the people of the Eastlands will celebrate my return with a son, then you are more a fool than me."

The king sighed again and stood, approaching his sister gently, almost like one would approach a child.

"The story has been spun, sister. You fled for the safety of your unborn child as the people celebrated the birth of a whore's son. The People of Riverna will look kindly on your fearless, maternal actions. You have seen the letter. The king already welcomes you back with open arms." King Leander placed his hands on his sister's shoulders reassuringly, and I saw her anger relax a little as her body untensed. Her brother must have had a lot of practice in pacifying his little sister. "You have had a hard time," he continued, "but it *will* be better now."

"This all could have been avoided if Henri had simply *told* me—" she said suddenly. I scoffed at this and realised when a dozen pairs of eyes turned to me that it had been aloud.

"He is a king," I explained as Odelia looked at me questioningly. "And a proud man in a difficult position. He was never going to admit to anyone, especially his young, handsome wife, that he was sterile and unable to have a natural heir," I continued. "It could be grounds for divorce and would become public knowledge, leaving the succession in jeopardy."

"But it seems like everyone knows already?" Odelia said darkly.

"Yes, there will always be whispers of your child's legitimacy. But if your husband accepts the child, then his word is law. There is no other strong claim to the throne of Riverna, and your King Henri made sure of that with the blood of his family."

"I wonder if he regrets that now, knowing he has singlehandedly ended his own bloodline," Odelia mused.

"Most likely, sister," said the king "but we will put it to rights, and soon our blood will hold the seat of the east and the west."

Chapter 24

"Come with me," Garrett ordered as the room began to empty. I held tight to Odelia, feeling a little unwilling to leave the girl in this state.

"You go," she said reassuringly. "My maids will be here, and they will see me to bed." I nodded and let go of her arm. I watched her stumble away, feeling uneasy until three young women came flooding through the doors to meet her. They had tears streaming down their faces as they each embraced the princess. I felt an odd stab of jealousy to see Odelia greet them so warmly. These girls were surely her creatures. No doubt they had grown up together and knew one another well.

"It doesn't matter if you are born well or not," I commented as I watched her. "We all have our roles to play."

"And which are you?" asked Garrett at my side. I turned and fixed him with a stare as passive as stone.

"Are you high-born?" he asked, unfazed. "I am almost certain that you are."

"I don't know why you are so interested," I commented.

"I am interested," he agreed. "You have painted the picture of a migrant orphan, who had no life before the workhouse. Yet you look very well in this armour." He tapped a knuckle against the cold metal of my shoulder plate. "You knew how to put it on," he said with a smirk.

"It's fairly self-explanatory" I answered too quickly. He shook his head and clicked his tongue

"It isn't. Not at all," he said, rubbing his chin. "You have worn it before."

"Stop being foolish!" I snapped. In my panic, my voice rose louder than I had meant it to.

My father, who was now walking past with Kohl beside him, stared at me with furrowed brow. I cursed Garrett under my breath, angry that my reaction had caught my father's attention. He approached and so did Kohl.

"Captain," said Father, addressing Garrett. "Who is this odd character that you have brought into our midst?"

Every muscle in Garrett's body seemed to tense up in the presence of my father. His back was straight, and his jaw clenched tight.

"Cera is the queen's knight," he answered curtly.

"Not yet she isn't," said my father as he looked me up and down, taking my measure.

"That's not for you to say, Celion," Garrett replied. It was clear from his tone that he disliked my father. Outwardly, my father appeared unbothered by this, but I knew that it would vex him that one of the king's favourites wasn't an ally. I bit down on the smirk that formed at the corner of my mouth, but my father noticed it.

"And who are you?" I asked before he could lash out at me.

"Lord Celion Flint," he said, raising his chin proudly. "My family is the oldest in all of the Westlands. I own more land that you have ever walked on in all of your days." He boasted. I rolled my eyes, and his jaw snapped shut in irritation. An action that used to intimidate me.

I met Kohl's gaze behind my father, and he looked uncomfortable. I didn't want to upset him or cause more trouble.

"Nice to meet you, Lord Flint," I said, as pleasantly as I could. My voice came out forced and odd.

"Let's go." Garrett took hold of my elbow and steered me away and out the door.

"I hate that man," I said aloud, letting the full venom of everything I felt flow out of me. As I did, Garrett yanked me fiercely to the side, and I found myself in darkness. My eyes adjusted, and I realised he had pulled us into a small alcove hidden behind a tapestry. I looked up at him questioningly.

"Don't you ever say that aloud again," he warned. His gaze was locked on mine, completely serious. When I didn't immediately answer, he gripped my shoulders and drew me in closer.

"I mean this, Cera. Do you understand me?"

"What?" I snapped, confused by this sudden display of aggression. I tried to jerk away and found that I couldn't, not an inch. I felt a sharp prickle of fear.

"Do not seek out that man, and do not go near him. Do not openly defy him or anger him."

"Why not?" I breathed.

"He is pure malevolence. He is powerful, and he has the king's ear in all things." None of this seemed reason enough for Garrett's excessive behaviour.

"He killed his own wife to save himself. He doesn't care for human life, and if you anger him, then even I cannot guarantee your safety."

I barely heard what he was saying. My ears were ringing, as disconnected from the conversation.

He killed his own wife.

So, my mother was dead.

He had sacrificed her somehow.

My beautiful, poor, meek mother. Who had always seemed to me like a mouse caught in my father's trap.

I had so easily recognised Odelia's panic in the council rooms because I knew that look well. It was the look my mother always wore. As though someone stood just behind her with a knife to her back, forcing her every move. Forcing her to smile, forcing her to eat, forcing her to play the part of proud mother and wife.

She had never stood up for me a day in my life. Yet I had loved her so dearly and craved her love in return. Now that I knew for sure that she was gone, I couldn't stop the tears. I looked up at Garrett hopelessly, hating that he could see me weak, but I had lost control.

Garrett jumped back from me as though I had burnt him.

"Cera?" His voice was barely a whisper, but it filled up this small space. I couldn't bring myself to answer him. I bit down on my lip so hard that I tasted the burst of blood. I couldn't hide my tears, but I wasn't going to sob in front of him. I shook my head wordlessly and let my failing body sink to the cold stone floor.

Garrett followed me, kneeling in front of me and placing his hand on the wall beside my head.

"Did I hurt you?" he asked, his voice low with barely concealed fury. He probably thought me pathetic now or easily scared. How many times had I exposed myself to him like this? I used to be better at hiding my feelings. I must have *been* better.

"Please. Stop," he said. I looked up and met his eyes as he brushed a tear from my cheek with his thumb. "I didn't mean to frighten you," he said, misunderstanding my tears. "But that *man*..." He spat the word, as though my father didn't deserve to be called human. "...He is a monster." I knew that already.

"What happened to his wife?" I asked.

Garrett hesitated, obviously still confused by my sudden change and reluctant to risk upsetting me again.

"It was a long time ago now," he started, "but he was accused of treason. He had been conspiring with the king's brother, who at the time was amassing an army, that had allied with the west in an attempt to take Nordia. Well, letters where found. Flint and his family were sentenced to death. His name was to be forgotten and his lands gifted to other nobles."

I remembered that well. I hadn't been affected at first, because I was in the guard. But my brother and mother were put on house arrest and confined to their rooms while my father had been locked in the tower.

Yet he had still managed to sneak notes and orders to me. Trying to get me to free him by planting evidence or murdering innocent people.

"He had a daughter," Garrett said slowly. I looked up, meeting his eyes, but he was unreadable. If mentioning me affected him, he didn't show it. "She was in the blood guard and bound to the king like I am."

"She tried to free him, but it didn't work out."

That was an understatement.

In the same week my father was arrested, the king died of natural causes, and his crown passed to his fourteen-year-old son.

And during that transition, something had happened. I could no longer be held by the bond. When I was sure of it, I had confided in my father.

What a fool.

My father had tried to manipulate me into carrying on as normal. So, every day I was ordered to carry out requests from the new, shell-shocked king. I couldn't blame him. He was only doing what his advisors ordered, following the demands in the same way I was expected to.

But his first order had been a simple one, to fetch him a lord that owed money.

As I had walked from the room, I realised I didn't feel the same desperate, maddening compulsion pushing against my body and forcing my legs to move.

In fact, I had dallied easily, and when I reached the door to the lord's rooms. I found that I was able to turn around and walk away if I wanted to.

But I fulfilled the request, out of habit and out of fear.

That man was slain there in front of me by the commander. I still recalled the wide-eyed look of horror on the small boy king's face as the commander split the man in two, splattering blood over us both.

That hadn't been the first time I played the part. But the requests got worse. The seneschal was desperate to destroy all his own enemies while he could and used the king's death to turn the halls of Nordia castle red with blood.

I didn't dare tell anyone what was happening, but fulfilling terrible orders that I was no longer forced to carry out through compulsion weighed heavily on my heart.

And then the last request came.

The request to execute my own family. Starting with my ten-year-old brother.

The king had looked horrified as he asked me to do it, hesitating and staring at the seneschal and commander for confirmation several times.

I knew I couldn't do it.

I had run to my father and told him everything. He advised me to hang tight and be strong, reassured me that his men would soon dispatch the new king and put the brother on the throne instead.

I didn't want to be a part of any of it. I knew in the end he would ask me to kill Leander, and I couldn't do that. That poor, terrified child who was in over his head.

Something in me snapped, and I ran. I ran and I killed anyone who tried to stop me… including Garrett's only brother.

That was the beginning of my cowardice, and I never stopped being a coward. I embraced it, and I encouraged it within myself.

A few months after my escape, I had overheard the news that the king's uncle was dead, so I knew my father's plans had never come to pass. I had just presumed that the executions were carried out as planned.

There would be no going back for someone like me, who left her own family to die.

"In the end, there was enough proof found that it had actually been his wife who was plotting against the king. She was in love with the king's brother apparently and wanted to be queen," he said this bitterly, and I was relieved to see that he didn't believe a word of it. Of course it wasn't true at all.

My mother had no ambition.

"She was buried near here actually," he said suddenly.

My heart leapt.

I needed to know where.

I opened my mouth to ask but hesitated. Would it be too obvious? Why would I even be interested. But thankfully Garrett continued anyway, as though he was telling the story for his own benefit now.

"Under the library, there is a magical tomb called the meadow," he explained. "It's beautiful. Many thought she should have a pauper's grave, but her family was wealthy, and she was the last of them. She had no brothers, so the name died. As a concession, they buried her there, where the rest of her family were laid."

I needed to go see her. I needed to apologise.

We sat in silence a moment until Garrett brushed the blood from my lip. I shivered.

"Let me take you to your room."

Chapter 25

My room turned out to be very similar to the barrack room I used to sleep in. There was a small bed with a straw mattress, a cupboard with a wonky door and a bathroom, which I was thankful for.

Garrett leaned in the doorway as I looked around.

"You have no things at all?" he asked.

I shrugged. "Only what I can carry."

"I thought as much," he said. "I asked a maid to fill your wardrobe. You have basic uniform, along with a full armour set, the same as the elite soldiers wear so that you look worthy of the princess," he continued.

"Thanks," I said, pulling open the wardrobe to inspect my new things. I could see rows of deep blue cloaks and thick leather outerwear. There were boots along the floor in various sizes.

"You aren't allowed weapons in your room yet," Garrett said as he observed me. "I know you have a dagger…"

I looked at him warningly. If he tried to take it from me now, then there would be a fight.

"Stop looking at me like that," he said. "I'm not going to take it, so just keep it hidden."

"As the queen's knight, should I be armed?" I asked.

"You aren't her knight yet," he said. "I will get you a blade tomorrow, and wear the full armour." He hesitated a moment as though he wanted to say more, but he shook his head. "Stay out of trouble"," he advised. "You seem to attract it." I wondered if he was thinking of my outburst earlier or my refusal to give up a dagger.

"Goodnight, Cera," he said. Without another word, he left me. I went to the door and watched him disappear down the corridor.

I wanted to call him back.

How foolish.

I stripped my armour off and made my way naked to the bathroom. There was a full-length mirror resting against the wall, and I purposefully avoided it. I knew I was in a state. How anyone could stand to be around me I didn't know.

There was a claw foot bath with taps, and I sent a thanks to the gods when steaming hot water erupted from them. I searched the well-stocked cupboard and found toiletries, towels and lotions. I tossed an herb pouch that smelt strongly of citrus fruits into the tub and then sunk in myself before the water had even filled halfway. I was desperate to be clean. I scrubbed myself from head to toe until I was red raw. It was blissful to be free of the days and days' worth of grime and blood. My hair was matted, so I washed it several times.

Once clean I wrapped myself in towels, brushed my hair out with a wooden comb, and collapsed onto the bed, I was asleep the moment I hit the pillow.

I dreamed of my mother, just her sorrowful, frightened face, disembodied, floating in darkness. Her mouth was moving frantically, but no words reached my ears. She seemed to bob there for hours as I watched on.

I felt an overwhelming weight on my chest, as though I was failing her. She was trying so hard to be heard, so why couldn't I just listen?

I awoke with tears on my face. I brushed them away hastily and rolled out of bed. Sunlight filtered in through my window, and I realised there were no clocks in the room. I could have slept for hours or days.

There was only one thing on my mind, however.

I needed to go to my mother's grave.

She had to know how sorry I was.

I gripped her talisman, seeking its comfort. It was cold to the touch.

When my father married her, my mother had been very wealthy. Her aging parents had no sons, and a wave of disease had wiped out her cousins. She was heir to all their holdings, and my father was heir in his own right. Together they could have been so powerful.

It was never enough for my father though. Celion Flint wanted the world, he wanted whatever he thought was his due.

Warde. That was my mother's family name. Centuries old, but it was a dead line now. Strange how both my mother and father were the rotting branches of both their family trees.

There was poison in the blood, and I wasn't sad to be the end of it.

I dressed carefully, choosing to wear the elite soldier uniform. It was similar to what I had worn in the guard, a navy-blue gambeson with silver buckles. I pulled on a layer of protective leather and then strapped the spotless silver arm guards over my forearms and the same on my calves and thighs. I sheathed my dagger into the belt that clipped around my hips. Lastly, I secured the bright blue cloak to the shoulder pads of the gambeson, using broach pins depicting the emblem of Nordia.

I dug around in the drawers and was thankful to see that some smart maid had thought of the kind of necessities a woman would need: sanitary products, hair ties and clips and a wooden toothbrush. I ran the comb through my hair again now that it was dry. I surveyed myself in the bathroom mirror, checking that the uniform was secure. I looked formidable and familiar. I rolled my shoulders anxiously, and the cape danced and swayed with me, catching the light. I looked like Celine. I squinted at my reflection, needing reassurance as a wave of paranoia rushed over me. The longer I looked, the more my refection morphed and transformed, hair from brown to dirty-blonde, eyes a bright pale blue, similar to the sky outside my window. Relieved, I blinked my stinging eyes until I could only see my true reflection. I needed to talk to Mags about updating the glamour so that I could see it too. While I was here, I would need more reassurance that the spell was working. If it failed me now, I would be as good as dead,

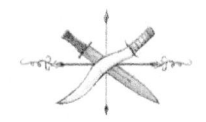

There were several libraries in the Nordia fortress, but I could guess the one Garrett had been speaking of. It was the oldest library in all the Westlands, a throwback from the archaic days when witches still held the throne of Nordia. It had been redecorated and renovated many times since its construction, but the bones were the same.

It had the atmosphere of a place of worship, and several guards stood watch over the doors.

They didn't flinch when an unfamiliar elite solder approached, however.

The doors were arched and carved from a thick marbled stone that looked as immaculate now as it ever had. It was spelled, because the doors slid open and shut easily despite their overwhelming size. Runes and sigils glowed orange above the rounded doorframe. I nodded silently to the guards as I swept through into the vast room. Even at this late hour, there were scholars sitting at the enormous rounded tables with large tomes spread out around them as they scratched away with their quills, translating and copying the histories and lessons of the past. The room was lit by fireplaces that were magically bespelled to never go out and never smoke. The flames were pure white and hard to look at directly.

The shelves were made from the same marbled stone as the door, and they stretched up into the heavens and along the length of the library. Some shelves were spiralling, others narrow and leaning. The hall was breath-taking. I felt a warm familiarity as I took it in. I had sought refuge in this place more times than I cared to remember.

It still had many secrets to share though.

I approached the desk to the left of the doors where several clerks sat, their heads buried in books. None of them reacted to me as I leaned over the desk.

"Where is the meadow?" I asked, hoping they would know what I was talking about.

The clerk closest slammed shut her book with a deep sigh.

"Follow me," she said. As she stepped out from behind the desk, I could see that she was missing the bottom half of her right leg. She balanced using a glowing purple cane that seemed fluid under the surface.

I observed that the craftmanship seemed to be the common style used by witches.

I followed the clerk for what was a mile at least. I opened my mouth to question her on how far was left, when she stopped abruptly beside a canvas on the wall.

"Here," she said, pointing directly at the oil painting. It was a landscape of a field covered in wildflowers.

"Here?" I repeated.

She nodded and tapped her cane at the painting. I could see that underneath in gold lettering was the word "Warde." My mother's maiden name.

"Step inside."

Step inside? Inside the painting?

I nodded along, not wanting to appear doubtful or worse, inexperienced, in front of the stern clerk.

So, without hesitating, I stepped right into the painting.

It disappeared, fading away around me and revealing a spiral staircase. I walked through and turned around, disorientated. The library was gone, replaced by a blank wall. My immediate thought was one of concern. I hoped I didn't have trouble getting back out again.

I walked down the narrow steps. As the name suggested, there was a meadow at the bottom. The ground below my feet was lush and green, with sprawling fields of wildflowers and flowering pink trees. The ceiling was spelled to appear like a sunny clear day, with clouds lazily drifting over. It was beautiful. I wandered through, noticing large erected stones as I went. Some were sculpted into the shape of people long dead while others lay flat with sleeping faces carved along the base. I searched the faces for a familiar one and was made breathless when I recognised my mother.

Her stone was a long box tomb nestled on the ground, and her full likeness had been sculpted on top of the lid. She looked peaceful, as though she was sleeping. Her name was engraved along the edge.

I ran my fingers over her eyelids and down the sides of her chiselled marble cheeks and felt my heart throb with the loss. It wasn't a new feeling. I had mourned my family these six years, but there was something so final about this morbid tomb.

"Are you here to pay your respects, child?"

I went cold and spun around at the sound of my father's voice.

He stood leaning against a twisted tree stump a few feet away, observing me impassively.

A familiar sickening anxiety began building in my chest as I watched him, standing completely still against the tree, observing me from hooded eyes.

People would often say my father resembled a snake. He was long and thin, almost too thin, with limbs that seemed too elongated for his body. Yet, he was elegant and moved with a captivating grace and swagger. But that wasn't why people would say that he was snake-like.

It was because one moment he could appear disinterested, pleasant, happy even and then the next he could strike without warning.

When this happened, his features would morph, like an invisible mask had evaporated, leaving behind his true face of madness behind. It was a face of pure chaos, and it was terrifying.

So, though his voice was agreeable and his stance was relaxed, I was keenly aware that a change could occur at any second. I clenched my jaw to hide the flinch as he pushed off from the tree and began to approach me.

My mind was racing, trying to anticipate what he would think of me being here, trying to decide how I would explain myself.

He walked off to the right and then the left, always forward but never in a straight line, almost as though he was trying to trap an animal.

"Lord Flint," I said, acknowledging his presence. "I have no one to pay respects to," I said firmly. "I thought it was a pretty walk." Was I overcompensating? Should I have waited for him to ask? Celion Flint knew how to read people, and right now, I was terrified that he had taken my measure.

He smiled slightly and rubbed a long finger over his bottom lip. "Is that so?"

"The morning grows long," I said coldly. "I have to get back to the queen."

"I am sure you do," he said slowly. The silence stretched, so I made to walk away.

"Stop, Celine," he ordered.

Celine.

I felt bile rise up in my throat, and for a moment I thought I would heave. My head spun, and I stumbled slightly, grabbing hold of my mother's tomb for balance.

"What did you call me?" I asked, trying and failing to sound unfazed.

"Celine," he repeated, smiling.

"That's not my name," I insisted. My trembling voice gave away my horror, but I continued in the farce, I *had* to. "Sorry, but you have me confused."

I knew you the moment I saw you," he said proudly. Dread filled me, but I refused to admit anything. He *couldn't* know me. He fixed me with a withering stare, as though he could see right through to my thoughts and was amused by my denial.

"You think I cannot recognise my own child?" His laugh was a bark that sent pure apprehension through me.

"I have to admit, I wasn't sure at first. I began to doubt my own fatherly instincts. But your appearance here has confirmed it."

I could have kicked myself for being so foolish. I had been hidden so long, and I put too much faith in my glamour.

"I knew you would return one day, Celine," he continued. His expression was manic, eyes wild with excitement and mouth pulled into a sneer. I took an involuntary step backwards in fear. "You made me wait longer than I expected," he chided. "I will forgive you though."

"I don't want your forgiveness!" I spat. "I want you to beg for mine!"

He laughed all the more at this.

"Why?" He asked. His eyes met mine, unblinking. "You should be thanking me with every breath you have, for all the rest of your days." He raged.

"You killed my mother!" I screamed. "Have you killed Cian too?" I demanded, terrified of the answer.

"All I have done I have done for you!" he countered, suddenly grabbing my cloak in his fist and yanking me up to face him. He was stronger than I expected. His face was contorted with rage now, his mask slipping completely. Was he angry that I wasn't overjoyed to see him? That I had taken so long to return? That I knew he had killed my mother? Or was it the old wound that filled him with so much righteous indignation? No doubt he felt himself very ill-used by me.

"I did everything for you, and you abandoned me to DIE." He screamed in my face, spittle bursting from his mouth. "You ungrateful bastard child," he continued. "What did that woman ever do for you? I would have seen you in a crown," he said, shaking me. "She was nothing to you, stupid girl." He continued, getting so close that our foreheads touched. I tried to pull away, disgusted by the proximity. He laughed and suddenly let me go. We both teetered back, and he fell to the ground, I onto my mother's stone.

"She wasn't even your birth mother, Celine. She despised you." He stood up and wiped the spit away from his mouth before turning back to me, his face a new mask of false sympathy. "Surely you knew that, my girl."

Surely I did not.

Chapter 26

"Who is then?" I asked, feeling all the fight slip away from me. How was it that he always seemed to get the upper hand? "If you are going to stand there and tell me my whole life was a lie, then at least tell me all of it," I implored, looking up at him from where I had stumbled, leaning against my mother's stone tomb.

"You don't deserve to know." He sneered, looking down at me like I was a snake in the grass. "I am disgusted with you," he continued. "After all of my hard work, all of the training and planning, after everything I had given up and sacrificed." He pounded hard on his chest, his face bunching up as if he was in agony, like it had been him who traded his childhood for a bloody sword.

Like it had been him who had his free will torn away and thrown back in his face and not I.

"You are weak and pathetic. Look at yourself!" he snarled. "You were born to be better than this, and I won't have you ruining my plans."

I sighed and let my head fall onto my knee. He was right. I was weak, weak and defeatist. All my strength and power, yet I still couldn't be rid of my own father.

"Dear daughter, hush now," he said, shifting tactics now that he could sense my exhaustion, ready to go in for the final blow. "Hush." He softened his voice so that it became a sickly shadow of what a real loving father might sound like. He crouched down and stroked my head. "You have been away from here for too long and have forgotten where your loyalties lay. You are home now though, and we can continue with our plan."

"Ah yes, the plan that you won't share with me?" I asked sarcastically, mockingly. His eyes flashed in an instant, and I found a dagger at my throat, the sharp point digging into my skin.

"With good reason, it turned out," He hissed. "Everything is finally in place, and I will make sure you don't fuck everything up again."

"What do I get out of this?" I asked, unbothered by the threat of steel. He clearly needed me for something, and as unhinged as my father was, he wasn't stupid.

"Help me, and I will tell you everything—who your mother is, *where* she is," he said, smiling like a hunter when he realises its prey is hooked. "I will tell you about your brother too. No one knows these things but me."

He had my interest, and he knew it.

"Is he alive?" I asked.

"I'll tell you, but first you must gain the trust of the king. Become Odelia's sworn knight, and I will tell you what you want to know." This seemed an odd exchange to me. It was something I had already outwardly agreed to, though I suppose no one knew better than my father my tendency to bolt when cornered.

"What's your plan?" I asked. "For me to seduce the king and give you a royal grandchild?"

He threw his head back at this and laughed heartily. I had a feeling I wasn't in on the joke. "No, nothing as foolish as that," he said eventually. He lowered the blade and forced it into the palm of my hand. "A gift, so you can remember this moment."

"But the crown is the end goal?" I asked, ignoring his words and letting the dagger drop to the floor. I didn't want anything from him. He picked it up again and slipped it into my belt.

" The crown?" he repeated "Why stop there?"

BOUND TO THE CROWN

I sat at the stone tomb for a long time after my father had left. Examining the dagger, twisting it in my fingers and memorising the weight of it. There was blood along the edge from where it had nicked me. The hilt was beautiful, carved from animal bone and hand-painted with the Flint family crest. The blade itself had a green hue that caught the light as I turned it in my hands. It was simple in its beauty, with no stones or elaborately decorated hilt guard. I sighed and placed it back into my belt, next to the one I already owned.

I stood, leaning against the tomb. I pressed my fingers to my mouth and touched the carved face of my mother.

"You are my mother," I whispered. "He can't take that away."

I heard soft footfalls behind me, and adrenalin pumped through my veins, I spun around, expecting to see my father returned, but instead it was Kohl making his way down the spiral steps and into the meadow. His eyes flared in surprise when he saw me. He looked around suspiciously.

"Cera?"

"It's me." I plastered a soft smile onto my face and approached him.

"What are you doing here?" he asked guardedly.

"I was on a walk and found myself here," I said, simply too numb to come up with a more elaborate excuse. "It's beautiful," I said honestly.

He raised his eyebrows and broke into a side smile that showed off the dimple in his lightly freckled cheeks.

"You are always turning up where you shouldn't." He laughed conspiratorially. "But at least you have a good eye. The meadow is a favourite spot of mine," he admitted. "This is lucky though, because I just saw Garrett, and he is looking for you. I'll take you to him before he turns the whole castle upside down." He rolled his eyes.

I groaned at the thought. "What does he want?" I asked.

"To start your training," Kohl explained. He gestured for me to go ahead of him on the stairs, and we walked in comfortable silence through the halls, both of us seeming distracted and lost in thought. I could only guess that he was preoccupied with worrying about the princess.

I couldn't help wondering what role he played in the guard. All members of the guard were elite soldiers, but they still had roles and skills that they were better at than others. I had excelled at combat, and I was nimble with a blade. But due to my age and small stature, I had often been tasked with assassinations. It was physically very easy for me, since I could slip in and out of almost anywhere, and most people weren't on their guard around a small girl-child.

Mentally, however, it had left scars.

"Have you gotten lost yet?" Kohl asked. "This place is like a labyrinth. I grew up here, but even I get turned about sometimes."

I thought about how he always stuck to the shadows when we were in Blackmoore castle, and I laughed out loud at the thought of him just being lost. "Is that why you always stay close to the walls?" I asked.

"Well, it's easier to know what way you have come from if you only need to go forward or back."

I nudged him playfully. In truth, Blackmoore castle was small compared to Tharnham Hold.

It was a maze of corridors and hallways, steps that sometimes led to dead ends where old walls and rooms had been blocked up.

I knew exactly where we were though and where Kohl was leading us.

Down.

Down into the meeting rooms.

There were designated rooms under the castle for all factions of the king's household. Soldiers, watchmen, kings-men, gentlemen and women, But the room I was being led to was one that the blood guard had claimed as their own. I felt my breathing coming fast and shallow as we walked down the familiar stone steps. I found myself trailing a hand down the wall as we descended, something I had been in the habit of doing. I had spent a lot of my time before missions here in these halls. I could almost predict every dip and curve of the old walls.

"Are you alright?" Kohl asked, suddenly turning to me. "I forgot how dark it was down here," he said apologetically. "We aren't fond of light in the blood guard," he continued. "And our eyes can adjust to almost any amount of darkness."

I knew this.

I didn't want Kohl to notice my abrupt change in mood, so I just laughed it off awkwardly. "It's okay, I am holding tight to the wall."

He nodded and came to walk with me, holding a steadying arm on my elbow, just in case. I pretended to stumble a couple of times to go along with the charade.

We reached the bottom of the stairs, and as we rounded the corner, we almost crashed into Maddie, who was dressed head to toe in a long black cape. She was checking over a leather tool pack full of thin, pointed instruments, counting them under her breath as she ran her fingers over them.

She looked up as we entered and gave Kohl and I a warning look. "Thank the gods you found her," she said.

"He's on the warpath." She grimaced then, turning to me. "How did you escape him?"

"Uh, I didn't do it on purpose," I said.

"Well, can you teach me, because I can't escape him for trying." She laughed.

I looked at Kohl questioningly. He shook his head.

"Well, off to do some skulduggery at our king's request," she said lightly, and without another word, she disappeared up the stairs like a shadow.

"What did she mean by that?" I asked.

"Hmm?" Kohl asked, distracted with scanning the room, no doubt for Garrett. "Skulduggery? She is probably on an assignment tonight."

"No, not that part… The part about not escaping Garrett for trying."

"Oh, that." He wagged his eyebrows up and down. "She was just being silly," he explained "They are engaged."

Engaged.

I felt like someone had physically kicked me in the stomach.

Several times.

"Are you alright?" Kohl asked. I nodded, numbly, sure that I had lost all the colour from my face.

"Kohl!" Garrett's voice was a bark that echoed all around the bones of the room, causing Kohl to jump and spin round guiltily.

"Where have you been?" Garrett demanded of me as he approached us. His face was lined with worry and annoyance, and his silver hair was twisted and standing up at odd angles, like he had been brushing his hand through it repeatedly.

"What happened?" he asked, softer as he took in my appearance.

"No idea," Kohl said. "She was fine a moment ago. Maybe it was all the walking."

Garrett looked unconvinced.

"I doubt it," he said as he led me to one of the nearest wooden benches. There were rows and rows of them in the cavernous room.

I found myself staring up into Garrett's blue-grey eyes. They were full of confusion and concern.

So, he had fallen in love with Maddie in my absence. I couldn't be angry. I had no right to that. If anything, I should be relieved that he found some kind of happiness.

What had I expected him to do? Pine over the woman who killed his brother and abandoned him?

Completely foolish!

"She was at the meadow," Kohl explained.

"The meadow?" he repeated "*Your* meadow?"

Kohl laughed. "It isn't *mine*," he said to me. "I just go there a lot. Its public, so feel free to visit whenever you want."

"Why were you there, Cera?" Garrett asked, his voice stern and low.

"I just went for a walk," I said meekly, trying to shake off this ridiculous feeling.

A few other guards had approached our bench now, drawn in by the spectacle. They all looked young, late teens at most.

"You're a bit fragile for a knight," observed one girl with free-flowing bright red hair. I noticed she was wearing a protective archer tab on her finger.

I didn't bother responding.

"Surely you can't let them swear her in, Captain," she said to Garrett.

"Get out of here, Grey," Kohl said. "She isn't a guard, so you can't put our standards on her."

I scoffed involuntarily at this. I was well aware I didn't look like much now, but I could keep up with the best of them. The redhead could be as sceptical as she wanted. Her doubt lit a fire in me, and I felt eager to prove her wrong.

I looked at the girl, fixing her with an unblinking gaze until she shuffled uncomfortably.

"Many have underestimated me in the past, archer," I said. "Don't be one of them."

She let out a mocking sound of dismissal and turned her back on me. I clocked her quiver and sling and inside it her bow.

Quick as a heartbeat, I drew my new dagger from my belt and tossed it overhand. It landed with a "thunk" in the upper limb of the guard's longbow.

She swore loudly and spun about, unsheathing her bow, nocking an arrow and pointing her weapon at me, the blade still sticking out from the top.

"That will mess with the balance," I observed, resting my chin in my hand casually. "You should take it out first."

"You won't look so smug with only one eye," the girl countered.

Garrett, who had been watching the exchange silently until this point, growled warningly and turned to the archer.

"What are you doing?" he asked. The girl blanched under his scrutiny but still held her arrow nocked on the rest and aimed directly at me.

"She threw a dagger at my bow!" she complained. "It's destroyed."

"I thought you were hinting for a demonstration," I said innocently.

"Sheath it," Garrett demanded as he pulled the dagger loose from the bow. The girl did as she was told, and after shooting me one last filthy look, she walked away.

"You aren't very good at making friends," Kohl observed. I couldn't disagree. I felt a little guilty now for the petty display.

"You are clearly fine," Garrett said. "Get up, it's time to test that aim of yours more thoroughly." He motioned for me to stand and held my dagger out to me. I reached for it, but he roughly pulled it back, his face going dark as he examined it. He looked up at me again, his eyes stormy, and his mouth tight-lipped in anger.

"I told you to stay away from him," he said, his voice a low rumble that vibrated in my chest. My cheeks flared hot as I realized the mistake. The Flint crest.

"Why do you have this?" he questioned.

"I- I stole it." I stammered.

"When?" he barked.

"Back in the kings chamber," I lied. "Before you warned me away," I added for good measure.

"Why?" he pressed, but his voice was already softer. He believed me, or he wanted to believe me.

"I told you. I don't like that guy."

He handed back the dagger wordlessly and gestured for me to follow him. I looked back at Kohl who grimaced and shrugged.

I was slipping.

Chapter 27

The wind whistled over and around the lanterns that lit the arena overlooking the Westlands. Garrett had taken us to the outskirts of the fortress, up a large mound that looked down on the towns below. The sun was getting low in the sky, casting a bright pink glow on the world. I took in a deep breath. The air smelt crisp and earthy.

I hadn't trained here when I was younger, and I wondered if it was a new setup.

As I waited for Garrett to finish prepping the equipment for whatever test he was going to force upon me, I scanned the horizon and the beacons of light dotting the landscape, and I felt calm and slightly embarrassed by my earlier outburst.

The ugly, familiar feeling of regret was beginning to loom over me when Garrett's voice broke me out of my thoughts.

"Was it necessary to break her bow?" he asked.

I bristled at his chiding tone.

"You aren't going to make much of a knight if you keep throwing your weapons away."

He was ridiculing me, but there was also truth in what he said. It was important to assert dominance when challenged, but I'd lashed out rashly, and I had a feeling that my ire hadn't been directed at the redheaded guard at all.

. The news of Maddie and Garrett's engagement had shaken me. I was jealous, with absolutely no right to be, but I was also happy for them. Happy and concerned.

I couldn't help thinking on what Mags had said about the crowns. Was there really a way to break the bond?

For everyone, not just for me?

With her help, could I make things right and destroy the blood guard?

Mags seemed to think so.

And if I did this, then Garrett and Maddie would be free to run off into the sunset.

It was the very least of what I owed them all.

So why did my throat go dry at the very thought of it?

"Ready?" Garrett asked.

"Let's just get this over with," I replied sharply.

"Very well," he answered, motioning to an obstacle course made up of aged, high steps, stone outcrops, iron netting and tall wooden podiums.

It was clear now that my surmising had been incorrect. This arena wasn't new, it was old.

Very old.

"A time trial?" I wondered.

"Don't tell me you've taken this test before?" he joked. "It may seem basic," he continued, "but swift movements and fast reflexes are just as important for knights as their swordsmanship skill or their armour."

"You've seen me fight," I said. "You know what I can do, so is all of this really necessary?" My impatience was growing, faced with the kind of course equivalent to what schoolchildren would attempt.

"It's to evaluate your skill." His smile once again belied a seriousness within it. "I have seen what you can do to an extent, but this is to get a more complete picture. Unless you think I should start you on something... simpler?"

I felt a desire to wrap my hands around his throat.

"This is fine" I sighed.

"Then, when you are ready?"

I set about jumping, running, sliding, climbing and dodging among the apparatus, hidden traps attempted to stop me in my path, but the obviousness of their placing was easy to discern, as ancient as the training ground was.

Notable grooves in stone and worn wooden indents told me all I needed to know. I wondered if I was making a mistake by showing my skill, but if I purposefully messed up now Garrett would know what I was doing and try to figure out the reason behind it.

As I pivoted past a swinging ball and chain, I couldn't help but think of how many other guards, knights and elite solders must have come before me, training for a place to protect the royal blood and some even of their own free will.

It left an oddly bitter taste in my mouth.

I reached the end without difficulty, The obstacle course was made to test the endurance, stamina and speed of normal people, and I was a member of the blood guard.

Garrett was awaiting me at the end, smirking like an idiot.

"OK, that was adequate."

I scoffed but remained silent. He was goading me, trying to get me to lose my temper like earlier.

"Now, let's see how you handle a bow."

As I moved forward onto the archery range, I spied ten different targets at varying distances before me.

One was placed up a tree, and at least two were stuck in hay bales, perhaps hard for anyone not able to see in the dark.

Garrett handed me a longbow, and silently stepped back.

I could feel him observing me, and the stillness in the air reverberated around us as I nocked an arrow and readied the bow.

"You may not be able to see all the targets because of the darkness, but try your best."

Almost sounded like encouragement.

I took a breath and felt the arrow brush my cheek as I drew it back.

Upon release, it silently screamed through the air towards its intended end. Before it landed, I nocked another arrow and released and another and another.

There was a cacophony of "thunks" as my arrows hit their marks, exactly as I had intended, and I saw what looked a little bit like admiration on Garrett's face when I turned to him.

"It's a shame you didn't have a bow earlier. You could've given her a run for her money." He smiled a genuine smile, and I felt a fluttering, nervous sensation within me as I smiled back. It was the familiarity.

The moment lingered in the air for long enough to be uncomfortable, so I hastily broke the silence.

"What now?"

"Now, I think, we should fight."

We made our way over the field towards a stone arena.

The area was completely empty, discarded rubbish and towels the only signs of recent use.

"Is there an actual reason we are doing this at night?" I asked. "Or did you want to be alone?"

"The less people who know of you and what you can do, the better…" Garrett answered stoically.

He turned his head to the sky.

"We should make this quick. It's going to rain soon."

"Go arm yourself," he ordered. I dug into my belt and pulled out my own little dagger.

"I have this," I said. He shook his head.

"No, a sword," he insisted. I shrugged, and sheathed it..

He hesitated a moment and then pulled a blade from his hip. I could tell right away that it was Haze, Vale's sword. I backed away involuntarily, not wanting to take that blade. Not after what I had done to her back at the riverbank. Not when I had washed her blood from my body only last night.

He held it out to me, hilt first.

"Take the sword, Cera."

"I can't," I pleaded. "It's not mine."

"Vale wasn't a sentimental person," Garrett said. "She would be furious to see her sword going to waste in my belt." I laughed.

Wasn't that the truth.

I couldn't think of a good reason not to take Haze, so I gripped the heel and slid it out of Garrett's loose grip.

"Thank you." I sighed.

"She called it Haze," he said. I nodded, not trusting myself to speak.

"Draw your weapon and come at me," he said as he unsheathed his own blade.

"If you're sure." I taunted.

I was going to enjoy this.

I lunged at him with my blade, going right in for the kill, knowing he would be able to parry it. He counterattacked, blocking the move with his sword and aiming his unarmed fist toward my abdomen. I twisted to avoid his and punch and danced around him. I swung for his left shoulder from behind, but anticipating my swing, he rolled forward to avoid the blow, turned and thrust his sword up at me from the ground.

I laughed as I swiped the attack away easily and swiftly kicked him in the head with the heel of my boot.

Garrett looked dazed for but a moment, then came at me again, lunging up to meet me.

Our blades crossed countless times, and their meetings rang into the air, clashing loudly and echoing around the arena.

For every lunge, there was a dodge. For every thrust, a parry.

We were evenly matched in skill.

"Enough," Garrett finally called.

"We're not done yet, are we?" I wheezed.

"I have seen enough."

He sheathed his sword and looked over to the doorway, as footsteps could be heard approaching.

It was Kohl.

"It would seem you are wanted," Garrett said, trying to hide his exhaustion.

"Have I passed this first round then?" I asked.

Garrett eyed me with a curious look,

"You have skill, but I'm watching you, Cera. I still don't understand why you are here, and we both know you haven't lived a sheltered life in a rent house all your days. The moment you or your witch do anything to endanger the princess, I will strike you down."

"If you can," I countered, playfully.

He smiled despite himself, and my stomach flipped nervously.

"And there I was thinking we were becoming friends," I continued.

"We could very easily be friends," he said, advancing on me and stopping so close I could feel his warmth. He bent close, his breath against my neck, and I couldn't help leaning in until his lips brushed the edge of my ear. "If you tell me why you are really here and where you really came from, then we could be the very best of friends." I shivered and stepped away, more shaken by his proximity than by his threat.

"Think about it," he added with a slow smile.

"I'm a rent girl. I already told you everything," I said, with no real conviction. To this, Garrett merely turned around and left, passing Kohl on his way.

"Watch her, Kohl," I could hear him say and then he entered the castle.

"What happened there?" Kohl asked pointedly.

"If I'm honest, I'm not too sure," I replied.

"The princess has asked to see you, Cera."

I slipped Haze into the empty sheath at my belt and sighed.

"Lead the way."

We made our way to Odelia's room through the southernmost passage of the castle, so as not to alert too many of our presence.

When we entered, she was sitting on the end of her bed, and worry filled her eyes. Her three maids sat on the floor around her, busy at various works. One was sewing, another reading aloud and the third was strumming gently on a small string instrument that looked similar to a harp. They all glanced up as we entered.

"How are you, Your Highness?" I asked.

She smiled weakly. "Sorry I called you so late, Cera," she apologised. "I couldn't sleep, and Kohl here told me you were probably awake also." Kohl nodded.

"I will leave you now," he said, disappearing into the shadows.

"Don't worry about it. You saved me, really. I was training with the knight," I said once he was gone and the door shut behind him. Odelia frowned at this.

"Its full night," she complained. "He should have waited until morning."

I shrugged. She stood up from the bed then and ordered one of her ladies to find me a chair to sit on. All three women stood and busied themselves with the task, eager to please their princess. They worked together, pulling one of the large embroidered armchairs over to the edge of the bed.

"I'm fine," I insisted.

"No, you must be exhausted after that, sit down." I did as I was bade and found that my whole body began to ache the moment I sank into the chair.

"I feel terrible," the queen admitted, shuffling over so that she was sitting in front of me on the edge of her bed.

"Why?" I asked. "Because of the letter?" She nodded. "I hadn't been silly enough to think that I would be staying here forever. I knew I would have to be married off again. It's my duty to forge stronger bonds for Nordia in this way. I never realised I would be going back there though." She sighed. "That man treated me like dirt. He locked me up and accused me of stealing a child." Her eyes blazed angrily, and her cheeks flushed red. "He swore it would be different this time and that I could take my ladies and Kohl and Marius along with me. But I am dreading it, Cera." She looked downcast, and I could see tears glittering as they rolled down her cheeks. "I promised you so many things, and I understand if you no longer want to be my knight," she admitted. "I will still pay you all the gold I promised, and if you want, you can disappear like we first agreed. I know you wanted to be free from the eastlands, and to ask you to come back with me in a mere nine months and with a child to protect also, I know it might be too much."

I was touched that the Princess had found time to think of me at all. She must have been worrying enough about her own fate since reading that letter.

"I was furious with my brother when I first read the letter," she said suddenly, her voice taking on an edge. "He has done some unseemly things since taking on Father's crown, but *this*. I was angry enough when he married me off to Henri, but at least I could understand it. And at the time, he had seemed just as sad to let me go as I was to leave… But now, the thought of going back makes me feel sick."

I could understand. She hadn't been well-liked or respected in Blackmoore, and it was a very different court to this one.

"It will be different this time," I said reassuringly. "You will have me." She stared at me then with so much hope that I had to bite down on my lip to relieve some of the worry.

I wasn't sure when I had decided, but I was sure now that Mags had been right. Odelia had come to me for a reason, and I was bound to her.

I had a feeble spark taking light in my heart, and spreading through my body, burning brighter the more I tried to dampen it down.

I couldn't live the way I had been living in Riverna, not anymore. Not when the chance to put some things to rights had fallen into my lap.

Maybe I could really do this.

I could free the guard, and then go with Odelia to the eastlands. The king would be easy to dispose of, and I could help Odelia set up as queen, with a faithful court of advisors.

Maddie and Garrett could marry and live as they pleased.

Mags would follow me anywhere.

The lady's-maid had begun strumming at her harp again, and the sound was soft and musical. I sat back a moment and shut my eyes, listening to the skilful player pick at the melody. I began to sing, a tune I had learned as a child from my mother. She would sing it to me to try to help me sleep when I had nightmares. A solitary tear slipped down my cheek.

"Can you sing the stanza, the one you sang at Riverna?" Odelia asked. "Kohl used to sing it to me. It was a favourite of his mother's," she explained.

I nodded and began to sing. The maid knew the tune, as she had probably played it many times over.

I woke with a start as some distant mechanical clock chimed out through the corridors. My eyes took a moment to adjust to the darkness, but I quickly realised that I still sat in the deep armchair in Odelia's room. Odelia herself was laying in the middle of her bed. It was so large and plush that she almost disappeared within the sheets. There was no sign of her ladies. It was still dark, so I couldn't have been asleep long. I stretched out my stiff legs, and after a quick search around to make sure nothing was amiss, I left the room. Odelia had three guards stationed outside of her door, I hoped they weren't easy to bribe. The people of Nordia seemed to really care for their princess though, so I felt confident in her safety.

Chapter 28

The moment I shut my bedroom door behind me, I knew something was off.

I couldn't put my finger on it, a perfume, a moved item, an open drawer that I had perhaps left shut? Something was different.

I took my father's dagger from my belt and stood completely still while scanning the room. It was silent and seemingly undisturbed, with my old clothes discarded on the floor in the mess where I had left them and my sheets pristine. The bathroom door was slightly ajar, leaving a small window into the darkness beyond. I crept forward, my footfall making no sound on the old floorboards and musty rugs. I pressed my back against the wall adjacent to the bathroom door and unsheathed my other dagger. Then, armed with both blades, I took a deep breath and kicked the door wide open with the back of my heel.

Silence.

No attacker raced out to ambush me.

My eyes were already adjusted to the darkness, so I didn't hesitate to enter the bathroom, daggers aimed to where an intruder's neck and abdomen might be.

But the small washroom was empty and as I had left it, long, dented claw foot tub, leaking sink and navy-blue towels.

Were my instincts off? Maybe the lack of sleep was playing with my mind, or maybe I was still rattled from the reunion with my father.

Wait.

"No," I breathed.

My father.

I spun around and flew back into my room, racing to my bed. In a frenzy of panic, I pulled back and stripped all the sheets and pillows away from the straw mattress, my heart pounding as I searched and searched. I began to think I was being too paranoid but then I saw it.

Sticking out between mattress and frame.

A forest green letter sealed with the Flint crest in a shimmering golden wax.

My father had worked quickly, no doubt trying to make up for the lost time that he believed I had stolen from him.

BOUND TO THE CROWN

In my childhood, I had received countless notes exactly like this one. They weren't the typical letter from father to daughter. They were instructions hidden in a code that he had taught me almost from the moment I could read.

I threw the pillow and blankets down onto the floor in disgust.

I ripped the letter open, curious despite myself.

Dear Knight to Be,

As the King's treasurer and member of the privy council, I thought it my duty to reach out to you and extend to you my most hearty congratulations on your new position.

Should you have any questions at all, please forward them to me.

With the warmest of welcomes,
Lord Celion Flint

If the note had been intercepted, then there would be nothing within it that could be seen as suspicious, unless you knew how to crack my father's code, as I did.

It was a letter instructing me to meet him in the Meadow at noon the next day. I felt sick to my stomach and couldn't help but regret, just for a moment, all the decisions that had led me back to this point.

I couldn't know what he would ask of me, but it wouldn't be good.

Damn him and the hold he had over me!

I wasn't going to do his bidding anymore. I needed to let him know this. The risk of him revealing my identity was a very real one, however, if he chose that path, then he would be stabbing himself in the foot as well. The king might be grateful to him for giving up his own daughter, and would no doubt reward him handsomely. However my father had other plans, I was sure of it.

He had always made it very clear to me that I was an investment and that I was meant for bigger things.

He never felt the need to share what those things were of course.

He may have moved on to other schemes by now, but I doubted it, and this letter seemed to confirm my doubts.

My mind was made up. I was going to free Maddie, Garrett and Kohl from the guard. Then I would leave with Odelia and never step foot past those black gates again.

Maybe I would raid my family's quarters first, and sell every single book he coveted.

I should have burned the one I kept, what a silly, romantic notion it was to have kept it at all. I dragged a chair to my door and jammed it under the handle so if anyone else tried to enter I would hear it. This time, I would make sure there were no secret entrances. I searched the walls, brushing my palms over every indent and corner, before dropping to my knees and repeating the process with the floorboards. I pulled and shuffled the heavy rugs until the air around me was thick with particles of dust that danced and sparkled in the low firelight.

Mine was a basic room, but any room in the queen's apartments could be equipped with secret doors, an entryway for lovers, for friends, or assassins.

I stood when satisfied and looked around at the dishevelled room. I wouldn't be able to sleep again now. I headed to the bathroom and filled the tub. The sound of water on tin was deafening in the silence, and I wondered how many people I was waking up as the noise reverberated below me.

The water was hot and healing, and I felt my muscles relax as I sank into the warmth.

I stared up at the ceiling and took in a deep breath.

What had I gotten myself into?

A series of preventable decisions had led me to this place, and now that I was here, I couldn't tell if I had done the right thing or just the stupid thing.

I would make the best of it though.

I was no closer to figuring out why the bond had failed with me so suddenly, and being back home was a barrage of memories and hurts. Anxiety was my constant companion.

I felt out of my depth.

Even with Mags here to guide me.

Spending every day with Garrett, pretending I didn't know him and lying to everyone was exhausting.

And in the forefront of my mind was fear. Fear that the bond could come back into effect as quickly as it had snapped. Without knowing why it happened, there was always the chance it could simply…unsnap. I had been so desperate to run that I hadn't taken the time to understand the why or how. However, if that were to happen, then it didn't matter how far away I was. If the King whispered for his guards to come to him, then I would have to come. Such was the power of the blood crown. When I served the old king, I had a list of orders that were a constant: to report to the crown every day, to never raise a hand in harm of him, to tell him of any traitorous plots.

But he was dead, and a new king had taken his place, so maybe those old orders were dead with him. I couldn't be sure though, the bond was to the crown, and it was endless… for most people. I had never heard of another person being free from it.

My last order was one that I had never completed… to kill my own family. It had been Leander's command but the old king's order. Either way it didn't affect me, however, would that order still stand if suddenly the bond began to tug at me once again?

I shuddered at the thought.

I hated my father, but I didn't want to kill him. For all his many faults, he was still the man that raised me.

I wondered if the roles were reversed, would he have any hesitation?

I liked to think that some part of him, deep down, loved me, but if it was love, then it was a complicated, twisted love and not as important to him as gaining power.

As a child, I had spent my days training with other guards and my nights training with my father. Guard work was physical, but my father's was spent thumbing through books. As I grew, he began to use me as a spy, I would memorise the maps of the castle and spend my nights slinking through tunnels, listening to court chatter, finding out who was allied with whom and placing those little green notes of my father's. I wonder who was doing that for him now.

I wouldn't let it be me.

Once bathed and dressed, I walked over to Odelia's rooms. I pressed my ear to the door and was rewarded with silence. She would probably be sleeping for a while still. The last few days had been traumatic for her, and her whole life had been overturned.

I was used to change and chaos, and sometimes it seemed as though I thrived on it. It wasn't that way for her.

I left her and went down to the library to visit the Meadow, cursing myself the entire way. Several times I turned around and decided to go sit with Mags instead only to change direction again.

I sat in the library for a few hours, listening to my stomach rumble and browsing through the shelves full of diaries and textbooks belonging to past kings-men, guards and citizens.

Just before noon, I spotted my father walking thorough the library towards the Meadow, the cape of his uniform dancing across the floors dramatically. He didn't even try to hide his comings and goings, so sure was he in his own ability to weasel out of any predicament.

I couldn't deny that it was a founded confidence.

I gritted my teeth together and slammed down the book I had been reading.

What was I thinking, coming at his call? It would be better to completely ignore the man.

And yet... he was still my father, and maybe... just *maybe* I could reason with him.

I stood, ready to follow.

"There you are," Garrett said. "Were you hiding again?"

For a moment I couldn't find my words as the captain of the blood guard approached me. He was wearing full Noridian armour, his silver booted steps echoed on the marble floor and his heavy blue cloak swayed with his broad shoulders. His white-silver hair was loose and falling choppily over his brows. It shimmered under the harsh light of the library.

"You are never where I expect you to be," he continued, almost to himself.

An old, familiar feeling of comfort rose up inside me at the sight of him, and I smiled warmly. The knight hesitated at this and stopped in his tracks, looking almost stunned. I watched as his gaze flicked to my mouth and back to my eyes in quick succession.

"You're in a good mood," he said eventually. "Let's see if that sticks."

"What do you mean?" I asked cautiously. He smiled slyly.

"After your display last night, I have decided to test you against some of the guard."

"Come on, follow me."

I hesitated as I placed my book back onto the shelf. My father was waiting for me, but I couldn't think of one excuse to give Garrett that would be sufficient to excuse myself from training. Besides, a part of me was thankful for the interruption. This conversation with my father would not be an easy one.

I followed Garett out of the library and through the castle halls, both relieved for the excuse, and anxious, knowing that my father would be made furious by my absence.

He walked fast, not looking back to check if I could keep his pace.

It was interesting to watch how the household reacted to Garrett. When I was a member of the blood guard, we were shadows at best. Attendants and courtiers alike would turn a blind eye towards us as we walked the halls, no doubt they thought we were hurrying around from one assassination or devious task to the next.

This was no longer the case with Garrett. His role as Captain of the guard and Knight to the king had advanced his standing to equal that of someone like my father. Attendants directed curt nods or half-bows his way as he walked past. Courtiers either greeted him friendlily or stared after him in awe, fear or lust.

There was once a time we could run full speed down these corridors without anyone sparing us a glance, but now Garrett commanded attention wherever he walked. The Knight led me down to the catacombs, and I ran my hand along the wall, as I always did, lost in thought. As we reached the bottom of the steps, I realised Garrett was watching me, his eyes flicking from my hands to my face, his face unreadable.

I hastily moved my hand, rubbing the damp away on my leggings.

"What are we doing today, then?" I asked him nervously.

"Sparring," he answered, monosyllabically.

We reached the ground, and I was taken aback by the large crowd gathered waiting for us. Guards sat on the rounded tables, eating breads, drinking from waterskins and tankards and chattering loudly.

That chatter died down quickly however, as all faces turned to Garrett.

"All ready?" he asked, his voice a loud growl in the now silent catacombs. Suddenly the halls erupted with cheers, jeers and table pounding. Several guards held their weapons aloft. Spears, bows, blades and axes glinted under the makeshift chandeliers, crafted from sizeable wagon wheels.

"Then follow," Garrett commanded, his booming voice easily heard above the din.

The guards all stood with a loud scraping-back of chairs and benches. I spotted Greta in the swarm and wove my way between people until I reached her. I grabbed her arm, and she started before realising it was me.

"Oh hello, you," she said, friendly. "You move like a shadow, you know," she continued with a sly grin, "You have slipped my net a few times. Where did you go this morning?"

"Only the library." I laughed, trying to hide the anxiety that flared in my chest when I remembered she had been tailing me. "It's no secret."

"I'm only playing with you," she said teasingly. "Don't be so serious." She gripped my hand in hers and ran ahead, forcing me with her until we caught up with Maddie, who acknowledged us both with a warm smile. She was holding a large axe in her hand, and I stared at the serrated metal with awe.

She had always favoured swords and bows when I used to train with her.

The sunlight was a shock to my eyes as we exited out of the secret tunnel from the catacombs to the gardens. Garrett led us over to the training green. It was nicknamed "The Arena" because guards would often spend their breaks or other leisure time there, sitting on the stone seats and watching other guards train. It could get rowdy, bets were taken sometimes, and I myself had sung there for entertainment more times than I could recall while drunk on ale and spirits.

I smiled at the memory but repressed it quickly when I realised Greta was watching me slyly.

A few people sat down on the stone benches right away, but I wouldn't be one of them. I didn't want to sit on the sidelines today. I wanted to have fun.

I unsheathed Haze. If Maddie or Greta recognised the sword as Vale's, then they didn't comment.

"Who is first?" asked Garrett. A dozen hands went up. Garrett pointed across at one, and as he walked onto the green, I saw that it was Marius.

"Oooh," Greta said, pulling air in through her teeth. "He's ruthless. I'll sit this one out." I was sure she had only said it to goad me, and Maddie's look of exasperation to her friend confirmed it. But I took the bait anyway and walked out onto the green, purposefully, hoping Garrett would ignore the other raised hands.

Marius looked me up and down and scoffed. His large chest was puffed out confidently, and he looked over at a group of men, who must have been his peers. They all jeered as he laughed. Garrett observed me, his face stony.

"No," he said, firmly as I approached. I pointed behind my head, for someone else to step forward. But I pushed his arm down forcefully, to the sound of a few indignant gasps.

"I want to show what I can do," I said. Garrett seemed to think about this for a moment.

"What can you do, renter girl?" he asked. He hadn't called me that in a while, and I rolled my eyes at him.

"Just watch and see."

He nodded wordlessly, and I stood to face off against Marius and his longsword. Marius stared down at me amused and then ripped off his shirt to expose a muscled torso. A few people wolf-whistled, and I laughed, caught up in the atmosphere.

"All ready?" Garrett called.

I braced myself, legs apart and sword raised. Marius did the same, mirroring my stance.

"Begin!"

Garrett's voice rang out over the arena. I attacked, aiming low and throwing my entire body down in an attempt to knock Marius from his feet. Despite his size, he was able to move back and out of my reach quickly. He wagged his finger at me, and I lunged again. My sword landed flat against his left side, and if this had been a real battle, it would have been a killing blow.

A few people let out cheers at this, and Marius seemed to look at me with new eyes. His face shifted from playful to serious, and he leaned forwards in a wider stance, ready to defend his honour.

We both moved at the same time, him straight towards me and I into a right feign. He tried to follow at the last moment as I changed course and spun around him. A fast swipe of my legs under his saw the guard falling hard onto his back. He gasped breathlessly and then smiled up at me, defeated.

"Again?" he asked as I held a hand out to help pull him up. I looked to Garrett questioningly, who nodded his consent. He stood at the side of the green, arms crossed over his chest. He had a slight smile tugging at the corners of his mouth, and I wondered if he was proud.

"Ready?" Marius held a hand up and went over to his friends. He spoke with them quickly before returning, a giant war hammer in tow. I looked at the weapon with no small amount of horror, but I wouldn't let it stop me.

I sheathed Haze and wielded my daggers instead.

"Ready?" Garrett called again. "Go."

This duel was much faster than before. I found myself having to jump out of Marius's reach several times to avoid the hammer. For every time I knocked him back, he knocked me back twice. I waited to find his pattern, and as he brought the hammer down towards me I kicked him, full in the lower abdomen. He fell to the ground with a howl. I moved to jump on him, when an arrow whistled passed me, stopping me in my tracks. It hadn't been close enough to hurt me, but I was taken aback. The redheaded girl whose bow I had destroyed raced to meet me with a broadsword. I parried her lunge and jumped away as Marius once again took up his hammer. It was two to one now. They both advanced, but I held off, standing my ground and waiting for the right moment to headbutt the redheaded guard.

Except I didn't get a chance, because as Marius's hammer crashed down towards me, it was intercepted by a long, silver blade. I lost my footing in surprise and fell to the floor. The redhead stopped and stood back immediately, her arms raised up in surrender.

Garrett, roared and deflected Marius's blade, redirecting the attack away from me. Marius stumbled under the Knight's strength and dropped to his knees on the trampled grass, defeated.

I stared up from the ground, open-mouthed and infuriated with the interruption.

"She is not a guard," Garrett growled angrily at Marius. "You took it too far."

"She can handle it!" Marius defended, and I felt myself warm to him. "She is as strong as a guard."

Garrett stared down at him warningly, his eyes blazing. Marius conceded, dropping his hammer and holding his hands above his head. Garrett turned and walked back to the steps while signalling for the next pair to begin their fight.

"Why did you do that?" I demanded. I got to my feet and chased him down. "I didn't need help."

"Didn't look that way to me."

"I had a plan. I knew exactly what their next moves would be. You embarrassed me by stepping in."

I spotted Kohl sat on the benches, and he signalled me to sit next to him. I brushed past Garrett, roughly hitting him with the side of my shoulder. His low chuckle only fanned my frustration.

"Why did he do that?" I asked Kohl huffily as I sat down next to him.

"He was worried." Kohl said simply. "Marius is huge, and Harriet has it out for you."

"Harriet, is that her name?" I asked, not really caring.

I sat with Kohl, watching the Guards spar until the sun hit its peak and became unbearable. The numbers began to dwindle, and I watched as more than one Guard abandoned a fight completely and walked away, stiff backed. I knew that walk and pained look. It only meant one thing, either the guard had been summoned by their King or a recurring order had triggered.

It was an odd feeling to see it in action after years away from it.

"We will have to leave soon," Kohl said suddenly. "The king asked us all to come to a meeting." I nodded.

"Look, don't hold a grudge. You aren't a guard, and I think Garrett is protective of you," Kohl said, sensing the anger that still vibrated under my skin.

"Why would he be?" I asked, doubtfully. Kohl hesitated and looked pained for a moment.

"Honestly, you are similar to someone he... someone *we* used to know. Your habits and the way you hold yourself."

My body went cold at Kohl's words, and I lost my breath. I was thankful of being spared a reply though as he stood up, looking frustrated.

"I have to go. I'll talk to you later," he said. I waved dismissively as he and most of the other guards, including Garrett, made their way back to the tunnels.

I sat until the arena had almost emptied, my mind lost in worry. Kohl couldn't have been talking about me, could he? I looked nothing like myself now, and I had changed so much in the last six years. I took a deep breath, realising that I had been shaking my leg aggressively as I let my mind wander.

I needed to put this to the back of my mind.

I needed a distraction, before my fears turned to full-blown panic.

Unfortunately I had the perfect one.

I watched for a few moments more, as some guards lagged behind to spar, obviously having not been needed at the king's side. I clapped when one guard felled another with an impressive headbutt. Then I stood and slipped away.

I had no doubt in my mind that my father would still be waiting for me. I needed to let him know that I had absolutely no intention of being his spy.

In my heart I already knew this would be a waste of my time.

I knew it, and yet I still couldn't help but hope that my father would listen to what I had to say, and for once in my life think of me as a person instead of a means to an end.

Our years apart clearly hadn't softened him, but perhaps he had missed me in some twisted way. Perhaps if I explained that I was no longer willing, or able, to be his puppet, we could forge some unique version of a father-daughter relationship.

It was doubtful.

No matter. He needed to hear me, whether he wanted to or not.

Chapter 29

I went straight to the library, using the front entrance of the hold for fear of running into Garrett again.

When I reached the painting, I could see that it was changed, with a figure standing in the middle.

So, it was enchanted to show when people were inside? I wondered.

I pushed through and walked down the spiral stairs, each step on the marble seeming to echo loudly through the enchanted room.

My father was waiting in the middle of the flower field. He turned and faced me as I approached.

"What do you want from me?" I asked quickly, letting it be clear how I felt about this summons.

"Let me speak it plainly to you, daughter," he began, not missing a beat. "So there is no room for misinterpretation." He ran his hand over my mother's tomb, looking down at her carved face with something like love. It filled me with a renewed rage.

"You are to gain favour with the king and become his knight, not Odelia's."

I wanted to say I was surprised, but I had expected something of the like. I suspected this would lead to another scheme, maybe a forced marriage between Leander and myself. He had encouraged me to flirt and use my body to gain information and trust from people since the moment I became a woman. If that was the case though, why would he waste time making me the Knight first? Gods only knew why he held back now. "Becoming Odelia's knight would be a waste of your time and your talent," he continued. "You are to stay here in Nordia with your family."

I ignored the surge of repulsion at his use of the word "family" as though any of this was being led by his desire to keep his family together.

"The king already has a knight, so how would that work?" I asked, thinking of Garrett. My father's mouth curled up at the corners, and his eyes sparkled in a way that made me feel as though he knew some obvious secret, and my not knowing it just proved that I was a fool. I knew that look well.

"It's more… complicated than that," he said eventually as he paced around in front of my mother's tomb.

"Is it?" I asked. "Or are you just being vague for the sake of it?"

He laughed sincerely at this. "I am being vague," he admitted. "But all will be clear soon enough."

"If this ends in your wanting me to *dispose* of Garrett, then give up that folly now. It won't be happening," I said firmly.

"No." He shook his head. "No need for that, not yet, not from you." He stopped pacing and stared at me "You can still be a knight to Leander, and that is your goal."

I watched the snake a moment as his eyes flicked around, unfocused on the world around him, too busy with his internal schemes.

"No," I said.

He looked up, his eyes narrowing as they focused on me.

"No," I said again. He rubbed his bottom lip and shook his head.

"You will not say no to me," he said, calmly, but I could see that familiar spark of fury and impatience growing behind his eyes. "I have raised you, I have waited for you, and you have betrayed me. You will do as I ask." I remained motionless, resolute.

"If you want to know anything of your mother or brother, then you will do as I bid." The tone of his voice was fluctuating in frustration now. He had been a patient man once, but perhaps time and my abandonment had sapped the patience out of him.

"Are you mad, Father?" I asked. "Good. I am mad too. If you think I have come all the way back to this prison of a land to once again be your puppet and your spy, then you are mistaken."

He laughed at this, humourlessly, threateningly.

"Let *me* make it clear now," I continued. "It will not be as it was before. I am not going to bind my future to whatever whim you have for me. My future is my own to choose, and if it ends with me in a dungeon for the rest of my days, then it will be because *I* chose the path that led there."

He was pacing now, and I could see clearly that he was not the same man I knew six years ago. He was changed, less in control of his emotions, easier to rattle. I liked it.

"You owe me this," he whispered. "You owe me all I have strived for, and I will see it to its end. You have no idea what I have done," he spat. "You stupid, silly girl. You have no idea."

"If I have no idea then it is because you kept me in the dark. I did everything you asked of me without question, without knowing or understanding why. Now here I am, a woman and not a child, yet still you share nothing with me but demands, and you expect me to be cowed by a delusional old man. I could kill you with no effort. Do you understand that?" I stopped, breathing heavily and revolting against the prickling tears that welled up in my eyes unbidden.

Maybe things could have been different between us if only he had treated me like an ally, like a daughter instead of a pawn to be pushed around the board.

"You dare!" he yelled, his calm snapping like a frayed thread. He approached me faster than I could have anticipated and backhanded me across the jaw. The force and shock sent me staggering, and I lost my footing and fell into the lush, damp grass.

"You have failed me time and time again." He spat down at me, his eyes wide and manic. "If you will not play your part, then I have no use for you, daughter!"

I let out a strangled cry of surprise as he unsheathed a longsword and held it to my throat. He had been cruel before and had never shied away from causing me pain, but this was something I hadn't expected of him.

He always surprised me.

"Let me go," I warned between gritted teeth. "I don't want to harm you, but I will not have my blood spilt by the likes of *you*."

He laughed at this and dragged me up from the floor.

"I brought you into this world. Wouldn't it be fitting for me to take you out of it?" he whispered.

"You didn't do shit." I hissed. "That was my mother."

"Ah, but which mother?" he pondered mockingly. "God rest their souls," he continued cryptically. I threw my head back to headbutt him, but this was a favoured move of mine, one he knew well and had already predicted.

My head connected with base of his sword hilt. Pain and light exploded behind my eyes, and I felt blood trickle down the back of my neck.

"That was stupid, Celine," he said callously. "You seemed so sure you could kill me just a moment ago, but how do you feel about it now?" He drew his blade along my cheek, and I bit back a cry against the sting.

"You will do as I ask you, Celine. Even though you cannot see it, I have your best interests at heart."

I scoffed loudly.

"You don't have a heart." I reached for my dagger in my belt only to stop dead as a shadow caught the corner of my eye. My father stilled behind me, and his hold on me tightened.

We were no longer alone in the Meadow.

"Garrett," I breathed.

"I didn't dare to hope it would be you." Garrett growled as he approached us slowly, sword raised out in front of him and pointed directly at my father.

My father's grip around my shoulders tightened still, and the steel at my side dug in deeper under my armour. I could feel his rancid hot breath on my check.

"Ah, yes." My father laughed. "My darling daughter killed your brother during her escape, did she not? I remember it well. Such a waste, such needless violence," he said. "You are an expert at betrayal, aren't you?" he said to me. I couldn't listen. My heart was racing, and I could barely breathe. This was everything I had been afraid of, everything I had been dreading.

Garrett's eyes narrowed in fury at the mention of his brother. I could see the pain clear on his face. It was etched into the lines around his mouth. I had caused this pain. I needed to tell him how sorry I was. He had to know how much I regretted Gallagher's death. I knew it wouldn't change how he felt about me now, but he had to know. I shut my eyes against the pain. Would he think back on our time together and be disgusted now? Would he feel betrayed all over again by my deceit?

"I am so sorry, Garrett," I said.

He didn't acknowledge me though, staring instead at the sword at my side. No doubt wishing it was he that held it.

"Did I say you could talk?!" my father hissed in my ear as he dragged his dagger across my throat, lightly enough that it wouldn't break skin. I gritted my teeth together tightly, trying to fight against the panic growing inside of my chest.

"Waste?" Garrett asked, looking at my father vehemently. "Yes, it was a waste. A disgusting, useless waste. Forcing children into servitude, making killers of those who have no taste for killing." He rolled his sword over his hand and pointed it directly at my father's chest.

"Do you think my brother would have stopped her?" he asked, his voice a low growl. "If his will had been his own, then Gallagher would have given his lifeblood to free any of the blood guard. Instead, he was forced by his binding to fight her, and in doing so, my brother *was* set free." He stepped closer still, and my father pulled me back, positioning my body in front of his own like a shield. He stumbled, and we both fell back onto the ground Garrett looked down at us both. His jaw was tight and his mouth a thin line, and I could see that he was anxious to spill blood. He could get it all over with right now, end my father's bloodline with one deft stab.

"I hold no grudge towards my brother's liberator," he continued. "Only to his true killer." With this, he bent down and ripped the blade from my father's hands, deftly handing it to me instead. I gripped the hilt, confused and hardly daring to hope. Garrett held a hand out for me, and I took it, letting myself be pulled up.

My father wasted no time. He was already up and running. I went to run after him, but Garrett placed a firm hand on my shoulder.

"We can catch up to him," I said.

"I wish I could let you kill him," Garett whispered. "He more than deserves it," he said darkly as he reached out and brushed back a strand of bloodied hair from my face. A shiver of awe ran through my body. "All I can grant you for now," he continued, "is the knowledge that his time will soon come."

Before I could answer this, Garrett drew back his sword, and with a feral roar, he let it loose into the air. It flew true and caught the hem of my father's cloak, causing him to stumble. He fell to the ground, splayed out and groaning.

Garrett and I approached. He turned, untwisting himself from his cloak. He tried to get up, but Garrett retrieved his sword from the ground and aimed it threateningly, a warning to stay still.

"You know you cannot harm me," my father spat mockingly.

"Not yet," Garrett agreed. "But will the King still order your protection if he knew that you had kept Celine's return from him?"

My father's eyes widened a moment in fear, but he quickly hid it behind a deranged smile.

"I am sure I could help him see the reason behind it."

"Perhaps you could. But not before *I* convince him to let me execute you."

"What do you want, knight?" my father asked.

"I want you to leave, get out of this land, forget whatever scheme you are plotting and never come back." My father laughed heartily at this suggestion, but Garrett kept his sword trained on his chest and didn't flinch.

"What if I tell you that my schemes could be your salvation?" he countered.

"Then I would rather rot here in misery," Garrett spat. "You have underestimated me, Lord Flint. I have been watching you for many years, and you're not as sly as you like to think," Garrett continued, walking a slow circle around my father, sword pointed threateningly just inches from his throat. My father tilted his head up and sneered "I didn't know I was so interesting to you," he said sarcastically.

"Oh, I have been very interested," Garrett said, unperturbed by my father's disdain. "For about ten years now, I have watched you, and I know exactly what you plan."

My father hesitated at that, looking at Garrett for a moment as if he had never seen him before.

"Don't bluff," he said eventually. "It's beneath you."

"I know *exactly* what you are trying to do, Flint." He crouched down then and grabbed my father by his thinning hair, forcing him to look into his eyes. "My spies have been gathering evidence against you for a decade, and now that your daughter is back, I have everything I need to ensure that you finally meet the executioner's axe."

My father spat at Garrett. "Lies," he said, as Garrett wiped his face with the back of his hand.

"You haven't been subtle, have you?" Garrett continued.

"So, what do you want?" my father asked. "The death of my entire line?"

Garrett shrugged.

"Your death certainly."

"Why tell me then?" asked my father. "Why not just hand this over to the king and be done with it all?"

"I have my own reasons," Garrett said, standing again.

My father laughed. "I see. You aren't content anymore with being a knight or a captain," he said. "You are aiming for the ultimate revenge!" He clapped his hands together. "I can applaud that. I can *respect* that," he said. "Have you not given any thought at all to how well we could work together on this?" he asked. "I could betroth my daughter to you? That would help in your plight gre—"

He stopped as Garrett kicked out, slamming his boot into my father's face. I heard the familiar crack of broken bone. Blood gushed from my father's nose, and he smiled a large bright red grin.

"Hit a nerve?" he asked. As he turned and spat a glob of blood onto the floor.

I was disappointed that it didn't give me more satisfaction. Instead, I couldn't help but notice how weak and old he had become. Hiding behind his large cloaks and bold sneer, I hadn't seen the lines, the frail bones, the thinning hair. I cursed myself for my foolish heart.

He had spent my entire life manipulating and threatening me, and even now, he had tried to throw my life away on a whim to Garrett. Betrothing me to the Knight without a second thought. He would do anything for his own advancement. It was a selfish streak that I sometimes feared he had passed to me.

Yet, he was still my father, the only father I had known. And though I disliked him, hated him, and had wished him dead, there was still an infuriatingly stubborn attachment to him that I couldn't part from.

"Stop," I whispered. Garrett turned to me apologetically. But his gaze shifted behind me, his eyes widening in surprise and… panic?

I spun around to find none other than Kohl, standing at the top of the staircase, observing the scene before him in complete horror.

"What is happening?" he asked. His voice was unsteady with emotion. "What the fuck are you doing, Garrett?" he demanded, suddenly furious. Advancing on us, he pulled his sword from his belt in one fluid motion. I intercepted him, pushing on his chest to slow him, but he looked ready to kill Garrett. I had to let him know what was happening. He must have thought we were betraying the guard or that Garrett was attacking me.

"Stop," I pleaded. "It isn't what it looks like." I shoved harder, and Kohl grabbed my hands. His eyes were confused and unfocused as he looked down at me.

"He is evil, Kohl. Trust me, the king will—"

He pushed me away with a grunt, and I stumbled.

"I won't fight you, Kohl," Garrett said, throwing his own sword to the ground and holding his arms up.

"You should have thought about that before you attacked my father!" Kohl yelled back.

Father?

My gaze flew to Garrett, and he looked at me, ashamed. He opened his mouth like he wanted to explain but couldn't find the words. He rubbed his hands over his face in frustration.

"Oh, Cera," he breathed, slowly starting towards me. "Cera, just let me explain first."

I stepped back, my entire body shaking as my father's hysterical laughter filled the Meadow.

"Father?" I repeated. Kohl looked from Garrett to me, his face full of rage and concern.

"Someone explain," he demanded. "Explain now."

I looked at him then, really *looked* at him. The golden eyes, the freckled cheeks and wavy brown hair. It all slotted into place in my mind like a puzzle, like I had been staring all this time at an optical illusion, and it had only just revealed itself.

Recognition sent me to my knees.

How had I missed it? How had my own brother been standing in front of me this entire time and I hadn't noticed?

Thoughts raced through my brain, scrambling to catch up and make sense of the revelation. Yet, a fast-growing rage began to rise up inside of me, overshadowing all other feelings.

My brother had been enlisted in the guard.

After everything I went through to try to save him from that fate.

And my father had let it happen, despite witnessing what it had done to me, even after promising me that Cian would have the estate and his own free will.

He had taken that beautiful boy and forced him into the same broken life he had forced me into. I stood and pulled the Flint dagger from my belt.

"I will kill you!" I screamed.

I ran full speed at my father, whose laughter died and choked away in his throat in fear. Kohl tried to intercept me, but I shook him off easily. Garrett stood in my way, and I didn't even attempt to avoid him. I crashed headlong into the larger man, sending us both sprawling to the ground in a painful crash.

"Get off of me!" I snapped as Garrett struggled to pin me.

"Stop, Cera!" he begged. "You have to stop."

I elbowed him in the stomach and felt his breath escape painfully at the force of the blow. I climbed up again and aimed the dagger at my father's neck. Garrett was there again, grabbing my wrist. I turned around and headbutted him square in the face. I couldn't even feel the pain. I was numbed by my emotions. Garrett barely flinched as a wound opened up above his eyebrow, and blood seeped unchecked.

"Stop," he gasped. "I am bound. I *can't* let you kill him."

I didn't care. My father couldn't get away with this. When I became part of the guard, it was in my Cian's stead, and Father had promised to protect him.

"You swore," I sobbed as Garrett pulled me away. "You swore you wouldn't enlist him!" My father looked almost sorry as I thrashed desperately against Garrett.

"I...I had no choice," he stammered eventually.

"There is always a choice!" I cried, my throat hoarse.

I slipped out of Garrett's grip again. My dagger was inches from my father when I felt the cold sting of a blade at my throat.

"Stop, Celine," Garrett panted. "I am bound to protect him. I was robbed of my brother, but I cannot lose you too."

I turned to Garrett. His sword hand shook as his blade flashed at my throat.

Please, he mouthed.

All at once, the flight left me, and I collapsed to my back on the floor.

"That was a low blow," I said. Garrett laughed weakly. I watched as he trained his sword on my father once again. But even the old man looked defeated and exhausted now. Perhaps he had not thought me capable of truly wanting him dead.

"What is your plan for me, knight?" he asked, spitting out the last word like an insult.

"You are to leave. Tonight," Garrett said quickly.

"And how would I explain that to the king?" My father asked. Garrett shrugged.

"That's your problem, not mine. But I am giving you until the stroke of midnight, and then from that moment, if I or one of my spies set eyes on you anywhere on these grounds, or indeed, anywhere in Nordia, I will tell the King, everything."

My father inclined his head. "As you wish," he said.

"Why did you call her Celine?" Kohl asked abruptly. He stood next to our mother's grave, and his face was hard, but I could see a spark of hope and confusion in those eyes. He used to be so expressive as a child. Maybe the Guard hadn't crushed all of that out of him yet.

I sat up and smiled weakly through the tears.

"I have missed you so much, Cian."

Chapter 30

"He will come around, Cera," Mags said reassuringly as she handed me a sweet scone filled with currants and raisins. I took it from her, but my mouth was dry, and I felt nausea well up in my throat at the smell.

"He wouldn't even talk to me," I said. "I'm not surprised," I admitted. "I completely abandoned him, then lied about my identity." My heart was conflicted, with the joy of learning that Cian was alive and the heartache of knowing that he was in the blood guard and that he hated me. It was no less than what I deserved.

I couldn't count the times I wished that I had taken him with me that day. I'd failed him so completely.

Mags rubbed my arm sympathetically, her golden bangles clinking together.

In the days since I last visited Mags's room, she had gathered more furnishings and comforts. Plush purple cushions embroidered with stars padded the otherwise cold, hard floor. Bright-coloured fabric draped from the ceiling, bright pink tulle and indigo velvet. The air was thick with musky incense smoke that curled up in cloudy ribbons from burning sticks or powders. I didn't ask how she was persuading people to bring her these things. Mags had always had a way of drawing others to her, plus I had overheard Maddie telling a young guard that Mags still had a lot of followers in the Westlands, people who were either terrified of her legacy and brought her gifts to gain favour and ward away evil or people who wanted to follow in her "evil" footsteps.

Mags sat in an ornate rocking chair, swaying happily as she knitted beside her small window.

It was full night outside, and a bright gibbous moon peeked out from behind thick clouds.

I wondered where Kohl was right now. I had so many questions. I wanted to know why he had changed his name and how he had found himself in the blood guard. As Father's only son, he should have been heir to the Flint estates. My heart throbbed just thinking about it.

After Garrett had marched my father out of the Meadow, I had tried to talk to Kohl, but all he had asked me over and over again was why I had left… and I couldn't risk telling him that, not yet. He was, understandably, furious and had walked away, leaving me alone in our mother's tomb. I had thought about following him, but what good would that have done?

"You need to give him time," Mags said, as if she could hear my thoughts.

"Mags…" I hesitated. "Did you know all of this would happen?" I asked.

"I did," she admitted without pause. I felt a stab of frustration.

"About my mother and Kohl?" I pressed. She nodded. Her purple eyes filled with compassion.

"Why didn't you tell me?" I breathed. "You met Kohl and knew who he was? How could you not tell me??"

"I never want to cause you pain, Cera, but there are some things that must play out a certain way," she said. "My power can be a burden sometimes," she continued. "I am cursed with the sight, but there are rules that even I cannot break."

I kicked out at a pillow in frustration. Mags had done so much for me, and without her… well, I would probably be dead.

However, the secrets she kept were stacking up against her in my mind. Her very reason for being in this tower room confounded me. In my lifetime, I had been manipulated by people more times that even I knew. Yet I still seemed to fall into the schemes of others.

A stab of shame at the insinuation made me rein in my thoughts. I trusted Mags. She had proved herself loyal to me a hundred times over. She hadn't acted selfishly in all the years I had known her.

My suspicious nature was making me paranoid. My father had taught me that no one acted out of love alone. It was a hard lesson to attempt to unlearn.

"You warned me that coming back here would be hard, but I didn't expect these constant blows," I admitted. "And now I have so many decisions to make," I said. "Odelia wants me to be her knight, but that will mean being bound to her, even if I *do* manage to free all the guards from the curse."

"You are already bound to that queen, Cera," Mags said, making it all sound so simple. "You are a nomad. Would it be so hard to follow her back to the Eastlands and see her settled? She may even take your brother as consort once her king has passed."

I looked at Mags suspiciously.

"Is that a premonition?" I asked. The witch simply shrugged. I sighed and rolled my eyes.

"She doesn't want that life, but there's no escaping it. With some confidence, she might be good at it," I admitted.

"I think she is very passionate, and the people of the East could do much worse."

It felt dangerous to think too much about what I would do after breaking the bond, firstly because I have no idea how to go about it and secondly because it seemed like tempting fate.

But really, what would be left in the Westlands for me?

I had no love for the Flint name, and I was almost certain that if Kohl were free to go as he pleased, then he would follow Odelia.

Garrett...

Garett was engaged to Maddie, and if I ended the bond, they could be truly happy together.

"Where will you go, Mags?" I asked.

She looked out the window, and her eyes caught the light of the moon. They glowed an unearthly colour, as though she could see something beyond what I could see.

"I might go home," she said, finally.

A knock at the door stopped me from asking where home was for her.

"Enter," she said. A well-dressed attendant stepped into the room, head raised high. "Princess Odelia has requested your presence in the council rooms, Lady Cera."

"I better go," I said. As I stood up off the floor Mags grabbed my arm, I looked at her questioningly.

"Come back after," she said, her voice low and her face serious. "Come back here." I nodded, silently, slightly alarmed by her tone.

I followed the attendant, shooting Mags one more look as she rocked in her chair. I felt a stab of guilt, knowing that she was here because of me.

The attendant shut the door behind me, and I followed him down the tower and out onto the battlements of the castle. The crisp night air took my breath away as it pushed against me. I walked over to the edge of the stone wall and looked down at the city of Nordia.

At my home.

The lights twinkled and danced, and I could almost hear the sound of drunken singing and laughter on the air. It reminded me of the rare night when myself, Garrett and Maddie had snuck out to drink.

"Is the view unchanged?" I let out a breath and turned to see Garrett leaning against the wall, arms crossed and looking over his shoulder at the capitol. The attendant approached him with his hands held out, and Garrett touched his palm with three coins.

"What are you doing?" I asked as the attendant shuffled away.

"The princess has called for you, but I wanted to speak with you first," he said.

"How is my father?" I asked. Garrett grimaced at the memory. "He is gone, escorted by three of my own men. They won't stop until they are at the border to the south." I nodded. I couldn't tell if I was relieved or sad. It was a little of both.

"I'm glad, really," I said, but my voice sounded off.

"I understand," Garrett said simply. "But now it is your turn to go, Cera." I looked up quickly, feeling like I had been stung.

"What?" I said. He nodded firmly.

"I don't know what act of foolishness has brought you back here, Cera, but it's not safe."

"Of course it's not, but I need to make things right."

"You did nothing wrong," he said. "If you have been waiting to be forgiven then here it is. I forgive you."

I couldn't believe this. I laughed humourlessly.

"I have a reason for being here, Garrett."

"I'm sure you think that," he replied. "I don't know what that witch has filled your head with, but there is nothing here for you except more pain."

"But what if I can free you?" I pleaded. "What if I can end the curse and destroy the crowns?"

He sighed and looked at me pityingly. It made me want to strike out at him.

"You can't. It's not possible," he said. "I know this to be a fact, I—"

"You don't know!" I yelled, walking away over the battlements, letting the wind rip the swear words and curses out of my mouth and take them into the sky. How had I ever loved this headstrong, impossible man?

"Cera." He grabbed the crook of my elbow and pulled me around. "It's folly," he pleaded.

"But I am no longer bound!" I admitted. "And if it happened for me, then it can happen for all of you. Don't you see, I—" He pressed his hand over my mouth, silencing me.

"I know you are not bound by Leander," he said slowly. "But what has freed you cannot free me or any other guard."

He sounded so sure. He couldn't be sure. He didn't know what Mags had told me! He didn't know that there was a chance he and Maddie could be happy. I peeled his fingers away.

"You have to trust me. I know I can do this."

Garrett placed his hands at either side of my face and looked deeply into my eyes.

"Cera, I don't care about being free, not if it comes at the risk of losing you. Knowing that you were out there somewhere in the world and living free from your father, free from the king, free from this job that was slowly killing you—" He paused and rubbed his thumb over my lips. "It has been the one thing that kept me going."

"Garrett," I whispered.

"So, promise me that you will leave."
"When?" I asked.
"Now. No, after the meeting, so that it doesn't attract attention."

I nodded, knowing his mind couldn't be changed.
Well, neither could mine.

Chapter 31

Garrett and I entered the council room together, and all eyes turned to us as the doors creaked open. After smiling reassuringly at Odelia, who sat next to her brother and chewed her lip anxiously, I couldn't stop myself from staring at the empty space of my father.

"You found the girl, but where is Flint?" asked the seneschal snappily.

"Not in his rooms," Garrett said.

"Something isn't right." The seneschal shook his head, appealing to the king. "Flint wouldn't miss a meeting."

"He wouldn't miss a chance," the general muttered under his breath.

"Enough," said Leander. "We will look for him later, but this can't wait."

The room quietened.

"As you all know, I have only taken on one new addition to the blood guard since my father... well, since the crown was placed in my care."

I hadn't known that, but it explained why I had seen no children in the catacombs. When I was in the guard children were being recruited as young as four years old.

"That is all going to change tomorrow night," the king announced. "The guard is becoming too scarce, and it is imperative that my father's legacy stays strong. Five children have been specially selected, and under the new moon I will add them to the blood guard."

The very thought made me sick to my stomach. Those poor children. I looked up at Garrett, but he wouldn't meet my gaze.

A few cheers went up at the news. Leander smiled, pleased with the reaction. "General, I place the honour of collecting and guarding the crowns in your capable hands."

The general bashed his fist to his chest plate and inclined his head. The announcement only strengthened my resolve to stay. I wouldn't be able to live with myself if I abandoned the guard again, not when Mags was certain we could break the curse.

I had left my brother to his fate once, and I couldn't change that, but I needed to prove to him that I wasn't just like our father.

"There will be a celebration and a public announcement afterwards," continued the king, "but until then, nothing must be shared outside of this room." He looked around, pausing on every face. "I don't have to explain why." I stared at all the grave, nodding faces and wondered what they all knew that I did not.

"The crowns will be held in the throne room, as is tradition," the king went on. "And I want no man, woman or child to enter from sun-up tomorrow to sundown. Is that clear?"

"How old are the children, brother?" Odelia asked, her voice full of concern.

"I hardly know, sister. Please do not start on with your ethics crusade. This is the way of things, and neither you nor I have the power to change it." Maybe he did not, but I would make it my mission to stop those children from being made into puppets and murders. Leander pushed his chair back roughly "That is all. Get out of here and back to your leisure."

I didn't know what it was, but something about this young king garnered some pangs of sympathy from me. He always looked pained and tired as he hurried about. Now that I think of it, he didn't seem to throw feckless revels or hold weekly public executions like his father had.

Still, I couldn't be entirely sympathetic to someone who could enslave children for the sake of "tradition."

I inclined my head as he brushed past me and out of the door in a blur, the general and seneschal following quickly behind him.

Garrett grabbed my elbow and leaned in close to whisper in my ear.

"I don't want you to think of any of what you just heard," he warned. "Come find me in the catacombs in one hour. Be packed and ready to go from there. Kohl will be with us, so you can say your goodbyes then." He hesitated and held tighter to my arm, looking at me in warning. "Can I trust this of you, Cera?" he asked. I wondered why he used my fake name, even now. Was it to protect me, or himself?

"Don't make me wait, I will come fetch you if I have to." With one last glace over his shoulder at me, Garrett slipped away out of view. His place was hastily taken up by Odelia. There was no sign of her three lady's maids.

"I suppose this all must seem a little barbaric to you?" She said, her face downcast, and I felt touched that she would care about my opinion on a tradition so proudly celebrated within their family. She looked down at her hands uncomfortably. "In all truth, I hate it myself. If I had been queen, I would have thrown those damned crowns into the ocean."

I smiled as overwhelming fondness for the princess rose up in my heart. I had no doubt that she believed what she had said, and even though I knew she probably wouldn't have been able to dispose of the crowns, had she been the eldest child and not her brother, the fact that she had thought it meant a lot. It reaffirmed in me that becoming her knight was something I could be proud of. I gripped Odelia's hands in mine and squeezed tightly, reassuringly. That was when I noticed that she looked close to tears.

"What's happened?" I asked, genuinely concerned.

"It's nothing," she said, her voice trembling. "Except... Have you seen Kohl anywhere?"

I bit down on my lip.

"I think something is wrong," she continued." We quarrelled a little the other night, and I haven't seen him since." I rubbed her arm reassuringly.

"Don't worry, I am sure he has just been busy with training. Garrett said he would be in the catacombs tonight," I said. Her face lit up at this. "I will talk to him for you."

I felt a stab of guilt, knowing that it was likely my fault that Kohl hadn't been around. He was still processing the forced banishment of his father and the sudden re-emergence of his sister.

Odelia nodded and dabbed gently at her face with a black handkerchief.

"I met the ladies who are to carry my child today," she said, suddenly brighter. "They are all cousins of mine. I was acquainted with most of them already, and I have quite a few you know," she continued. "My parents were first cousins actually." She drifted off, as though lost in thought about them. I wondered what kind of father that hateful king had been. "It must be hard for a mother to give up a child," she said eventually. "But I assured them all that I would be the best mother I could be. I am looking forward to it actually."

I could only imagine how it would be, Odelia visiting the expectant mothers, bringing them cakes and embroidered clothes for their children and thinking up baby names, perhaps oblivious to how each mother would be praying for their child to be born a girl.

Odelia squeezed my hand resiliently before letting go. "My mother hated the crowns too. She was the heir to her father, destined to rule, but my *father* was the one who took the crowns. His own father had been a youngest son," she recalled. I had known all of that, but she would not expect me to.

"I'm going to be a better parent to my son than they were to me," she said resolutely.

I could easily believe it.

Odelia let out a large, exaggerated sigh and smiled at me wistfully before making her way out of the chambers, she was quickly surrounded by her flock of maidens. I made a mental note to see if any of them could go back with her to the Westlands.

When the room was empty, I snuck out myself and made for the tower room over the gatehouse. I knew I didn't have a lot of time and that Garrett would be furious when he realised I had no intention of leaving. But how could I leave now?

The crowns would be on display all day tomorrow. If I didn't at least try to end the curse, then I would never be able to live with myself.

It was too much of a coincidence for me to pass this up.

There was only one guard stationed at Mags's door, and as I approached, I realised he was asleep, leaning up against the stone wall, his legs braced in a wide "v" stance. I hovered a moment, unsure of what to do. I contemplated taking the keys from his belt, but if he woke up, that would cause all sorts of trouble. Instead, I jabbed him roughly with the tip of my finger. With a loud, vulgar snort he woke and stumbled to the ground.

"Uh, can you let me in?" I asked. He looked up from the floor, his face covered in drool and pink with embarrassment.

"Uh, yes, go on inside," he said as he quickly jumped up and unlocked the door for me.

I walked into the smoky room to see Mags facing away from me, looking up out of her window.

"Did he fall asleep again?" she asked, her voice sounding oddly faraway.

"Yes, but I woke him. Was that the right thing to do?" I asked, wondering if I should have left him to his sleep and let Mags escape.

"Where would I rather be than here?" she said dazedly, reaffirming my belief that she could read my thoughts, at least to some extent.

She seemed to snap out of some kind of trance then, jumping in the air and spinning around excitedly to face me.

"It's happening?" she asked, her face lit with an inner glow as she predicted what I was about to tell her.

"Tomorrow night," I said, presuming she was talking about our plan.

"Then you must go in the day at the first signs of light," she declared, and she hastily made her way over to me, stepping over cushions and gifts of flowers and chocolates that her admirers must have sent.

"What do I do?" I asked.

"It's simple, Celine. Just take the crowns from the podium. One will have the incantation for the blood bond and the other to break it." She so rarely called me by my real name that it felt strange to my ears and made my heart skip in anxiety. I looked to the door nervously as excitement and adrenalin thrummed in my chest unbridled, threatening to overflow.

"I wish you could come with me," I admitted. "I'm worried about getting something wrong. I'm no witch."

"While I have been trapped in this room, I have been reserving and gathering my power. If we plan this well, then I will be able to transport myself to your side, but it would be brief, very brief," she said, as she pulled a piece of yarn off her finger.

"Wear this ring," she said. I held my right hand out to her immediately, but Mags pushed it away.

"The other hand," she said, taking my left and sliding the knitted ring onto my index finger. It was soft and rainbow coloured. I felt a warm heaviness settle around my finger, as though the ring was made from some type of metal, and not yarn.

"What do I do?" I asked.

"Just call my name."

"Will this really work?" I wondered. "Have you seen into the future, Mags? Can you share with me just one word of certainty?"

"Nothing is certain in this world, my girl, but I have every confidence that this will play out the way it is meant to."

This wasn't as reassuring as I had hoped, but it was no more than I had come to expect from Mags. It was hard to have as much faith as she did. Her enthusiasm seemed to fill me with more apprehension, though I was sure she was trying to do the opposite. She made this whole task sound so simple, so self-explanatory. Fetch the crown, read the spell. But surely if it was that easy, other guards would have tried it before?

But then, other guards were bound to the king's every word, and for some unexplainable reason, I was not.

"And what of the king's general? He will be watching over the crowns," I said.

Mags looked at me meaningfully. "You must do whatever it takes to get to them, Celine," she said. "It's the only way to free your brothers and sisters of the guard."

I had to agree. Maybe I would be able to disarm him long enough to get the crown.

"Go to bed now, Celine," Mags said kindly. "You will need your sleep."

I nodded at her reassuring smile and left the tower room, feeling nervously optimistic. I stepped over the guard, who was fast asleep again.

As I walked along the battlement I stared down into the dark, wondering if Garrett would be waiting for me somewhere out there right now.

I walked the rest of the way to my room with a heavy heart.

Chapter 32

I woke with a start as the chair that I had jammed under the door handle flew violently across the room to smash with a clatter against my bed. I jumped up and pulled my father's dagger from under my pillow just as Garrett strode into the room. I tensed as I took him in. His face was twisted with barely concealed anger. He slammed the door shut again and paced a moment before approaching me.

His body towered over mine. I could see his shoulders rise and fall, and he breathed fast shallow.

For a moment I contemplated making the first move and striking out at him, but I couldn't do it.

I had known Garrett since I was seven, and I had never seen him look this angry and out of control.

"What are you doing?" he said eventually. "Do you have a death wish Celine?" My name in his mouth sounded almost foreign to me after all this time, but his voice sent a thrill through my chest.

Garrett looked back and pointed to the chair that was now laying in pieces on the floor. "Do you think that will keep the king out if he were to realise who you are?" He walked over to my wardrobe and began pulling clothes from the rails and shelves.

"What are you doing?" I asked.

"You need to leave," he said. "Get up and get out now." He searched around the room until he found a large saddlebag and began to roughly shove clothes inside. "I have paid off your door attendants," he said. "They won't breathe a word of your departure or my part in it. Not if they value their lives."

"I have door attendants?" I asked. Garrett stopped and looked up at me as though I was insane. "Yes, meant to guard you against intruders, and I managed to pay them off with a measly three bronze coins each."

He looked at me meaningfully. "Imagine what it would take for them to slit your throat in your sleep."

"And why would they do that?" I said, standing and taking the bag from Garrett's hands. "No one but you and Mags know who I am."

"Mags?" he asked, his eyes wide. "You told the poison witch who you are?" His face darkened in disbelief.

"I didn't need to tell her," I said, emptying out the bag and letting my creased clothes fall to the floor in a messy heap. "She already knew who I was when she found me." Garrett sighed at me and ran a hand through his tangled silver hair. I didn't know what to make of this. I had been so sure he would want me dead before, but here he was, concerned about me, anxious for me to leave. It filled me with an odd and dangerous hope.

"Listen, Garrett, I'm not going. For once in my life, I'm not going to run away. I need to figure out why the bond no longer forces me to obey."

'I have bought you about half an hour, plenty of time to escape," he said, ignoring me. "If I were you, I would get out of the west lands completely and go north."

I stared at Garrett in silence as he said all of this. I knew he meant well, but that didn't stop the anger.

'I know you have no faith in me, Garrett. Gods know I have caused you more pain than I could ever expect you to forgive, but I cannot go. I have to try to fix this. I have a plan, and I think it could free us all." If my words surprised him, then he didn't show it.

"I don't know what plan you have, Cera," he said, his voice low and dangerous. "But it will not work." He was calling me Cera again. Had the earlier use of my real name been a slip or was he distancing himself from me? I honestly couldn't tell.

Suddenly he leaned in, his eyes blazing. His mouth moved close to my ear, and his breath there sent a traitorous shiver down my spine.

'I am trapped, Cera, and I will never be free from it. Do not throw away *your* chance of freedom for a mad witch's folly.' He stood back and moved away, kicking the remains of the chair in frustration.

'I *will* make you see sense," he spat over his shoulder before leaving the room.

I collapsed on the bed and let go of my dagger. I had been gripping it so hard it hurt to release it.

Let him be mad at me. Come tomorrow morning, this would all be over. He would be free from the crown, free to be with Maddie, and I would be free of my shame.

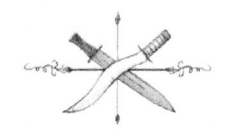

The moment the sun crested above the city line, I was awake and dressed. I paced around my room a while, going over all the things that could go right or could go wrong today.

I clutched the thick-knitted ring that Mags had given me and slipped it over my finger. When the time came, all I needed to do was say her name and she would be there to help me. I knew I had to plan it right, or she would disappear again before the curse was broken.

The walk up to the throne room doors was an uncomfortable one. The usually bustling hall was empty of people. The intricately detailed carpet that let up to the navy doors of the throne room was just as I remembered it, faded blue and scuffed from years of wear. I stopped and leaned against one of the large columns that lined the room, hiding from the glare of the guards at the end of the hall and regretting my choice.

I had thought this would be the best place to start. Sometimes the easiest approach worked out. I was beginning to sense that this wasn't going to be the case today.

"Who goes there?" a guard yelled in warning. I came out from behind the column and stepped as close to the doors as I dared.

The guards looked down at me, perplexed.

"The throne room is closed today," the guard on the left said. "What is your business?"

"Nothing, I was admiring the great hall," I said pathetically.

"Admire it another day," the other guard said less tersely. At least they didn't see me as a threat. I commended myself on the foresight of wearing the plain navy gambeson instead of my full armour. I nodded and walked away, feeling deflated.

I had known that wouldn't work, but I was resistant to the other option.

I needed to find a secret way into the throne room. And the only way I could think of finding that was with my father's maps.

With a heavy heart, I took the stairs up to my father's apartments.

The name Flint was carved over the doors in large lettering. It had once been gold, but it was faded now.

There were no guards at the door, but when I tried the handle, it was locked.

I pulled my old dagger from my belt, the one I kept with me always, and with a twist and a firm tug, I yanked the hilt from the blade. Hidden inside the handle was a small bronze key. Further proof that I had one day planned to come back here and make right what I had done wrong.

I unlocked the door and sheathed my blade once more.

The nostalgic smell of home hit me as I stepped inside, it was a dusty smell, of books and herbs and something indescribably familiar. It reminded me of my mother, or the woman I had thought of as my mother, if my father was to be believed.

I walked through the dark rooms with purpose, refusing to linger over old memories, until I reached the library. Our family library was small but impressive, and I had passed many hours in here with my father.

I didn't have time to waste getting sentimental, so I began to shuffle and thumb through the shelves and cases. I had seen a book with the throne room in it before, but I couldn't remember.

"What are you doing?"

I jumped and spun round to find Kohl... Cian sitting at the bottom of the spiral steps that led up to the second floor of the library, watching me with interest and caution in his glittering golden eyes.

"Hi," I said gently.

"I asked what you were doing."

"I'm looking for a book." "What book?"

I hesitated a moment, fully planning to lie to him, but I thought again. Surely there had been enough lies and secrets in this family. I owed him the truth. I wanted our relationship going forward to be different to the one I had with the rest of my family.

"I'm trying to find a map," I said. "I need to get into the throne room, and I know there is a passage, but I don't remember the way."

Cian seemed to process this, then he stood up, walked towards my father's desk in the corner of the room by the bay window. He opened a draw and pulled out a large roll of aged paper.

"All the plans for the castle are drawn up here," he said. "But you don't need that. I know the way around this place better than anyone."

"Really?" I asked. "I thought you told me that even you get lost sometimes." He shrugged and put the scrolls back into our father's desk.

"I only said that to make you feel better."

I smiled warmly. "Lead the way then." I faltered. "You can't come into the room with me though, Cian. It's important."

"So, you're up to something then?" he asked "I thought you were. I'm still having trouble wrapping my brain around the fact that you are Celine. I remember her... you, being so quiet and stoic... and sad. You were always busy and running around after Father. Sometimes I resented you because he never seemed to have time for me. But then you left, and Mum was locked away... and I joined the guard. I understood you more then."

"I always tried to protect you," I said. "But in the end, I just couldn't do any of this anymore. You have no idea how much I have regretted leaving you here," I said, desperate to explain. "They wanted me to kill you and all our family. When I left, I wasn't thinking straight. I was just so desperate to be free. That's no excuse, but..." I trailed off, not knowing the words to say to make things better between us.

It seemed unreal that I was here, speaking with Cian right now, after years of believing he was dead. I could see the similarities between this man before me and the small boy I had known. The same messy hair and rounded face, the shadow of freckles along the bridge of his nose and large, open smile. It was hard to reconcile the two though after being gone so long. I felt the ache of guilt and loss in my chest. I had missed so much, and we had no relationship now. There was once a time I was the one he ran too when he was scared or sad. But now I am just the sister that abandoned him.

"It doesn't matter," he said, making his way to the door. "You can't change the past."

Wordlessly I followed him out into the corridor, down the stairs and through more corridors, like a labyrinth that went back on itself. Finally, we descended down into a cellar packed full of barrels of wine and crates of glass bottles. He slipped behind a shelving rack and moved a wooden panel to reveal a small space behind the wall.

"It looks abandoned," he explained. "But servers still use this tunnel when the king holds festivals. It's quicker than the main route."

I followed him into the dark, my eyes adjusting to the change in light. The space grew almost too small to push through at times. I wondered how attendants managed to get squeeze through while holding large decanters of wine.

Finally, Cian pulled back a large tapestry that opened up into the corner of the throne room behind a column.

"Here you go," he said. Kohl hesitated a moment. "Are you sure you don't need me to come with you?"

"No," I insisted. "I will see you after though."

"After?" he prodded. I just nodded and checked that my daggers were secure in my belt. I hoped I couldn't need them, but I wasn't naïve enough to believe it.

"Good luck then," he said curtly. "And be careful. It would be good if I had enough time to forgive you before you disappear again."

I chuckled awkwardly at this. I hoped so too.

"Hey, Cian?"

"Hmm?"

"Why did you change your name?" I asked.

"I changed it when Mum was killed and Dad shipped me off into the guard. I didn't want anything to do with him anymore. He clearly didn't want me to be his heir. Fuck the Flints."

I felt the same, but then he was a Flint, so we couldn't all be bad.

"I will call you Kohl."

"No, call me Cian," he said. "It makes me feel like I have a family again."

He smiled weakly at me, then turned away before I could say anything. My heart felt full and hopeful. Maybe we would be able to forge a new relationship after all.

BOUND TO THE CROWN

With our mother dead and our father on the run, we were all the family we had left.

I took a deep breath, focusing anew. I needed to get through this. I had to break the curse and release my brother from the guard.

It was time.

Chapter 33

I could hear my heart thundering in my ears as the blood rushed too fast through my adrenalin-filled body.

The throne room was empty: empty of people and empty of the usual garlands and ornaments that decorated it. Only the wide navy carpet remained. It led up to the marble dais where the twin thrones of Nordia were seated underneath a canopy of velvet and gold. Two identical cabinets, each with a large, ornate bronze base and clear crystal display case, had been moved to the top of the dais. Inside them, sat upon a blue velvet cushion that had faded with age, was a twisted, cursed crown. I stepped closer cautiously, feeling both in awe of and disdain for those twin crowns and the history behind them. I hadn't seen the crowns since I was seven years old and the king himself had placed one upon my head.

BOUND TO THE CROWN

I remembered that day perfectly. I could see it when I closed my eyes, playing out in my mind like a story.

I had stood alone in centre of the outer ward on the hottest day of that year. It was midsummer, and I wore a thick yellow dress that my mother had ordered especially for the ceremony. She hadn't spared a thought for how warm it would be, but her heart had been in the right place.

The sun had been scorching and uncomfortable on my back, and the sweat had beaded on my forehead. I couldn't wipe it away though. My father had warned me that morning that no matter what happened I was not to flinch, cry, run away or show any sign of weakness at all. And as I was more afraid of him back then than the king I knew nothing of, I did as I was bidden.

The courtyard around me had been full of people, guards, servants, and members of the court, all dressed up in their finest, proudly showing off any medals, sashes and accolades that had been gifted them.

My mother, father and Cian, who was only a babe, had all stood back against the curtain wall, half hidden by the shadow of the busy battlements above.

My mother had smiled at me weakly and held my baby brother aloft so that he could see me, his round bonny face scrunched up as he began to fuss. I had looked to my father then. His face had been stern and hard, and he had frowned and mouthed something to me between gritted teeth. I had hurried to look away and stand tall, so afraid of angering him.

The king had made no strong first impression on me, but I remember feeling confused as to why the commoners behind the ramparts would cheer deafeningly every time he opened his mouth. I was sure they had no idea what he was saying, I could barely hear, and he had stood only a few feet away from me.

There had been other trainees all around me, the people that I would grow up with. None of them had looked at me, and I remember feeling a stab of jealousy at how straight and proud they all stood. Unmoved by the heat of the crowd. Some of them barely older than me, all evenly spaced apart in their blue trainee robes, heads facing forward, faces blank and arms at their sides. Would I look like them in a few years, a few months?

The one nearest me had been a boy with moonlight white hair, cropped short and jagged to his head, but I could see that it was wavy. He didn't look much older than my seven years, nine maybe? He was tall though. All the other trainees were tall and broad. I had been besotted with Garrett from the moment I saw him.

I didn't fit in with them. Anyone could see it.

I hadn't been the usual type chosen for the blood guard.

BOUND TO THE CROWN

I had heard the maids whispering that morning when they were dressing me. They had meant for me to hear. My father was being punished. At first I hadn't understood because we had won the war with the Westlands, and it had been my father's strategies as war councillor that had done it.

But the king's favourite brother had died during a morale visit to the front line that my father had planned himself.

I overheard my governess telling a maid-servant that If the war had not been put to rest that very same day, my father and all of us in the house of Flint would have been executed.

Instead, I was being initiated into the blood guard. My father's firstborn child and heir.

It was considered an honour to be chosen.

Really it was a punishment. Everyone could tell. They had made bets on how long I would last, but I thought back then that I would prove them all wrong.

Initially I had liked the idea of joining the guard, more than whatever life my father had planned out for me. I had already seen the letters on his desk from lords all around the Eastlands, asking for their sons to be betrothed to me. Becoming a warrior sounded infinitely better than becoming a child bride.

I hadn't been afraid when the cannon boomed from up on the battlements, nor when smoke bellowed above me in a dark cloud. I had watched mesmerised as a clutter of black birds flew over the battlements and around the castle turrets. I had stared as they glided out of sight, past the gatehouse and over the crowds of commoners beyond. I'd envied them the freedom and power to go wherever they wanted.

The king's seneschal, Amon, who had been an old, gangling man with wild white hair and staring blue eyes even then, had slapped me sharply across the back of my head. Scolding me for daydreaming, he had warned me to pay attention to my betters.

The king only laughed though as he approached, holding the twisted crown aloft in his hand. I remember what he said so clearly.

"Let her have her last daydreams, Amon." He had chuckled, his eyes glittering with malice and excitement. "Allow her to her last taste of freedom while in my presence."

I shuddered back to the present, not wanting to linger on the vision of those eyes, nor those words.

I could see the general standing on the first step of the dais in full Nordian armour, complete with a sash of medals from various battles and accomplishments, looking very much the same as he did the first time I met him in the king's chambers.

As I stepped out into the middle of the hall from my hiding place, he took my measure. His eyes widened slightly in recognition, and he gripped the hilt of his sword at his waist, but he made no other move, and he didn't seem surprised to see me here. The general showed no other emotion, and the silence was taut as we sized one another up.

I felt my strength falter for just a moment as I watched him, knowing already in my heart that I would have to fight him.

He stood and waited for me to say my piece.

"If I swear to you that I will not take them away from here and that what I do is for the good of Nordia, then will you let me hold the crowns?" I asked.

He seemed to let my words sink in before firmly moving his head from one side to the other.

No.

"I want to free the blood guard. I want to break the curse. Won't you let me do that?"

"Freeing the guard is not for the good of Nordia," He stated, his voice gruff and firm. "The blood guard makes Nordia strong. They are feared not just on the isle but throughout the world. They are unbeatable. Even if it were possible to do so, why would I want them disbanded?"

"At what cost though?" I countered.

"At the cost of a soldier. This is what we sign up for. It is not a curse, but a gift."

Part of me felt annoyed at his response. He wasn't a part of the guard, and he couldn't truly understand what it meant to have your free will stripped away.

"I am going to take the crowns, general. I don't want to fight you."

"If you want them, you will have to spill my lifeblood upon this dais first," he said sternly, pulling his blade from its sheath.

I took up my daggers, one in each hand, but they weighed heavy in my grip. It was always a hard thing, to kill someone who held no ill-will towards you. I felt my hands tremble slightly, as revolution made my stomach twist.

"That isn't what I want," I admitted.

"Then turn around and leave."

"I can't do that!"

"Then fight me, Queens knight."

Reluctantly I approached him with my weapons gripped tightly. My first mistake was not immediately moving in for the kill. The general was a seasoned fighter and could tell my apprehensiveness in an instant. With a jolt of movement, he was upon me, blade pointed squarely in my direction. I barely had time to weave out of the way and felt his sword scrape across my stomach, I spun around, hoping to counter his move, but gasped as I saw him pirouetting into his own follow-up and bringing the weapon down at my head.

I raised my daggers in defence, not able to dodge this attack. The blades clashed together, the sound reverberating around the hall. The general planted his boot directly into my torso, pushing me away with such force I careened across the floor, abruptly halting only when my body met a column.

I winced but only momentarily. I didn't have time to spare as the general advanced for the killing blow again. I ducked as he struck the column, and I quickly ran out of his arm span.

If I didn't anticipate his next movements and match his intent, then I wouldn't see this day through.

I faced the general as his quick footfalls echoed off the marble. He was approaching rapidly with a serious but strangely empty look on his face.

He had to do this. It was his duty.

But he wasn't enjoying it either.

One of us needed to end the fight.

Without hesitating, I launched one of my daggers at his face, throwing it through the air with a light flick of my wrist. He effortlessly swiped it away with his sword, something I anticipated. I attacked while he was distracted, aiming low when his blade was high.

He looked shocked as I stabbed my dagger deep into his leg, just behind his knee, twisting it so I felt his bone dislodge, pulling it out, and dodging away.

He roared in pain and clutched at his leg. His hands came away red with blood.

I could still end this without killing him, I panted to myself.

The general, realising what I was trying to do, steadied himself on the injured appendage and glared at me sullenly.

"You'll have to kill me," he insisted.

I couldn't resign myself to it just yet.

He was only doing his duty.

I didn't want his life's blood on my hands.

The general came at me again, with more vigour than before, like a man possessed.

I was taken aback. His knee would be causing him excruciating pain, but he was still after my life.

I glanced at my dagger on the floor across the room and sidestepped the first strike he launched at me by rolling toward it.

Or so I thought.

He feinted the attack and twisted around, meeting me at my destination and sinking his sword into my right wrist as I reached out for my knife. I screamed as he pushed the blade down and clean through. I felt the world reverberate and dissolve around me, as my eyes could only focus on my now limbless arm.

The pain echoed around every fibre of my being, and my heart was pounding so hard in my chest I could hear only it and nothing more. Dark red blood spilled onto the white marble, the shock of it making me feel faint.

Was this it? Was I going to die here, having failed everyone?

I felt the general readying another attack.

Time seemed to be going too slow, and the numbness was seeping in.

He approached leisurely this time, assuming I was done. That I could no longer fight.

That was his mistake.

"I'm sorry." The general's voice was mournful, not victorious.

The instant he lunged at me with his blade aimed for my chest, I made my move. I met his sword with the dagger in my left hand, forcing him to follow though and lose his balance as his weight shifted to his injured leg.

He crashed to his knees above me, within arm's reach, and in quick succession, I dropped my dagger, grasped his collar, and pulled my head up with such force that when it connected with his, I felt his skull crack.

He screamed something unintelligible as his sword fell from his grip, and he grasped at his forehead. I reached for my dagger again with my left hand and placed it at the general's throat, who was writhing above me.

He stopped, as if on command, and opened his eyes.

"What is your name?" I asked, feeling broken and full of fatigue.

"Farrant," he replied.

I hissed in a breath as the excruciating pain that ran up my arm threatened to force my hand. I didn't want to kill the general, but I needed to end this fast.

"Yield to me Farrant, please?" I begged.

He shook his head, and I saw him reach for his sword again with his other hand.

"It doesn't have to be this way!" I pleaded.

"If you get the crowns, I will be worse than dead. I will never yield to you."

"Then I'm sorry, Farrant," I sobbed. I needed to act now, I was losing too much blood, and my hold over him wouldn't last. If he attacked me again, I would lose.

In one fast, well-practiced movement, I slit his throat.

Chapter 34

The moment the general's body fell to the ground, twitching as his lifeblood spilled over the dais, I screamed Mags's name.

I needed her here, to stop the bleeding, to tell me everything was going to be alright, to say the spell. Nothing happened at first, and I looked down at the tattered band around my finger, wondering if I had damaged it too much during the fight.

Every second was agonising, and my head was spinning into a faint. I had no idea what to do, I had to try to slow the bleeding. I shifted over to Farrant and tore at his cloak, I was too weak to pull it from his shoulders, so I tied it just above my wrist as tightly as I could using my left hand and my teeth to pull it taut. The room spun, and I felt my body sway back. I let myself drop to the floor for only a moment before hoisting myself back up.

The cloak helped, but it wasn't enough.

I heard fast, loud footsteps on the marble and turned to see Greta running towards me.

She must have been tailing me this whole time. Her face was slack with horror as she dropped to the floor beside me and lifted a canteen to my lips. I drank the burning liquid gratefully. It felt reviving.

"I couldn't intervene," she explained. "I wasn't expressly ordered to protect him, but I could do him no harm."

"Thank god you weren't." I laughed weakly, knowing that a fight against them both would have been almost impossible. It was my own folly though. If I hadn't been so reluctant to kill, then I would have been able to take the general out with little trouble, and I would still have my hand.

"Can your witch fix it?" she asked, pointing to my wrist. I shook my head.

"No idea," I gasped. At the mention of Mags, I remembered something though. It was a long shot, but I was desperate now.

"Can you get the pouch from around my neck?" I asked Greta. She complied instantly, pulling both my talisman and my pouch over my head.

I unwrapped my wrist, gasping at the pain.

"Please, gods, let this work," I panted. "Pour it on, Greta."

The guard did as she was asked and yanked open the pouch before upending the powdery contents over my wrist.

I screamed soundlessly as agonising, searing pain shot up through my arm. The powder fizzed and bubbled, hissing violently. It burnt like flames, tearing through my body mercilessly.

Everything went black in my vision as I lost consciousness. I woke again, seconds later as Greta threw the burning contents of her waterskin over my face. I gasped and tried to wipe it away with my dominant hand, only to remember that I no longer had that appendage.

The pain had mercifully faded now. I examined the stump to see that the powder had completely cauterized it and magically closed up the wound.

"Fucking witches!" I laughed hysterically. That damned hedge-witch.

Thank the gods for her and for Kohl who had retrieved the pouch for me.

I was able to think more clearly now and realised we were running out of time. I used my teeth to rip the frayed ring from my hand and put it to my lips. "Mags, its time. Hurry you, witch!"

Greta and I exchanged anxious glances until finally burst of pure white light filled the room.

At the same time, I could see the doors at the far end of the room slowly opening as the guards outside came to investigate the yelling. My heart pounded fiercely in panic. Everything was happening too fast and yet too slowly.

"Mags!" I screamed as her form began to appear in front of me. She was slightly opaque as though she wasn't actually standing in front of me.

She looked at the chaos around me, at my limbless wrist, at Greta by my side, and the guards by the door. Her purple eyes were so dark they were almost black.

"Quick!" she cried desperately. "Give me the crowns, Celine, I cannot take them from the case myself." Greta stood to retrieve them herself, and Mags let out a cry of warning.

"No!"

Greta and I stilled.

"Only she can do it, stupid girl."

I hesitated at Mags's tone, but I knew she was only feeling as desperate as me.

I shuffled on the floor towards the glass cases, pulling myself up the cold, hard steps. Greta placed a steady arm under my elbow and helped to hoist me up. The crowns were so much smaller than I remembered them being in my childhood and were made from aged wood. In my distorted memory, they had seemed to be made of sparkling gold.

Without hesitation, I took the crowns up one after the other and began to hobble back to Mags.

I held them out for her to take.

Then, my job done, I let myself sink back to the floor with Greta supporting me.

I could hardly believe that this was almost over, that after all these years of pain and regret I could put the blood guard behind me.

Maybe I would go to the Westlands with Odelia and Cian, or maybe I would stay with Mags, helping her in her shop, spending my days drying herbs and traveling from village to village. It would be nice to let Mags take the lead for a change. It would be nice to relax.

Mags had the crowns cradled in her hands, and I let the tears of pure overwhelming relief cascade down my face.

I clasped my wrist tightly, and I couldn't help but feel like my hand had been a worthy sacrifice for the annihilation of those cursed crowns. Maybe when I got back to the west, Freddy could lend me the use of one of her magic hands. I almost laughed at the thought.

Mags stood above me now, looking as beautiful, and otherworldly as she always had, and I was so thankful for her.

I smiled up at her through the tears.

"You do it," I said. "I trust you."

"Yes," she said. "A trust I earned with patience and time." Her voice sounded weird and faraway, just as it had when I visited her in her room the night before.

"Yes," I agreed, suddenly feeling faint again from the blood loss.

"It was a long time," she said again almost to herself.

"My grandmother made these crowns, did you know?"

I shook my head, not able to understand the revelation.

The room was beginning to spin again, and my brain felt foggy. I looked down at my wrist in alarm, feeling as though I was seeing it for the first time. I stood, faster than Greta could stop me, and held my arm out towards Mags. I lost my balance, crashing down onto my side.

"Stop moving," Greta scolded.

"Can you fix this?" I slurred at Mags, still waving my arm at her.

I could see shadows at the corners of the room now, and angry voices echoed around my ears, some yelling my name and others unintelligible.

At the centre of it all stood Mags. Looking down at me pitifully.

"Say the spell," I said, but my voice was weak and barely made a sound. Mags smiled slightly and shook her head at me, as though I was hilarious.

"Hurry, witch! She is going to pass out. Do what you came for!" Greta snapped as the guards approached us, swords raised. She jumped up to try to hold them off. But in a flash of white light all three, Greta, and the two guards, fell to the floor, silent. I stared, open-mouthed as blood seeped from Greta's body. I could see no obvious wound, but there was so, *so* much blood. Panic rooted me in place.

I looked up at Mags, horrified and shocked.

"Did you do that?" I whispered, my voice cracking. "Why?" Mags's turned to me, her purple-black eyes empty of emotion. I had never seen that look on her face before.

"I will mourn you, renter girl," she said simply.

In a flash of bright white magic, she vanished.

Taking the crowns with her.

Chapter 35

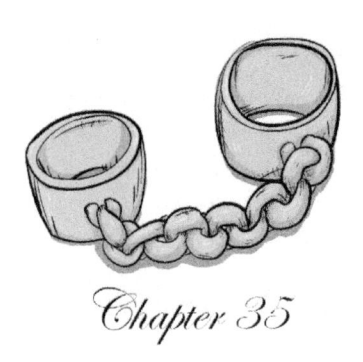

I could hear a constant drip-drip-drip from somewhere in my dungeon cell. The floor was wet and had soaked through into my clothes, and the cold was steeping into my very bones.

I couldn't feel my legs anymore. They were dull from sitting on the wet floor. The stump at my wrist thrummed with a constant pain. Every now and then I imagined I could feel my fingers moving, but it was a trick of my mind.

I knew I should stand up and walk around to get some heat back into my aching body, but I felt too numb and hollow to care.

Mags had betrayed me.

My Mags.

I couldn't comprehend it, and I couldn't reason with it.

Yet I was down here in the dark, in pain, starving and freezing, because of Mags.

Mags, who had been nothing but nurturing towards me, who had become a beacon of light in my otherwise black world. Who had saved my life more times than I could remember.

It didn't make sense. I replayed old memories shared with her in my head over and over again to try to pick them apart and root out the evil in them. To find the obvious display of self-interest and insincerity that must have been present in every single interaction we had shared.

But try as I might, I couldn't find it.

Not in the golden evenings spent walking through forests together, gathering herbs. Not in the nights drinking and laughing. Not in the hours when she held me while I came undone from my own guilt and trauma.

She had taught me so much about the world that I hadn't known, about what plants were toxic and what ones could heal. Were these lessons all lies? Could I trust the things she had taught me now? Maybe mugwort wouldn't heal a sore stomach, and maybe it would be poison.

Empty heartache danced through me in waves, and I pulled my legs close to my chest in comfort and moaned. I knew this self-pity served no one, but this betrayal was worse than any I could have imagined.

I expected this sort of thing of my father. He had always put his own needs first, but he was open about it and had never been any other way, yet Mags. I just couldn't accept it. Foolishly, I tried to figure out what trick had been played on her, what terrible thing must have forced her hand. Because I couldn't imagine Mags... my Mags, betraying me cold-bloodedly for a crown. Not Mags who had happily abandoned everything she owned and followed me on whatever whim I entertained.

But then, why had I never thought that strange before? No one in all the lands was completely selfless. What reason did she have to follow me around and keep me out of trouble? I had thought it was attachment, love even.

I laughed aloud at myself for being such a fool. How could a trained killer be so weak and gullible, even until the end.

She had killed Greta.

No one had confirmed her death as I was dragged down to the dungeons, but the look on Garrett's face when he discovered us in the blood painted throne room said it all. It was disappointment, it was fury, it was loss.

I had made such a terrible mistake, four lives taken, and all for nothing.

I could hear a soft footfall echo through the dungeon and the jangle of keys on a chain. I shifted back into the farthest corner of my cell, hoping the darkness would keep away any visitors.

Slowly, Garret came into view. His silver boots were still red with blood from the throne room, and the sight of It made my stomach heave painfully. I couldn't bear to look at him.

I didn't want to see him, I didn't want to hear any of what he had to say, I wanted to be left alone to rot in this dungeon alone. It was more than what I deserved.

"I've come to get you," he said, his voice was as cold as my cell. Had he been ordered to execute me for my crimes? I wondered if he would be happy to do it now that he really knew the extent of my cowardice and stupidity. The general, Greta, the two guards and Gallagher, all dead by my hand. The bodies were stacking up against me.

"My princess has asked to see you," he continued.

"What?" I gasped, my voice a hoarse whisper. I grimaced in pain at the effort—my throat was still raw from screaming.

Garrett observed me calmly. His face was unusually pale, his hair unkept and tangled. He was wearing the same clothes that he had worn the day before when he found me in the throne room after Mags had left.

"You are free to go," he said.

"How is that possible?" I croaked, completely stupefied. "Doesn't she know who I am or what I have done?"

"No," Garrett said firmly. "No one does, and it will be kept that way. Do not breathe a word of the truth of it, even to me… especially to me." He crouched down low so that he could speak more softly.

"Everyone who knows the truth is dead, save you and the witch," he whispered.

"But you and Kohl both know my identity. Aren't you bound to report me?" I asked, thinking of Vale and how she had struggled to apprehend me, even until her dying breath.

"No, Cera. The curse of the crown is nothing to the bonds of blood. It cannot be used against direct kin. This is why the guard usually only accepts one child from a family. Kohl cannot be ordered to act against you, just as the king or queen cannot initiate their own siblings, parents or children into the guard."

I hadn't known any of that. Part of me realised that there had to be something put in place though, or the king could enslave his family and change the outcome of the regency. That still didn't explain why Garrett had not reported me.

"You aren't my kin, Garrett." I reminded him.

"No," he said. "No, I am not," he continued with a sad smile. He stared into my eyes steadily. "When I became guard to the King, it was agreed that I would deal with my brother's killer in any way I saw fit. Free from the bonds of the crown."

Ah, the contract,

So that was why he bargained with the King to become his Knight, to get revenge on me in any way he chose. To make sure that it was he who landed that killing blow and not another.

"Well, out of all the hands in Terravetus, I would rather my fate be in yours," I admitted.

He was pensive a moment and opened his mouth as though to say something before thinking better of it and standing. "Come," he said, his tone one of command. "My princess wishes to see you and then the Crowned King has plans to reward you for your valour before you leave."

"My valour?" I asked, confused. Garrett pulled a ring of keys from his hip and unlocked the cell. He pushed upon the heavy metal bars and helped me to my feet. I wobbled unsteadily as I tried to reach out with my missing hand. A shock of loss shivered through me anew as Garrett took a hold of my arm and directed it back down.

"Yes," he said. "You, Greta, the general and door guards all fought bravely against the poison witch. And although you were not successful, the king believes he owes you some thanks and an apology for not taking the threat of the witch more seriously. Perhaps if he had, she would not have been able to kill her guard and escape with the crowns so easily."

Was that the tale that he had spun? One of courage in the face of an unbeatable enemy?

So not only did I have to stand in front of the king and pretend to be someone else, but I also had to pretend that I hadn't caused the loss of two crowns that been in his family for hundreds of years.

Those crowns were now in the hands of the poison witch, and the fault was mine and mine alone. Only the gods knew what she was planning to do with them.

I stared at Garrett, hopelessly ashamed for not trusting in him.

"Don't," he said. "At least there will be no more guard, for a while."

"What does she want with them?" I asked, genuinely confused.

"Who knows. Only royal blood can use them," he said. "I don't know how she was even able to hold them," he added, as though to himself.

"You said I was leaving?" I remembered as Garrett led me through the halls of the dungeon. Several prison guards inclined their heads in greeting to the Captain as we passed them on their watch.

"You are to be knighted, and then you will escort the princess back to Riverna," he said.

"But what about the crowns? Don't we have to try to get them back, to destroy them or... something?" I blurted.

"I will be seeking the poison witch, and you are to go to the East. And I hope by gods that you never come back."

The remark stung deeply, and I swallowed against the lump that rose up in my throat.

"When am I going?" I asked, resigned.

"As soon as you are knighted," Garrett said.

"So soon, but what about the child? Has the King abandoned that plan?"

Garrett stopped and turned to me, his arm still supporting me under my elbow as though he thought I would crumble to the floor at any slight breeze. He hesitated a moment, looking over my head to guess whether or not the prison guards were in earshot.

"The princess is with child," he said, eventually. "She is with child and anxious to leave for the East. I think it is more for your sake than anything."

"The princess... is?" I faltered, doubting my ears.

"With child," He repeated. "Odelia is pregnant."

I remembered how tearful she had been only two days before and how insistent that she would be a good mother.

"She said they had quarrelled..." I recalled, trailing off as I met Garrett's grey eyes.

"Congratulations," he said, stone-faced "You're going to be an aunt."

Epilogue

The afternoon sun bore down on my back, its hazy golden light glinting off of my Noridian armour, blinding onlookers and forcing them to shield their eyes behind a raised hand or a decorative fan.

I stood in the centre of the outer courtyard. King Leander was giving a speech from his place atop a hastily built podium. Odelia was by his side, dressed in a deep red gown with her hair braided up in the Riverian style. She stared down at me with a mixture of anxiety and fondness. The corners of her mouth were turned up into a sad grin, and her hands were clasped tightly out in front of her. I could tell she was trying hard not to wring them together.

Cian stood behind me, I didn't turn to see him, but I knew he was there, along with Garrett and the rest of the blood guard.

BOUND TO THE CROWN

I watched as Odelia descended the podium towards me, the knight's contract in her hands, and pen for me to sign it with. Her stare was glassy and preoccupied, and she stumbled slightly on the wooden steps.

I smiled encouragingly at her as she approached, and I held my left arm out to take the contract from her willingly.

Instantly I could see the trepidation in her eyes fade away to be replaced with a sparkle of hope.

When I joined the blood guard all those years ago, I had no idea what I was getting myself into, I had blindly followed the orders of those around me. I had let the people I trusted and respected manipulate and bend me to their own wills.

But now, I would become Odelia's Knight with my eyes wide open and a resolute plan in my mind.

I would protect my queen and Cian's child unto the ends of the world and beyond. I would find Mags and destroy those cursed crowns. My days of running and hiding were behind me.

Now I would prove my worth, and gods help Mags, Henri, my father, or anyone else who dared try to stop me.

SIMONE NATALIE

BOUND TO THE CROWN

Simone Natalie lives in a little English town with her Husband, three boys, and a plant eating cat named Nova.
She has been burying her head in books since before she could read them, and writing since before she could spell
(That one is still fairly tricky, actually)

You can find Simone on Amazon, Facebook, TikTok and Instagram.

Printed in Great Britain
by Amazon

26018297R00238